THE MIND AND BODY SHOP

By the same author

KRIPPENDORF'S TRIBE

Frank Parkin

THE MIND AND BODY SHOP

ATHENEUM New York 1987

Originally published in Great Britain by William Collins Son & Co. Ltd.

Atheneum
Macmillan Publishing Company
866 Third Avenue, New York, N.Y. 10022

Library of Congress Cataloging-in-Publication Data

Parkin, Frank.
  The mind and body shop.

  I. Title.
PR6066.A69535M5   1987   823'.914   86-25953
ISBN 0-689-11895-3

First American Edition

10 9 8 7 6 5 4 3 2 1

Printed in the United States of America

To Siu-Mi

CONTENTS

Michaelmas

1

It was the first day of Michaelmas term and acid rain was falling on the campus. It seeped through the cracks in the roof of Senate House and formed a complex network of puddles that ran from the main piazza to the fenced-off artificial lake. It fell on students huddled in bunches on the library steps waiting for the doors to open. It fell on learned professors scurrying to seminar rooms and lecture theatres or to the university snooker hall. It fell also on the Vice-Chancellor as he dismounted from his moped and parked it in the diagonal space reserved for it. He hurried along the greasy duckboards leading to Admin II, removing his bicycle clips and crash-helmet as he went. Before going through the swing doors he paused to shake water off himself like a dog. Lecturers, students, secretaries and administrative personnel filed past him in both directions. Some of them said, 'Good morning, Vice-Chancellor,' as if they might have meant it; others looked away in embarrassment, fear or loathing.

'Good morning, Sheldrake, morning, Poulter-Mogg,' he replied, reciting the names on their identity discs. Who the devil are these people? he wondered. Surely they aren't all on the payroll?

He spurned the lift and bounded up the stairs two at a time, causing people walking down to stand aside to avoid his swinging crash-helmet. On the mezzanine floor he had to stop for breath. He sat on the bottom step with his head between his knees, sucking in air through his nose and mouth like a small woman giving birth to a large baby. Presently he felt able to stand upright. He plodded slowly up the remaining two flights to his office, holding on to the handrail.

Once inside his office he took off his damp tracksuit top and wiped the mud off his trainers with a university prospectus. He sat down behind his glass-topped desk and examined his diary. It was going to be another busy day. At ten-fifteen he was seeing a consortium of antiquarian booksellers; at eleven he was due to receive a student delegation to listen to complaints about the allegedly poor quality of tented accommodation behind the sports field; at noon he was lunching with a local hotelier in the hope of persuading him to donate some crockery and cutlery to the university refectory in exchange for an honorary doctorate. From two until four he was chairing a meeting of the Big Five universities to try to hammer out a solution to the problem of academic espionage. At six he was broadcasting a welcome address to first-year students on Radio Free Campus; then he was free until the evening charity concert in aid of the unemployed professoriate.

He looked at one of the dials on his shatterproof wristwatch. If he dealt with his correspondence quickly there might just be time for a quick work-out on the wallbars. He reached for his micro cassette recorder with one hand and eased the damp crutch of his tracksuit trousers with the other. Putting his mouth needlessly close to the microphone he began dictating in an indeterminate regional accent.

'Memo to all Heads of Departments: It has again been brought to my attention that certain junior lecturers have been failing to clock on for the afternoon shift. Professors will, in future, validate the timesheets of their junior staff as well as countersigning all claims for overtime payment. Furthermore, to conform with the policy in other institutions of higher learning, productivity bonuses will now be determined by departmental performance over the calendar year, not the academic year as hitherto. The question of paying teaching staff a small retainer during vacations will be considered at the next meeting of the Senate Subcommittee on Wages and Conditions, together with the vexed question of the chalk allowance.'

The Vice-Chancellor pressed the pause button and leaned back in his swivel chair. Should he say something about last year's examination results, or leave it to the Senate Subcommittee on Illiteracy? He picked up his solid glass paperweight and turned it in his hand reflectively; it was in the shape of a sauce bottle and coloured cherry red with a triple white stripe running from top to bottom. This was the symbol of the multinational company sponsoring the university in the current quinquennium. The same symbol appeared on the breast pocket of the Vice-Chancellor's tracksuit top as well as on the flag flying from the library roof. The sponsorship flag had once been in the flamboyant colours of a well-known merchant bank before the directors grew dissatisfied with the university's rating in the Academic Index.

The intercom buzzed. 'Yes, Miss Pollins?'

'I'm sorry to bother you, Vice-Chancellor,' a timid voice said. 'It's a quarter to ten.'

'I know it's a quarter to ten, Miss Pollins. Is that what you rang to tell me?'

'Professor Hambro's waiting to see you, Sir. His appointment was at nine-fifteen.'

The Vice-Chancellor groaned aloud into the intercom. 'Hambro? First thing in the morning?' He checked his diary and saw to his dismay a pencilled entry between the sign of the full moon and an autumn gardening hint. It said, 'Hambro: bollocking.'

'All right, I suppose you'd better send him in.'

Seconds later there was a perfunctory knock on the door and then the domed head of the Professor of Metaphysical Philosophy appeared around it. There was no sign of an accompanying body.

'Come in, Hambro, come in,' the Vice-Chancellor said, smiling like a dentist. 'Park yourself down.' He flapped a hand in the direction of a narrow sling of synthetic leather suspended across a low frame of tubular glass bars.

Douglas Hambro stared down at it in perplexity, as though having been asked to guess its real purpose or recommended retail price. He shuffled his small feet, turned his back on it,

11

and then lowered himself into it from the knees as if in simulation of a Presbyterian schoolmistress using a Moroccan public lavatory.

'Fag?' the Vice-Chancellor asked, proffering a plywood box decorated with painted seashells and containing two menthol cigarettes and the stub of a panatella. 'I've jacked it in myself.'

'Thank you, Vice-Chancellor, I shall stick to my pipe.' Because his knees were now at a slightly higher level than his head it took Hambro several minutes to extract his pipe, tobacco pouch, matches, pipe-cleaners and tamper from his various pockets. While he was filling the bowl with scented shag the Vice-Chancellor said, 'I expect you know why I've called you in?' He propped one foot on the corner of his desk and looked at it with apparent interest. 'I've been going through the Philosophy accounts. Enrolments are down again, they're even worse than last term's. You're going to be the only department in the entire university running a deficit. Even Catering Studies looks like breaking even.' Though only just, he admitted to himself; they would have been in trouble if they hadn't won the fast-food contract for the military detention centre.

Hambro sighed heavily as he peered up between his spreadeagled knees. 'It's not for the want of trying, Vice-Chancellor, I do assure you. The difficulty is, you see, moral philosophy doesn't really lend itself to a purely commercial approach. It is quite different from cheese or linoleum in that respect. And in certain other respects, too, of course.'

The Vice-Chancellor screwed up his face. 'Balls,' he reasoned. 'Anything can be sold if it's properly presented. What you've got to do, Hambro, is think of philosophy as your merchandise. Regard it as a commodity, just like any other. One of the most valuable lessons I learned when I was East Midlands sales rep for Consolidated Tractor Fuels . . .'

Hambro allowed his mind to disengage while the Vice-Chancellor rambled on about the techniques of high-pressure salesmanship in a buyers' market. How, he asked himself for the hundredth time, could the balance of the universe have been so upset as to make such a conversation possible? It seemed relatively few years ago that the university was a comfortable backwater of quiet learning and modest scholarship. He could still vaguely remember it as it had been before privatization. That was the time when students entered the lecture theatres without passing through coin-operated turnstiles. In those days he was not required to preface his seminar on the Stoics with a message from the commercial sponsors. Nor was he responsible for sweeping up the room afterwards. After all these years he could still not get accustomed to adding the suffix Inc. to the name of the university, nor to renting his office on a monthly tenancy. He could not even look forward to the prospect of his imminent retirement now that the pension had been abolished. His gloom deepened as his gaze fell upon the newly-installed exercise bicycle and the now familiar wallbars where the panelled bookshelves used to be.

'What I'm driving at, Hambro,' the Vice-Chancellor was saying, 'is that you've got to think about your subject in an entirely different way. You need to open up your mind to fresh ideas, like any good entrepreneur.'

Hambro ran the flat of his hand back and forth across his shining pate as though wondering whether hair had unexpectedly sprouted overnight. 'My department is not averse to innovation. We did try to incorporate the Eastern mystic tradition into the framework of logical positivism.'

The Vice-Chancellor beat Hambro's words away with the back of his hand. 'No, no, no, that's not what I mean.' Doddering old fool, he thought: no wonder he can't get across to the ordinary buying public. What could you expect of a man who tucked his handkerchief up his sleeve and who allowed the waistband of his thermal underpants to show above his trousers? 'My point is that you've got to try and see philosophy from the consumers' angle.'

Hambro sucked spittle thoughtfully through the stem of his dormant pipe. 'Hm. Consumers.' He uttered the word again, experimentally, as though pondering whether it could be an anagram for a more familiar term.

'Consumers are the people who buy the product you're selling,' the Vice-Chancellor explained wearily. My God, he thought, this man may be an Old Etonian but he wouldn't have lasted ten minutes at Consolidated Tractor Fuels. Just look at him, slumped in my best chair like a sack of turnips tied in the middle, sucking on that filthy pipe, ash all down his front, the buttons of his woolly cardigan fastened up the wrong way . . . How can I be expected to run a modern university with duffers like him on the payroll?

'The fact is, Hambro,' he went on, 'Philosophy has got to earn its keep, just like any other subject. The days of the ivory tower were over long ago. It's not all that difficult to adjust to the real world. Your colleagues in other departments have shown what can be done with a bit of ingenuity.' He strode athletically to the far wall and rolled down a coloured sales chart that hung beside his framed Diploma in Laundry Administration from the Pontypridd College of Commerce.

'Look for example what Professor Grimaldi has done for the Politics department.' He pointed to a green dotted line that rose in a steep curve like the markings on a malaria chart. 'In less than four terms he's turned it from a loss-maker into one of our most profitable concerns.'

Hambro's voice squeaked in protest. 'Yes, but he's managed that by serving as political adviser to military despotisms. But for him, half the dictatorships in Latin America would have fallen long ago.'

The Vice-Chancellor seemed not to hear. 'Look at Jurisprudence. Young Tench-Overton has worked miracles there. He looks set to win the Faculty shield for the second year running.'

'Yes,' Hambro muttered, 'by acting as legal consultant to the Mafia. He spends half the academic year in Palermo.'

The Vice-Chancellor's voice took on a harder edge and his accent became more noticeably regional. 'The point

14

is, Professor Hambro, they, unlike you, are now running prosperous departments. They're a credit to the university. You've no call to get snooty about colleagues who are subsidizing you.'

Hambro squirmed about in agitation in his low-slung leather seat. As he did so, it gave off a succession of spluttering rasps, causing the Vice-Chancellor to glower at him reprovingly. In order to clarify the origin and nature of these sounds, Hambro at once proceeded to wriggle his buttocks energetically, thereby producing a more sustained series of explosions.

The Vice-Chancellor stared at him in disbelief. The revolting little tyke, he thought; what the hell's he been eating, refectory food? He hurried across to the window and flung it open demonstratively. Damp air flowed into the room accompanied by the whine of electric drills, the thudding of steam hammers, and the agonized roar of mechanical diggers. He remained at the window looking down at the huge yellow machines plying to and fro across the muddy site of the Khomeini Centre for the Propagation of Islam. Imported marble slabs were being winched into position, watched by three men in dark suits and steel helmets. Nearby, partly concealed by scaffolding and flapping sheets of tarpaulin, gleamed the white walls of the mosque. The sight of this, and the activity all around it, made the Vice-Chancellor's pigeon chest expand with pride. The Khomeini Centre, with its vast endowments, would almost certainly have gone to Oxford if it hadn't been for his own powers of persuasion and Oxford's reluctance to allow the Sheldonian to be used as a Shi'ite seminary. More fool Oxford, he thought, as he watched two tractors racing each other through the mud; that place was out of touch with the times. No wonder half its colleges were up for sale. He turned unwillingly from the tangible signs of his own university's progress and renewal to face the equally tangible sign of its degeneration and decay who was now polluting his office.

'The fact of the matter is, Hambro, we can't go on carrying

Philosophy as a passenger any longer. I'll give you till the end of the present academic year to get your department on a sound economic footing. I can't say fairer than that, can I? If you're still in the red at the end of Trinity term . . .' he drew a finger across his throat, 'you'll go the same way as Classics and Maths and English.' He opened the bottom drawer of a steel filing cabinet, giving Hambro a sudden twinge of apprehension that he was about to be offered a small glass of sweet Cyprus sherry from a wine box. Instead, the Vice-Chancellor took out a manila folder and tossed it on his desk next to the October issue of *Heart Attack Monthly*.

'I've been discussing your case with the professor of Marketing Science. His bods have designed a sales programme specifically for your needs. I want you to follow it to the letter. Okay? As I keep saying, Hambro, it's all a question of the right mentality.' He pointed to the wall chart with his bottle-shaped paperweight. 'If you really set your mind to it you could put Philosophy where it belongs—up there among the market leaders.' He passed the folder to Hambro. It was marked 'Confidential: Consumer Research Survey (Philosophy). Itinerant Sales Strategy for Lower Income Groups.'

He reached for his crash-helmet. 'I must be off. I've got a meeting with some local book dealers – I think we've finally found a buyer for the History library.' He put on his tracksuit top and bicycle clips. 'I'll let you see yourself out.'

Hambro was struggling to raise himself out of his chair. Each time he pushed down with his small feet the tubular glass frame slid backwards across the carpet tiles. Soon he found himself gliding alongside the exercise bicycle.

The Vice-Chancellor shook his head in wonderment. Who would ever believe it? An old man riding about the room in a chair like a great big kid. He checked that he had his keys, his security pass and his bleeper. He turned in the doorway to catch a final glimpse of Hambro slithering back and forth alongside the wall below the framed lithograph of Adam Smith.

16

2

Dr Hedda Hagstrom buttoned up her long white coat as she picked a path between the stacks of concrete pipes and drums of yellow cable obstructing the forecourt between Experimental Psychology and Admin II. She wore two velour sweaters beneath her coat because of the heating economies and knee-high Gucci boots because of the mud. The bottoms of her cashmere trousers were tucked inside her boots, over-hanging the tops in the Cossack fashion. Often she wore her platinum blonde hair in a single, tapering plait tied at the end with a black velvet ribbon, but today she had it drawn up from the nape and stacked on her head with the aid of metal combs. She paused for a moment on a low hillock of mud surrounded by puddles, as though trying to decide the easiest route between them. Instead, she splashed her way through them in a direct line to the duckboards leading from the entrance of Admin II to the annexe at the rear.

The annexe had once been part of a manor house, and various Acts of Parliament still gave protection to its rotting beams and scorched thatch. A Victorian extension had been built on one side and an Edwardian extension on the other, both of which were dwarfed by the cantilevered concrete block of the main building. A commemorative plaque above the door stated that the manor house had, at different times, been occupied by a minor Lakeland poet, a Wildlife Trust, and a ladies' cyling champion. Some of the original mullioned windows were still intact, but others had been replaced with aluminium frames. None of them opened because of the subsidence.

Hedda Hagstrom clattered up the narrow wooden staircase kicking mud and water off her boots as she went. The stairs led to a low-ceilinged room with chairs arranged along three of its asymmetrical walls. All the chairs were occupied and some people were squatting uncomfortably on the sloping floor. The low buzz of conversation ceased as Hedda Hagstrom swept into the room.

'Sorry I'm a bit late,' she said unapologetically. 'We had a spot of trouble in the Psychology lab – one of my chimpanzees has been playing up. I suspect he's been got at by Animal Liberation.' She took a bunch of keys from her pocket and unlocked a fireproof door. A sign hung from the handle saying 'University Counselling Service and Abnormality Treatment Centre. Tuesdays, Wednesdays and Fridays. Emergencies by Appointment.' The door opened into an unheated room that was bare of furniture except for a kneehole desk and two slatted chairs. Pale grey light came through a dormer window. Pinned on one wall was a faded poster of the Queen sitting sideways on a horse. Beside it was a notice appealing for student volunteers for the Surrogate Motherhood Unit.

Hedda Hagstrom shut the door behind her and wiped the chair with a paper handkerchief before sitting down. Another completely wasted morning, she thought resentfully. Three hours listening to social incompetents groaning on about their self-inflicted problems. What a grotesque misuse of her time and talents when there was vital work to be done in the lab. She watched her breath vaporize in the chill air. Still, she was better off than some of her colleagues; think of poor old Myerscough who now doubled up as lecturer in Hispanic Studies and car park attendant; or McGinty in Biology, who spent three afternoons a week in the boilerhouse. She reached for the top dossier on the pile in her in-tray and simultaneously pressed the buzzer.

There was a barely audible knock on the door.

'Yes,' she intoned.

Nothing happened for several seconds and then the knock was repeated, this time a little louder.

'For God's sake come in,' Hedda Hagstrom pleaded.

The door opened by degrees to reveal a short young man

18

with a stoop. He waited to be told to sit before sitting. His feet did not quite touch the floor.

'How can I help you?' Hedda Hagstrom asked doubtfully. Where do these people come from, she wondered. The circus? The young man crossed and uncrossed his legs and wiped the palms of his hands on his elbows. He mumbled into his chest as though speaking into a concealed microphone. 'I've been getting these fits of depression. I keep bursting into tears for no reason. It happened again yesterday during a seminar on Human Personal Relations. The professor ordered me out.' His head sank lower and lower on his chest until Hedda Hagstrom found herself looking at a crown of tangled hair. 'Now I've started wetting the bed again,' he mumbled.

Hedda Hagstrom moved her chair away a little. 'Bed-wetting? At your age?' She wrinkled her nose in distaste. 'You're a university student, you should be able to control your sphincter.'

The young man nodded his head without raising it. 'I know I should. I used to be able to, before my troubles began. It's costing me a fortune in mattresses.'

Hedda Hagstrom opened the dossier in front of her and riffled through the medical reports, psychiatric profile, examination results, bank statements, campus parking tickets, photocopied laundry lists, and a swimming certificate for the hundred metres freestyle. The psychiatric profile ran to four foolscap pages. My God, Hedda Hagstrom thought, as her practised eye picked out key passages, no wonder he's such a mess. She unclipped a silver propelling pencil from the pocket of her white coat, laid it on the desk, and began manoeuvring it about with her fingertips. When it was precisely midway between the out-tray and the in-tray, she said, 'Tell me about this dog of yours. It could be at the root of the problem.'

The young man raised his head and looked at her directly for the first time. 'Dog?'

'According to your file you enjoy a relationship with an

19

Airedale terrier called Binley that isn't altogether healthy. You can be perfectly frank with me. I'm used to hearing the most appalling things.'

'I've never had a dog. My mother said there wasn't room for one in our caravan. She let me have a goldfish instead.'

Hedda Hagstrom frowned, consulted the psychiatric profile once more, then checked the name on the front of the dossier. 'Are you Shirley Mendip?'

'No, I'm Colin Lumsden.'

Hedda Hagstrom closed her eyes and tossed the dossier aside. The bank statements and freestyle swimming certificate fell to the floor. 'You should have *said* who you were. I might have given you a completely wrong diagnosis.'

Lumsden stared miserably at the sisal matting. I can't seem to do anything right lately, he thought. On Thursday he'd been reported to the campus police for putting bent coins in the lecture theatre turnstile, and the day before he'd been ejected from the library for standing on the first two volumes of a medical encyclopedia in order to reach the third. He just wasn't cut out to be a student.

'Right,' said Hedda Hagstrom, 'let's start again from the beginning. We've established that your name is Colin Lumsden, that you're not fixated on your dog, that in fact you don't possess a dog or any other domestic animal other than a goldfish. Is that correct so far?'

Lumsden nodded in confirmation, deciding not to reveal that the man in the caravan next door had since swallowed the goldfish in order to win a bet.

'Good, now we're getting somewhere.' Hedda Hagstrom realigned her silver propelling pencil until it was exactly parallel with the edge of the desk. 'These crying fits you've been having, and the bedwetting – when did they begin?'

Lumsden replied without having to think. 'October the fifth.'

Hedda Hagstrom flipped back the pages of her university diary. 'The Science Faculty jumble sale? I fail to see the connection.'

'It was the day I flunked my exams. Nothing's gone right for me ever since.'

Hedda Hagstrom scribbled a note on her jumbo pad. 'Ah. Yes. What degree are you reading?'

'I'm doing the Certificate in Social and Economic Forecasting. The trouble is I'm useless at it. None of my forecasts ever work out. I didn't even predict the result of the Ebbw Vale by-election, even though the Tories won it by a landslide.' He pulled at the loose skin on the backs of his hands as though trying to remove a pair of surgical gloves. 'I didn't want to do the subject in the first place. I wanted to take the Diploma in Warehouse Management, but my mother wouldn't let me. She runs her own clairvoyant practice in Porthcawl and wants me to continue in the family tradition.' His thin voice trembled as he talked about his examination failure and his mother's reaction. 'She was absolutely livid. She said I've brought the family name into disrepute. She refuses to have anything more to do with me until I've passed the re-sits.' He took out a greyish handkerchief, blew into it copiously, inspected the contents, and folded it away. 'Now, to cap it all,' he choked, 'my girlfriend's packed me in. She didn't even have the decency to tell me. She just left me waiting like a wally outside Senate House. I had two complimentary tickets for the ladies' wrestling.'

Hedda Hagstrom was busily making notes on her pad: spring onions, water chestnuts, fennel, black peppercorns, deodorant refill (verbena), suede cleaner, airmail envelopes . . . The silence caused her to look up. 'Do go on, Mr . . . er . . . Lumsden. Why did your girlfriend leave you? Maureen, was it?'

'Janice. She complained about my bedwetting. She said that sleeping on a rubber sheet brought on her impetigo.' He cleared an obstruction at the back of his throat and swallowed it. 'I don't know what to do,' he gurgled. 'I'm a failure at my studies, my mother's disowned me, my girlfriend's jilted me, and my sheets are always damp. My life's a total mess.' He covered his face with his hands. Presently

21

his shoulders began to shake to the accompaniment of whimpering sobs.

Hedda Hagstrom averted her gaze from this unseemly lack of composure. She rose from the desk and went to the dormer window. Low clouds had gathered above the campus. Seagulls wheeled and dipped in the wind. They circled over the refectory, squawking and pecking one another, before turning quickly back to sea. The sea itself was just visible in the distance through the gap between Experimental Psychology and the Hayek hall of residence. It looked curiously brown and lumpy, like an instant pudding mix left too long on the stove. The sight of it filled Hedda Hagstrom with profound melancholy, reminding her of wasted childhood days playing on a beach with bucket and spade when she could have been mastering statistics or Basic. If only she had been blessed with parents capable of appreciating her enormous potential, instead of the humdrum couple who bought her dolls and party frocks and made her play with the ordinary children next door. Given the right home environment, the right motivation, she would most likely have been a child prodigy at something—the cello, perhaps, or bacteriology, or astrophysics, or possibly all three. She would long ago already have received the awards, distinctions and academic honours she so desperately coveted: Fellowship of the Royal Society, Nobel Prize for Experimental Psychology, an entry in the *Guinness Book of Records* (Academic Supplement), a guest appearance on the Dirk Oesterbroek Celebrity Show . . . And it would all have come so effortlessly, the natural culmination of innate, but properly fostered, gifts. Instead, the road to international recognition and acclaim was studded with obstacles, stuck as she was in this godforsaken place, starved of facilities and resources, denied the esteem due to her, and where she was forced to squander precious hours cooped up in this squalid rabbit-hutch listening to endless tales of woe. She suddenly remembered Lumsden. She turned to see him stroking the lobe of his ear and sucking his thumb, rocking to and fro.

22

'So,' she said, resuming her seat, 'are you feeling better after your little weep? It's quite good therapy, if you don't mind the embarrassment.' She pressed both palms flat on the open dossier, as though absorbing its information through her pores. It took her a little while to be quite sure that the spaces between her fingers were exactly equidistant.

'I'm so unhappy,' Lumsden simpered, first extracting his thumb from his mouth and wiping it on his lapel. 'What can I do?'

Hedda Hagstrom's pale blue eyes visibly softened as she leaned across the kneehole desk. Her low voice was resonant with professional concern. 'Have you ever considered suicide?'

Lumsden blinked, sniffed, coughed and nodded, almost simultaneously. 'I've thought about it once or twice when I've been really down. The last time was when my mother ridiculed me in public for not forecasting the collapse of the Japanese economy. She'd already seen it coming in her tarot cards. It's times like that I think about it.'

Hedda Hagstrom shook her head slowly in mild remonstrance. 'It's not much use thinking about it. You need to be more positive. Part of your problem is that you're far too passive. You let things happen to you instead of making them happen. You'll get nowhere with that attitude.' She opened a drawer in the desk and took out a bundle of illustrated booklets held together by a stout rubber band. 'Take one of these manuals, it'll show you the most reliable methods to use. They've all been scientifically tested in my lab.' While Lumsden was riffling through the pages she closed his dossier, drew a red diagonal line across the cover, and put it in the out-tray. She reached for the next dossier on the pile in the in-tray and scanned its contents. Another tedious case: a third-year student of Acupuncture complaining of uncontrollable sadistic impulses.

Lumsden got to his feet. He did not seem much taller standing up than sitting down. 'Thanks for all your help, Dr Hagstrom, I really appreciate it.'

Hedda Hagstrom smiled her counselling smile. 'I'm glad to be of service. That's my duty, three mornings a week.' She pointed to a tin box that might once have contained layers of chocolate biscuits. 'It's twelve pounds fifty for the booklet. Cash only, I'm afraid.'

3

The pale October sun flickered intermittently behind a bank of cloud, like a lightbulb in a faulty socket. Presently it went out altogether as the sky darkened from dove grey to battleship grey. Rain began falling on the campus for the tenth consecutive day. A brisk wind blew in from the sea. It flung the rain against the mullioned and replacement windows in the annexe of Admin II and against newly erected billboards advertising an anti-depressant that could be taken as a bedtime drink. Students huddled beneath shared umbrellas as they made their way across the duckboards from one building to another. Most of the men wore suits with collar and tie and most of the women wore dresses or knee-length skirts, but quite a few wore *chadhors*. There was no visible blurring of the genders, even from behind.

Although it was early in the afternoon lights were coming on one by one in the Hayek hall of residence. Denise Mason closed the curtains of her study-bedroom on the eighth floor and switched on the bedside lamp. Despite its red tasselled shade it failed to cast an intimate glow on the distempered concrete walls and ex-RAF furniture. On the wall above the single divan hung a rectangle of locally-made batik that Denise had won in the Arts Faculty lottery, together with a cheeseburger voucher. Light operatic music played by the band of the Security Police came from a small transistor tuned in to Radio Free Campus. Later the music gave way

24

to an urgent appeal from the Medical Centre for organ transplant donors.

Denise took off her dress and seemingly inadequate brassiere and folded them over the back of a chair. She had a flat stomach and a protruding navel that looked as though it served some useful function. There was a tiny, moon-shaped scar on her left breast just below the more recently acquired cigarette burns. She sat on the chair and began struggling with her white wellingtons.

'No, keep them on,' said her Moral Tutor. He was fiddling with his monogrammed cufflinks on the other side of the divan. 'But not, of course, your tights,' he added. He took off his shirt and hung it on the coat-hanger that he had himself provided for the purpose. He had the brisk orderly movements of a man used to working to a tight schedule. He was lying undressed on the divan by the time Denise had taken off her wellingtons, peeled off her tights, and then replaced her wellingtons. 'What about my panties, Mr Poulter-Mogg?' she enquired, mindful of her Moral Tutor's unpredictability in these matters.

Poulter-Mogg pushed his vestigial lips forward as he gave the question due consideration. 'Off, I think. There isn't a lot of time. I'm chairing a meeting of the Senate Subcommittee on Professional Ethics at three-fifteen.' There was only one item on the agenda, he recalled: one of Professor Hambro's junior lecturers accused of misappropriating the chalk allowance.

Denise disposed of her disposable paper panties and knelt at the foot of the divan. She gripped her Moral Tutor's big toe between her thumb and forefinger and said in a childlike falsetto, 'This lickle piggy went to market, this lickle piggy stayed at home . . .'

Fifteen minutes later he was getting dressed again. She noticed that he invariably first put on his long, black cotton socks, black suspenders and black brogues as if deliberately to accentuate the Fetta-cheese whiteness and texture of his flesh. He stood with his legs wide apart, catching drips in a

25

coloured tissue. Denise had heard it rumoured that he was always applying for jobs at other universities but that none of them would take him, either because of Mrs Poulter-Mogg or because of his bogus degree. In some ways she felt she quite liked him, even though he was a stickler for discipline. At least he always paid her promptly, not like some of the lecturers she could name. While he was buttoning up his waistcoat she summoned up the courage to say, 'I don't mean to be a pest, Mr Poulter-Mogg, but did you manage to put in a word for me to the Dean? You said you'd try.' She was huddled on the divan with the covers wrapped around her and her chin resting on her knees.

'The Dean?' Her Moral Tutor glanced at her quizzically as he shook the creases from his pinstriped jacket. 'You mean about being improperly dressed in the computer lab?'

'No, I've already paid the fine for that. I meant about bribing the examiners.'

Poulter-Mogg flicked at minute specks of fluff on his sleeves and wide lapels. 'Ah, yes.' He pressed his thin lips together until they disappeared. 'I'm afraid the Dean took a very dim view of that episode. You may have to face a disciplinary tribunal.'

'But that's not fair,' Denise protested. 'Everyone here does it. The examiners *expect* it.'

Her Moral Tutor stamped his foot hard on the floor, not in anger or expostulation, but to correct the hang of his trouser leg. 'My dear Miss Mason,' he said equably, 'there is a certain protocol to be observed in these matters. It was quite improper of you to pin dollar bills in the front of your answer book. Examiners are sensitive people. It was the sheer crudity of your action that caused such deep offence.' He consulted his gold pocket-watch, tutted, smoothed back his hair, and made a final adjustment to the knot in his Greenpeace tie. 'Let's fix a time for our next tutorial.' He took out his university diary. 'Shall we say next Wednesday at two forty-five, here as usual?' He pencilled an entry without waiting for her reply. 'Good. I can just fit you in between an emergency meeting of the Illiteracy Subcommittee and my lecture on the Dissolution of the Monasteries.'

As soon as he had gone, Denise took a shower in the communal washroom, powdered herself with jojoba talc, manicured her nails, flossed her teeth, plucked her eyebrows, put on her Annabelinda dress, and took the goods lift to the basement. She made her way through a labyrinth of dark and dusty passages that were silent except for the hiss and rumble of mysterious pipes that ran along either side. Before long she came to some stone steps leading down to a darker passage that looked like the entrance to a disused tunnel. She edged her way forward, feeling the dripping walls with her fingertips. She was soon able to feel, but not properly see, a metal door set back into the wall. She knocked twice, counted to three, and knocked five more times in rapid succession.

'It's me, Baxi,' she whispered hoarsely. 'Denise.'

There was the sound of a key scraping in a lock. The door opened just wide enough for her to squeeze through into the small box room or large broom cupboard that served as Baxi's illicit, though rent-free, accommodation. The room was lit by a kerosene lamp hanging from a meat-hook in the ceiling. It cast lambent shadows across the mossy walls and on to the unrolled sleeping bag that occupied most of the available floor space. The remainder was taken up with stacks of printed questionnaires.

'Nice timing,' Baxi said. 'You can help me fill this lot in.'

Denise took up a blank questionnaire and read aloud in a singsong voice. 'One. What is your opinion of the Admiralty's decision to lease the Cinque Ports to the Chinese Navy? Two. What is your view of the Chancellor of the Exchequer's proposal to scrap the Wealth Tax and double the Budgerigar Licence Fee?'

Baxi handed her three ballpoint pens, each of a different colour. 'Just tick the boxes marked Agree, Disagree, Don't Know. If you can't make up your mind, toss a coin.'

Denise removed a pile of soiled paper plates from the

sleeping bag and squatted on the rolled-up Oxfam overcoat that was doing service as Baxi's pillow. 'Aren't you supposed to get members of the public to fill these in?' she asked.

Baxi made a noise with his lips like a child's balloon collapsing. 'What, at the rate Hedda Hagstrom pays? Too uneconomical.' He ticked three Don't Knows and one Disagree and added another completed questionnaire to the pile. 'Besides, it's no use asking the punters for their views. You can't have uninformed minds shaping national policy.' He exchanged his red fibre-tip for a green rollerball. 'Doing it my way brings results. I reckon it was down to me that the Police Federation came out in favour of legalizing pot.'

By the time the refectory dinner klaxon sounded far above them, they had filled in more than half the questionnaires and tied them up in bundles of fifty. Baxi made a quick calculation as they waited in the queue for a choice of paella and chips, chop suey and chips, or spaghetti carbonara and chips. 'I'll soon have enough to pay for next term's fees, allowing for decent tips in the Senior Common Room bar, and if I get that nice little earner cleaning out the guard-dog kennels.' He picked at something on the surface of his closely-cropped head. He could not afford to visit the barber more than twice a year, so that his hairstyle was in a permanent state of transition between Roundhead and Cavalier. 'I might even have a quid or two to spare for a textbook.'

They sat at a table by the wine automat. On top of the machine stood used plastic beakers containing dregs of Yugoslav white, Spanish red, and Portuguese rosé. Baxi poured all the dregs together until he had a beakerful of light brown liquid. He held the beaker to the light, swirled the contents, sampled the bouquet, sipped, rolled the liquid around his tongue, swallowed, and nodded in appreciation.

'Are we going back to my room?' Denise scraped her untouched spaghetti carbonara on to the remains of Baxi's chop suey.

'Why? What's wrong with my place?' He helped himself

liberally to the free supply of salt, mustard, ketchup, olive oil and horseradish sauce.

'It's too cramped for fucking in properly,' Denise complained. 'It's all right for you, I'm the one who has to lie on the stone floor.'

Baxi sucked in loose strands of spaghetti, causing the ends to flick bright red sauce across his cheeks. 'I thought you liked it standing up.' He wiped his cheeks with a scrap of bread from a previous meal and ate it. 'Either way, we'll have to finish the questionnaires first. I need the cash.'

Denise's full lips came forward in a pout. 'Money, money, money, that's all you ever think about.'

Baxi continued eating his only meal of the day and said nothing. It's all very well for her, he thought, with her British Telecom shares and the Krugerrands given to her by her rich socialist parents for passing her Advertising prelims at the first attempt. He had never met her parents but knew her father was a celebrated lawyer who had made a fortune in the defence of unpopular causes. His own father, by contrast, was a tenor saxophonist who sometimes played with the London Philharmonic but more usually in the pedestrian subway of Baker Street station. Baxi occasionally helped him out in the vacations by playing the zither while Mrs Baxi collected the money in a cloth bag. His parents would have liked him to play with them on a permanent basis, but Baxi knew it would never work out because of his father's artistic temperament. He slit open his bread roll, filled it with chop suey and horseradish sauce, then wrapped it in a paper napkin for his late supper.

The rain had almost stopped as he and Denise walked hand-in-hand between the puddles in the main piazza. They continued on, past the north face of Admin II, round Senate House, and up the slippery embankment that led to the highest point on campus. Far below them, the lights around the small horseshoe harbour twinkled with deceptive gaiety. Out at sea an oil tanker hooted and was immediately answered by another.

'I'm driving into town tomorrow,' Denise said. 'D'you fancy coming for the ride? I'll treat you to a movie if you're nice to me tonight.'

Baxi shook his bullet head. 'Not tomorrow, it's a full day for me. I've got Psychology 201 all morning, window-cleaning in the afternoon, and a zither recital on Radio Free Campus in the evening.' He turned up the collar of his summer jacket against the cold. 'Renaissance man had nothing on me.'

They stood in silence watching the dipped headlights flashing along the arterial road. There was no sound other than the wind soughing through the scaffolding around the Khomeini Centre; then came the undulating wail of the muezzin calling the faithful to prayer in the Portakabin mosque.

4

Margery Hambro pressed the butterknife fiercely against thin slices of brittle toast, causing them to disintegrate into small black fragments. She banged the plate hard on the table in front of Hambro, followed by another, larger, plate banged equally hard but containing a curl of charred bacon and something that looked remarkably like a rubber fried egg from a joke shop.

'Breakfast,' she said informatively.

Hambro was engrossed in the obituary columns of *The Times*. He muttered something half aloud as he read the eulogy on the life and accomplishments of an old academic rival whose death, though not in itself distressing, was a further reminder that he himself was now in the obituary league. Who, he wondered, would they get to write him up? Skeffington? Bulkowski? He, after all, had already been asked to prepare preliminary drafts on them. Perhaps the three of them should get together to ensure fair play?

'Tea.' Margery slammed the teapot down on the ornamental tile as though having taken a violent dislike to its Florentine design.

Hambro gave a curt, derisive laugh from behind his newspaper. In tones of rising incredulity he read aloud, '. . . A scholar of the very highest rank, revered by students and colleagues alike for his unswerving intellectual honesty, unimpeachable professional integrity, and unfailing courtesy and charm.' He lowered the newspaper only just enough to be able to say over the top of it, 'Unswerving intellectual honesty? Hah. No mention, you notice, of his expulsion from the Royal Metaphysical Society for repeated plagiarism. Unfailing courtesy and charm? This was the man who responded to criticism of his paper at the Heidelberg symposium by letting off a fire-extinguisher over the Neo-Kantians.'

Still reading aloud, he released one hand from the newspaper in order to unfold his linen napkin and tuck it into his shirt-front as though settling down to a heavy lunch in Provence. The same hand then inched its way across the tablecloth in search of the milk jug. It stiffened upon encountering instead a litre carton. 'Dearest,' he complained, 'what is this disagreeable object doing on the breakfast table? We are not Americans.' He put his newspaper aside and was surprised to see his wife kneeling beside the empty dishwasher with her face buried in her hands. Drops of what he supposed to be tears were falling through her fingers on to her frilly pinafore. 'Is something the matter?' he enquired. 'Surely that machine hasn't broken down again? You'd be far better off doing the dishes by hand.'

Margery folded herself into a large, misshapen ball and rolled unevenly across the kitchen floor. She came to a rest at the wire vegetable rack and began pounding her fists on the aubergines. After some initial hesitation Hambro removed his linen napkin, folded it neatly in its silver ring, and went across to her. He stood bending over her with his hands planted on his knees like a judge at a horticultural show examining a potentially prizewinning entry. Unexpectedly,

31

Margery began throwing onions, tomatoes, aubergines and green peppers in all directions.

Hambro stared at her in distress. 'Dearest, if you've had second thoughts about the ratatouille . . .'

Margery swung at his ankles with a five-pound bag of Maris Piper. 'I hate you, I hate you! Hate, hate, hate you!' she screamed unambiguously.

Hambro stepped quickly back, squashing a beef tomato under the heel of his carpet slipper. He wondered what he might have done, or omitted to do, to provoke this latest outburst. Had he again failed to recognize her in the street, or inadvertently lit his pipe with her origami? Perhaps he had forgotten their third wedding anniversary? Last year he'd confused the date with the Wittgenstein centenary. 'I appear to have upset you,' he observed. 'I do apologize. What exactly did I do?'

Margery dabbed at her eyes with an oven glove shaped like Mister Punch. 'You know very well what you done,' she sobbed. 'It's what you always do.'

Hambro wiped tomato flesh and seeds off the sole of his slipper with a wodge of kitchen paper. 'Could you be a little more explicit?'

Margery blew her nose into the oven glove before saying, 'You showed me up again last night in front of your fancy friends. Just like you always do.'

Hambro groaned internally and resumed his seat at the breakfast table. A green pepper had landed on his plate, sending congealed bacon fat over the obituary columns of *The Times*. He picked up the pepper gingerly by the stalk and wondered what to do with it. 'What am I supposed to have said or done this time?' he asked wearily.

'It was when we was having dinner at the Poulter-Moggs,' Margery blubbered. 'You introduced me to everyone as your cleaning woman. You didn't even say cleaning lady.' She pulled strands of wet hair from her mouth. Her hair was straw-coloured with dark roots and ends that seemed as if they might easily snap off. 'You kept on scolding me in front of everyone—first for tilting my soup plate the wrong way, then for saying mirror instead of looking-glass. You even told them I preferred drinking tea from the saucer even though you know I haven't done that for ages.'

Hambro closed his eyes and gripped his temple between thumb and middle finger. 'Dearest, we didn't dine at the Poulter-Moggs last night,' he pointed out reasonably. 'We didn't dine with anyone last night. We haven't dined out since you embarked on your pomegranate diet.'

'Yes we did,' Margery insisted. 'In my dream we did. I can remember every detail. You were really horrible to me – I'll never be able to show my face in front of them people again.'

Hambro concentrated hard on the plate in front of him until the shrivelled rasher of bacon became an Archimedean point external to the moral universe. 'These things only ever happen in your dreams. It really is quite important not to confound them with reality.'

Margery looked up at him from the floor. 'They're real enough to me, that's what matters. It's not as if I'd made them up.'

Hambro's voice took on the didactic tone he used when lecturing to Catering students on the is/ought distinction. 'A person cannot be held culpable for misdemeanours committed in someone else's dream. Bulkowski's recent monograph on Other Minds . . .'

'Someone else's dream?' Margery cried. 'Someone else?' She sat bolt upright among the imported vegetables. 'I'm not just someone else, I'm supposed to be your rotten wife, though I know you still think of me as your cleaning woman.'

Hambro stirred his undrinkable tea and drank it. He felt the same despondency that he always felt in the presence of the Vice-Chancellor. 'I assure you, I no longer think of you as my cleaning wom . . . lady. Three years have elapsed since you ceased your activities for me in that capacity.' Or was it four? he suddenly thought. It seemed much longer. His first marriage had lasted twenty-seven years, but already it felt shorter than his second. He could not recall his first wife ever accusing him of wrongdoing in her dreams or throwing food about the kitchen. Nor, for that matter, did she wear rollers in her hair when going to the shops or knit woolly covers for the lavatory seat. He was slowly coming to realize that in many ways she had been the ideal partner, despite her fondness for methylated spirits and, in later years, her unshakeable conviction that she was an extraterrestrial being.

'I don't know why you married me if you're so ashamed of me,' Margery persisted. 'I should've listened to me dad, he's dead against mixed marriages.'

Hambro spread his small hands in supplication. 'Sonia, I am not ashamed of you. Your humble origins do you credit.'

'Then why did you get me those elocution tapes?' Margery demanded. 'And why did you give me that second-hand copy of Fowler's *Modern English Usage* for me birthday?'

'It belongs on every bookshelf.'

'It's the third copy you've bought me. I haven't read the first two yet.' She reached up for the handle of the broom cupboard and hauled herself to her feet. 'And stop bloodywell calling me Sonia. I'm Margery, got it? Margery.' As if to signal that their conversation was now concluded she switched on the radio, turned up the volume, and listened with apparent interest to the shipping forecast and gale warnings for Tyne, Cromarty, Fairisle and Dogger. A few minutes later she tuned in to the pirate pop station and joined in the singalong while she cooked herself a plate of scrambled eggs, bacon, fried tomatoes, black pudding and chips, followed by waffles and hot chocolate sauce. She was gobbling up the remains of some ginger shortbread when Hambro shuffled off into the back garden.

He stood on the step for a moment breathing in the heavy autumn air. Sticky yellow leaves covered most of the lawn. Inedible apples from the neighbour's tree had fallen among the rose bushes and were beginning to ferment. The scent had attracted a few surviving wasps. They droned about listlessly as though conscious of having no further part to play in the natural scheme of things.

Hambro drew aside the delicate branches of the cotoneaster that overhung the path around the rockery. The late honeysuckle was still in bloom though the leaves around the lower stem were brown and shrivelled. He picked off bits of dead wood and crinkled leaf in a desultory fashion before ambling down to the brick outhouse at the foot of the garden. He unlocked the door and replaced the key in its secret niche above the jamb. The moment he stepped inside he was filled with a profound sense of tranquillity. It was as though within this small space the precarious world of order and meaning had been preserved miraculously intact, impervious to the clamour and disarray pressing on the outside walls. Here was the one place he could be the person he really was.

He sighed with contentment as he made himself comfortable in the rickety bentwood chair that had once belonged to George Orwell during his Hampstead period. Humming quietly to himself he took out his pipe and scraped the bowl over the chipped saucer that Orwell had also used as an ashtray while typing the final draft of *1984*. Block-mounted photographs covered one entire wall: Orwell as a boy of three in naval uniform; Orwell feeding his goat; Orwell talking into a BBC microphone; Orwell's chest X-ray; Orwell's dog on Southwold beach; Orwell's sister; Orwell's sister's cat; Orwell's sister's cat's feeding bowl. Each photograph was neatly labelled and numbered according to a code. The code in turn referred to a filing system housed in wooden cabinets on either side of the window. The drawers of the cabinets were labelled St Cyprian's, Eton, Burma, Paris, Hampstead, Wigan, Catalonia, Jura.

Hambro reached for his index cards and proceeded to write detailed entries for the three most recent acquisitions to his collection of memorabilia. These were a dummy packet of gravy powder from Orwell's grocery shop in Wallington, the red and black ribbon on which Orwell had typed the final version of *A Clergyman's Daughter,* and a size twelve and a half army boot that Orwell had probably worn on the Aragon front. When each of these items had been duly labelled, recorded and cross-catalogued Hambro placed them on the open shelves among the rest of his collection. He sat for a long time simply looking at the many priceless objects, though now and again he would reach for one and turn it reverentially in his hand or alter its position in the display on some aesthetic or classificatory whim. There was still much scholarly work to be done to show the full significance of these artefacts to their original owner's literary creations. So much to do and so little time left to do it in, he thought ruefully. And the necessary time would be even more difficult to find once he became Dean of Faculties. His heart dipped at the prospect of endless committee and sub-committee meetings spent discussing shareholders' grievances, library thefts, accusations of academic espionage, and sponsorship schemes. Perhaps he could persuade the Vice-Chancellor to let a younger man take it on? Poulter-Mogg, possibly? Or the Regius Professor of Cosmetic Surgery?

It was past eleven when he thought of checking the time. His spirits sank even lower at the thought of having to return to the world outside and at the realization that he was already fifteen minutes late for his lecture on Remedial Logic to Chiropody 201.

5

Hedda Hagstrom's classic profile was only marginally disfigured by the notional smile she conferred upon the Vice-Chancellor as he came bounding into her laboratory.

'Just a routine visit,' he wheezed. He shook water off his coloured sporting umbrella and looked around for somewhere to hang, lay or prop it. A shallow puddle quickly formed around his jogging shoes. 'I like to see for myself what's going on at the frontiers of science, ha, ha.'

Hedda Hagstrom relieved him of his umbrella and motioned to one of her male laboratory assistants to mop up the puddle. What could be the *real* purpose of this unscheduled visit? she wondered. She shielded the combination lock of her wall-safe with a cupped hand as she twiddled with the knob and shut away the galley proofs of her book on paranoia. Was he going to ask her to serve another stint as telephone receptionist in Admin II? Maybe he wanted her to take over the boilerhouse while McGinty prepared his Reith Lectures? How insufferable that her career could be impeded by this awful man with dirt under his fingernails who insisted on pronouncing the p in psychology.

She led him through the humming corridors of the experimental wing, showing him into rooms full of rats running around in mazes while explaining the scope and character of her current research in words he might understand.

'I've just completed a project designed to test the limits of human psychological endurance.'

'Ah. Good, good. Who funded it, the Marine Commando?'

'The Post Office. They wanted an economy job, so I had to use hens.'

She ushered him into a dimly-lit room in which two chimpanzees were strapped in front of a screen showing video recordings of breakfast television. One appeared to be asleep or dead and the other was showing signs of acute emotional distress.

'It's not yet official,' Hedda Hagstrom said in a confidential voice, 'but the news is I've been awarded the OPEC contract. It's worth ninety thousand dollars.' They went through a swing door into a general office divided into glass partitions.

'Ninety grand?' The Vice-Chancellor gave a long low whistle, causing a plain typist to turn round. 'To do what?'

'They want me to show that exposing children to leaded petrol fumes increases their IQ.'

The Vice-Chancellor faltered in his stride. 'Won't that be difficult? Supposing you can't prove it?'

Hedda Hagstrom looked at him as though he had broken out into Creole or iambic pentameters. 'The grant is conditional on my proving it. These people don't throw their money away.'

The Vice-Chancellor grunted in comprehension of this basic principle. Ninety thousand dollars, he thought; surely some of it could be earmarked for the helicopter pad on the roof of Senate House? 'Let's hope you get the result they want.'

Hedda Hagstrom held open a door for him to pass through. 'If I don't, someone else will.' She steadied him by the elbow as he stumbled on the low step. 'It's really all a question of experiment design. The answers you get are dictated by the way you ask the questions. I showed that in my project for the Scotch Whisky Cartel.'

The Vice-Chancellor's face clouded over in bafflement. 'That must have been before my time.'

'I managed to demonstrate that the growing taste for vodka was directly responsible for the increase in the communist vote. As a result, the government banned the sale of it in depressed areas.'

The Vice-Chancellor inclined his head in admiration, scratched his armpit and unconsciously smelled his fingers. 'Excellent. Well done. That's what we're here for, to give customer satisfaction. Thank goodness someone here understands the function of a modern university.'

They waited for the lift. The Vice-Chancellor kept his thumb pressed on the call button until it came. His face fell at the sight of so many students jammed inside. The campus seemed to be crawling with them – the library, the lecture theatres and seminar rooms, the refectory and the snooker hall – they were like cockroaches in the central heating. Crammed in among the steaming bodies he felt more strongly than ever that the very concept of student had become outdated. Their fees made up only a small proportion of

38

total revenue, so that the resources and personnel tied up in teaching them would be used far more constructively on contract research for foreign governments and the multi-nationals. Besides, the university would be a much better place without them; there would be fewer germs, fewer social diseases, more parking space. The Hayek hall of residence could be refurbished and let out as holiday apartments, or converted into executive suites for visiting sponsors. The entire campus could be re-modelled as an entertainments and leisure complex; there could be hang-gliding off the library roof, a windsurfing school on the artificial lake . . . the possibilities were endless. Just give me another five years, he thought, and I'll do for this university what I did for the East Midlands division of Consolidated Tractor Fuels . . .

'This floor, Vice-Chancellor.' Hedda Hagstrom used her elegant thigh to prevent the lift door shutting on him. Why, she wondered, was he always scratching his crutch in public? She led him along the echoing corridors of the Cyril Burt wing to a long laboratory with a one-way window. On the other side of the tinted glass a dozen or so students were seated at computer terminals. Each of them was wearing a rubber neckband, the size of a clerical collar, to which delicate wires were attached.

'What are they up to?' the Vice-Chancellor whispered unnecessarily. He pressed his face against the glass, causing his nose to flatten out.

'It's our language-teaching experiment. Each time the student makes a grammatical error the computer administers an electric shock. The more serious the error, the higher the voltage.' She bent over the instrument panel and made a small adjustment to one of the settings. 'It's surprising how quickly students can master a new language when there's a strong incentive to get it right.'

The Vice-Chancellor was pulling at the seat of his tracksuit trousers with both hands as though trying to release some living thing trapped inside. 'Absolutely. Incentive's the name of the game.' He seemed pleased with this observation, and

39

repeated it. 'Would it work for any of our other subjects? Fisheries Science? Laundry Administration?'

'Oh yes, almost anything. It's got great potential in primary schools. The Ministry of Education wants us to carry out a pilot scheme on slum children.' She gave a summary of the commercial application of the system, in home, factory and office, and reported the keen interest shown in it by the South African police. As they were about to leave, a shrill cry rang out from the other side of the glass screen. Hedda Hagstrom glanced at the dials on the control panel. 'It's poor Gutteridge,' she smiled. 'Still having trouble with the Spanish subjunctive.'

They took the lift to the basement and went to the front of the coffee queue in the departmental common room. At the Vice-Chancellor's behest they sat at a table partially concealed by an unattributed metal sculpture of what appeared to be a one-legged dwarf climbing up or sliding down a parking meter.

'There's something I've been meaning to have a chat with you about,' the Vice-Chancellor said. He leaned forward in his chair and dunked a Garibaldi biscuit in his paper cup as if to show he could do two different things at the same time.

Here it comes, Hedda Hagstrom thought, the real reason behind his visit. She pressed her knees together protectively. She would rather resign than take over the boilerhouse. If the worst came to the worst she could ask for her old job back with the Institute of Psychological Warfare.

'I like the way you run your outfit, Dr Hagstrom,' the Vice-Chancellor said, slurping his coffee. 'I wish there were more like you in the university, instead of all these damned intellectuals.'

Hedda Hagstrom smiled in relief and appreciation. Perhaps he's not totally moronic after all, she told herself, despite his inability to read without moving his lips, and his tendency to dribble when excited.

'You may not have heard yet,' he continued, 'but the Dean

40

of Faculties wants to take early retirement at the end of Lent term. I gather his wife wants him to help out in her kissagram shop.' He paused melodramatically and added, 'I'd like you to succeed him.'

Hedda Hagstrom could barely contain her astonishment. Dean of Faculties, one of the most powerful posts in the entire university! She felt a tremor of erotic excitement at the mere thought of commanding so much authority. It would mean easier access to money and resources, which meant better research opportunities, which meant more publications, which meant wider international recognition, which meant . . . She bit the inside of her lip to prevent the physical sensations from surging out of control.

'In the normal course of things,' the Vice-Chancellor was saying, 'the post would automatically go to the Deputy Dean. But you know who *that* is.' He fished about in the bottom of his cup for a lost segment of biscuit.

'Isn't it Professor Hambro?'

'Exactly. And I don't intend having that old twat as my right-hand man.' He spoke with a vehemence that caused heads to turn and eyes to be lifted momentarily from learned psychology journals and the daily racing tips. Lowering his voice, he went on, 'The official opening of the Khomeini Centre is due at the end of Trinity term. Right? It's the Dean of Faculties' job to plan and organize the whole affair. It'll be the biggest thing the university's ever taken on. Half the Middle East will be turning up.' His voice dropped to a stage whisper. 'We couldn't have Hambro running a show like that. In the first place he'd make a total balls-up of it. In the second place he's a Jewboy. If the wogs found out they'd go bananas.'

He fell silent as Baxi hovered around them with a trolley laden with dirty crockery. All his pockets were bulging with scraps of food, giving him the appearance of someone suffering from a rare glandular disorder. The Vice-Chancellor waited for him to go before returning to the matter in hand.

41

'Would you be willing to take the job on, if I can swing it? I'm banking on you.'

Hedda Hagstrom lowered her heavy eyelids. 'Certainly, Vice-Chancellor, if you think it's for the general good.'

'Terrific. That's great.' He propped his foot on the metal sculpture and scraped mud off the sole of his jogging shoe. 'I can't see there'll be any real problems. Hambro's bound to put up some resistance, I expect the old fool fancies himself as Dean. Luckily, he's making such a cock-up of his department that he's in no position to win support.'

Hedda Hagstrom gave a sigh of mock commiseration. 'Yes, he's a strange man. He's really his own worst enemy.'

Wrong, thought the Vice-Chancellor, bending his plastic spoon until it snapped.

6

The New Palm Beach housing estate lay in a deep hollow of poisoned ground between the nuclear-waste disposal plant and the army firing range. Birch saplings had been planted at twenty-yard intervals along the pavement, each one protected by a stout cage of corroded iron. Nothing grew on the trees, but bicycle tyres and pram wheels hung from the branches of some, and others had been painted with aerosol sprays. Small children roamed about in packs. They ran screaming down one side of the street, and back up the other, throwing moveable objects at passing vehicles. They swarmed over parked cars, and jumped on the roof of the mobile vasectomy van, tearing at windscreen wipers while kicking the coachwork with their roller skates. All the streets on the estate were named after the Pre-Raphaelites.

Hambro tried to breathe in only small amounts of the sulphurous grit-filled air. 'All set, Skillicorn?' he said morosely. 'You take Rossetti Avenue and I'll take Burne-Jones

Crescent.' He looked away to avoid seeing the depressingly enthusiastic smile that would almost certainly illuminate the face of his junior lecturer in Philosophy.

'Jolly good, Sir,' Skillicorn piped. He was a lanky young man whose angular wrists protruded several inches beyond the cuffs of his sleeves. His arms and legs were never quite still, conveying the impression of someone permanently warming up for an athletic event. His fresh pink face now broke into the smile that Hambro feared to see. 'Troops into action.' He gave a kind of military salute and went gangling off across the communal scrub. He skirted a gang of children playing on a rubbish tip, shielding himself skilfully from their missiles with his pigskin briefcase. Hambro watched him until he had safely turned the corner into Rossetti Avenue before commencing his own round.

The front door of number two Burne-Jones Crescent had neither bell nor knocker. Hambro first rapped tentatively on the glass panel, then rattled the flap of the letterbox. The door was opened while his fingers were still inside the flap. He found himself face to face with an oblong woman holding a mixing bowl and a wooden spoon.

'Good morning, Madam,' he intoned, raising his deer-stalker. 'I've called about the problem of Mind.' He held his presentation kit in readiness. His instructions were not to reveal its contents until the psychologically decisive moment. 'You will, I trust, already have received through the mail our advance literature and trial cassette. Did you manage to listen to the sample lesson on Epistemology in the Home, or examine the pop-up illustrated brochure?' He allowed a strategic interval to elapse. 'I'd be glad to answer any questions, conceptual or otherwise.'

The woman shifted her mixing bowl from one arm to the other. Hambro felt with a strange certainty that her arms would be heavily tattooed beneath the flounced leg-of-mutton sleeves.

'We aim to cover most of the salient aspects of the mind/body problem,' he assured her as he peered into the mixing bowl. 'As well as, of course, the theory of identity and the meta-language controversy.' He now flipped open the cover of his presentation kit and drew her attention to the stylized drawing of a human brain divided into red and green hemispheres. Immediately below was a photograph of Bertrand Russell sitting astride a bicycle and looking worried, as though wondering which way the pedals turned.

'Would you, perhaps, be interested in the Location of Pain, or in the Berkeley fallacy?' Exactly on cue, Hambro turned the page to reveal a caricature of a whiskered clergyman kicking a table and wincing.

The woman looked at the drawing and sniffed, seemingly unimpressed by its draughtsmanship and symbolism. She then cocked her head to one side like a cage bird listening to a human voice imitating a cage bird. 'Is it about the gipsy camp?' she enquired. 'I've already signed the petition. Filthy bleeders,' she added, gyrating her wooden spoon with sudden vigour.

Hambro stared down in desolation at his mud-spattered galoshes. He felt very tired and much too old for modern academic life. The four years to his retirement stretched ahead like a prison sentence. Four more years teaching a subject in which he had long ago lost all interest and for which he had no commercial aptitude. To make matters worse, he still hadn't thought of how he could avoid becoming Dean of Faculties. The last thing he wanted was to take on extra burdens just when his name was being put forward for Honorary President of the Royal Eric Blair Society . . . With a conscious effort of will he put these thoughts from his mind and applied it to the matter immediately in hand. He took a measured breath and delivered without pause the sales message specially prepared for him on the everyday uses of logical positivism.

'Next term,' he concluded, in the same monotone, 'which is to say Lent term, we shall be offering courses at the intermediate, preliminary and remedial stages. Each course leads to the award of a tastefully designed diploma. Fees are payable in easy weekly instalments or by university savings stamps.' He took from his kit a facsimile of the intermediate diploma and handed it to the woman. Make sure that the prospective customer actually *holds* it, the marketing experts had insisted. To Hambro's relief she took it without demur, first handing him her mixing bowl and wiping her hands on her apron. She held the simulated parchment close to her face, inspecting the huge red seal, copperplate lettering, and megalomaniac signatures.

'Very nice,' she decided. She picked at the red seal with her fingernail. 'How much?'

Hambro coughed. 'Actually, the diploma itself is not really for sale, not as such.' He gave the contents of the mixing bowl a perfunctory stir. 'However, on successful completion of the course . . .'

'I usually give something,' the woman said. She scrabbled about for coins in her apron pocket. 'Except to that Muslin lot. They been on the cadge again for a new mosque.' She took the mixing bowl from Hambro, pressed two silver coins into his palm, and closed his fingers over them. Before he could explain the nature of her error she waved goodbye with her wooden spoon and closed the door, gripping the Intermediate Diploma in Mind firmly between her knees.

Shortly before noon he met Skillicorn at the junction of Holman Hunt Drive and Millais Walk.

'How's it going, Sir?' his junior lecturer called from the other side of the street. 'I've had a fantastic morning.' His scrubbed face shone with zeal as he waved aloft a sheaf of completed enrolment forms. He came loping over on his wobbly legs. The tail of his corduroy shirt was hanging out at the back and there were smudges of mascara and pink and scarlet lipstick on his collar and all around his ears and neck.

'These young housewives,' he enthused. 'I've never known anything like it, they're absolutely wild about the subject. We must be the first linguistic philosophers they've seen out here in ages.'

7

The mellifluous sounds of recorded stringed instruments wafted through the scented air of the department store. They floated above haberdashery and men's toiletries, drifted through to rainwear, and swirled around the chandeliers in ladies' garments. Behind the lingerie counter a salesgirl was chewing gum while rearranging piles of jumbled micromesh tights and miniature panties. Directly above her head hung life-size blow-ups of these same garments being modelled by sulking girls in acrobatic postures.

Margery Hambro circled the counter for the third consecutive time. She paused once or twice to finger the bikini briefs like a penniless child at a sweet counter. At the age of thirty-four she felt much too young to be on the wrong side of the deep divide between women who wore panties and women who wore bloomers. She waddled over to the skirt racks to look at the autumn fashions. All the skirts were in the shape of elongated tubes with heavy-duty zips running from waist to crotch. She selected three from the outsize rack and took them into the changing room.

In the neighbouring cubicle two schoolgirls were giggling as they tried on maternity smocks. Margery hung her flowery taffeta dress on the single hook provided and stepped into the largest of the three skirts. She sucked in her stomach, held her breath, and forced the waistband by degrees over her thighs. After some intense manoeuvring she managed to get the waistband over her left hip-bone and part of the corresponding buttock. She was breathing hard and would have liked to rest for a moment on the three-legged stool but could not now bend at the knees.

'Everything all right, Madam?' called an assistant through the curtain.

46

'Fine, thanks.' She gripped the waistband in both fists as though preparing for a judo throw. She closed her eyes to concentrate her mind and gave a sudden upward tug of great force. There came a sound as of an Australian rugby fifteen breaking wind simultaneously in the showers. She found herself holding two jagged strips of beige polyester. Seconds passed before she let out an agonized cry and proceeded to tear the two strips into many smaller ones and stamp on them in her stockinged feet.

Presently she gathered the strips up and set them out on the sales counter like the pieces of a jigsaw. 'I'll take this one.'

'Certainly, Madam.' The assistant's face gave nothing away as she checked the pieces to see that none were missing and folded them in tissue. 'Is it just the one?'

'Yes, the others were too big.'

She took the escalator to the rooftop restaurant and ordered a pot of Darjeeling, two slices of bilberry cheesecake, two milles-feuilles, two pineapple doughnuts, and a side dish of clotted cream.

The waitress re-set the table for two.

Fifteen minutes later, Margery beckoned her once more. 'Same again, love.'

While she was biting into her third pineapple doughnut she reflected again upon the unfairness of life. How could she have developed such an appetite and grown so . . . large in such a short time? Three months ago she was easily capable of clipping her own toenails and of plugging in the Hoover without crawling on all fours. She could even get out of the bath without holding on to the taps. To reassure herself that her memory wasn't playing tricks, she took from her handbag a photograph of herself and Duggie walking arm-in-arm on Southwold beach shortly after their engagement. She looked tanned and slim in a bright summer frock; she was smiling joyfully into Duggie's eyes as he scanned the obituary columns of *The Times*. She must have been happy then, it was written all over her face. Where did it all go wrong, she

47

asked herself as she wiped a smudge of clotted cream off Hambro's trouser leg. And why did she keep stuffing herself with fancy cakes when there wasn't anything to celebrate?

She paid the bill, left the waitress an excessive tip, and took the escalator to what had once been called the basement but was now called the lower ground floor. As though by chance she found herself in the babywear department. She went from counter to counter inspecting the carrycots and bath toys and fluffy hats with names embroidered on the front. Everything seemed so lovely and hygienic. She noticed that pram shades and woollen bootees were on special offer for one week only. She bought two pairs of blue bootees and two pairs of pink and then went back for a carton of disposable nappies.

When Hambro returned home that evening he found her weeping in front of the television. He glanced at the screen expecting to see Humphrey Bogart saying his last farewell to Ingrid Bergman, or the clubbing of baby seals. Instead a rubicund man with a giant rosette pinned to his lapel was complaining volubly about the government's broken promises on fatstock quotas.

'Dearest, you mustn't let these people upset you,' Hambro counselled. 'They'll say anything in the heat of a by-election.'

Margery snorted into a blue tissue, rolled it into a ball, and tossed it into the brass coal scuttle among the many others. 'Oh, Duggie,' she whimpered. 'Oh, Duggie.'

Hambro recoiled at this distasteful familiarization of his name. Why did she persist in addressing him as though he were a domestic pet or a sporting personality? She had never once done that in all her years as his cleaning woman.

'Duggie,' she repeated, 'help me. I need help.'

Hambro felt a stab of panic. Oh no, he thought, she's been stealing prams again. Or shoplifting from the babyfood counter. Why did she keep doing it? The larder was already full to overflowing with miniature tins of beef and tomato purée.

'You haven't been, ah . . . removing things from Mothercare?' He tried not to sound too censorious. After all, she wasn't wholly to blame; that sort of thing ran in her family for three generations on both sides.

'No, honest. I just keep feeling down in the dumps all the time. I been miserable every day this week except Tuesday, or was it Monday, when I nearly won the bingo prize in *Methodist Housewife.*' She held out a hand in supplication. 'Duggie.'

Hambro fidgeted with a loose button on his lambswool cardigan. He felt disconcerted by the outward display of deep emotion. Emotions should be confined to the privacy of one's own soul, not hawked about before the public gaze. It was a precept he himself had always strictly observed, even during his prep-school days on that bleak Northumberland moor. Not once had he blubbered when his monthly food parcel failed to arrive on time or when his teddy bear had been emasculated. Even on the blackest, most traumatic day of his life when, in the confusion of changing trains, he discovered that he had left the pith helmet from his Orwell collection on the Birmingham express, he had waited stoically for the carriage to empty before beating his head in anguish against the antimacassar.

'Why am I like this, Duggie? You should know, you're a professor.'

Hambro puckered his brow in contemplation of the problem. 'It could be your blood-sugar level,' he hypothesized. 'It may have fallen too low since your pomegranate diet.' He gave her a comforting pat on her outstretched arm. 'I'll make you a hot milk drink, that normally bucks you up.' He hurried with relief into the kitchen and began fumbling about with saucepans and chocolate powder. He studied the instructions on the back of the packet with scholarly care, translating the metric measures into imperial equivalents with the aid of pencil and paper. While he was trying to work the kitchen scales the milk boiled over. He mopped it up with a tea-towel depicting a map of French vineyards and started all over again. Twenty minutes later he had succeeded in combining

49

warm milk, sugar, and chocolate powder in their designated proportions and transferred the mixture to a Coronation mug.

He returned to the sitting-room to find Margery kneeling beside the button-back leather chair and stabbing it repeatedly with her crochet needle. 'I'm pretending it's you,' she giggled. 'It's a lovely feeling.' She drove the steel needle in up to her fist. At her side was a tangled skein of soft wool and a knitting pattern for a baby's winter bonnet.

Hambro looked on in deep distress at the sight of white stuffing protruding through the punctures in the dark leather. 'Actually, I'd rather you didn't do that,' he said. 'I'm rather fond of that chair, it was a gift from my wife.'

Margery looked up at him, her cheeks quivering. 'I'm your rotten wife,' she pointed out. 'Me, me, me!' She drove the needle in fiercely with each repetition of the personal pronoun.

'I was referring to my former wife,' Hambro explained. 'That is to say, your immediate predecessor. She bought it to commemorate my appointment to the Chair of Metaphysics. She felt that an actual chair would be an appropriate symbol for the purely figurative one.'

Margery buried her face in the soft leather seat and appeared to be tearing at the buttons with her teeth. Hambro leaned forward and touched her tentatively on the shoulder, as though to inform a passenger on a bus that her hat was on fire.

'Sonia, here is your hot milk drink. It is advisable to drink it before it forms a skin.'

Margery got to her feet with surprising agility. She snatched the mug and flung it inaccurately at a framed photograph of Hambro as a young man sitting outside a Left Bank bistro, next but one to Jean-Paul Sartre. She rushed upstairs, slamming the doors behind her one by one.

Soon the house fell quiet except for the wheedling voice of the by-election candidate now proffering his own solution to the fatstock problem. Hambro unlocked the french windows and went unsteadily down the garden to his outhouse sanctuary. He sat in the semi-darkness waiting for his hands to stop shaking. When he felt able to hold a pen he preoccupied himself with cataloguing the two newest additions to his collection, both from Orwell's period in wartime London: an air-raid warden's whistle, minus the pea, and a discoloured teaspoon to which was attached part of the chain which had once secured it to the zinc counter of the BBC staff canteen. Hambro gave the spoon a stir in an imaginary cup. There was still some controversy over exactly how many sugars Orwell habitually took in his tea. He turned the relic this way and that, half convinced that the evidence needed to settle the issue was staring him in the face.

Before long he felt his concentration wavering. Again and again his thoughts kept returning to the Sonia problem. Through his tiny window he could see her bedside light burning in the master bedroom. What would she be doing – reading the comic strip in *Methodist Housewife*, watching her favourite puppet show on the portable black-and-white set, or knitting more redundant baby clothes? Their marriage, he felt bound to admit, was not a conspicuous success. Perhaps he was partly to blame. Marrying her had certainly not been an easy decision to take, though at the time the choice between mere personal inclination and high moral example seemed clear enough.

He took from the wall a picture of Orwell wearing a battered, tailor-made jacket and smoking a handrolled cigarette. He stared at the ravaged face and into the feverish, all-seeing eyes. 'You at least understand why I did it,' he murmured, as though addressing a priest in a confessional. 'My gesture was a small one compared with the sufferings and humiliations you endured to transcend the class barrier.' He shifted his position in the rickety bentwood chair, thereby dislodging the folded strip of paper wedged beneath its shortest leg. 'The trouble is,' he sighed, 'I seem to have made a serious blunder in that regard. The fact is, my wife appears not to be of pure plebeian stock after all. Although she herself is, or rather was, a cleaning woman, almost all her closest kin, and her father in particular, are somewhat . . . disreputable. Much of their time is spent helping the police with their enquiries.' Orwell's eyes stared back at him, deep-set and judgmental. The thin lips seemed to be biting the flimsy cigarette in two. 'What it amounts to,' Hambro continued, 'is that I appear to have married inadvertently into the lumpenproletariat instead of the working class proper. It's all terribly upsetting. No wonder we're not hitting it off too well.'

He continued discussing his problem late into the night. When he returned to the house the bedroom light was still burning and the television was flickering imageless and silent. Margery was lying face down beneath the covers. A Channel Four booklet on the comparative advantages of breast and bottle feeding lay open on the bedside table. Hambro gave a malarial shudder and put it out of sight.

'Sonia,' he said softly. 'I've been thinking matters over. It might, after all, be advisable for you to seek professional counselling. Perhaps we should try and get to the bottom of your outbursts before the neighbours start complaining.' The hump beneath the eiderdown changed shape, and Hambro found himself addressing it directly. 'That is not to say, of course, that I endorse the claims of psychological medicine. My views on that subject are still the same as those set out in my early monograph, *Freud or Fraud?*'

The bedsprings creaked as the hump dissolved and reconstituted itself in a different form. Hambro stroked it as though it were a much-loved but ailing domestic pet. 'I'll make an appointment for you with the university specialist.' He gave a dry, faintly sceptical laugh that seemed to have been produced by the act of loosening the knot in his Old Etonian tie. 'We shall see whether our famous Dr Hagstrom is all that she's cracked up to be.'

8

Synthesized organ music hummed through the loudspeaker of Radio Free Campus. It soothed the passengers in the lifts and the queues in the refectory and lulled the readers seated among the open stacks of the library. In the crowded bar of the Senior Common Room it went unheard above the whine of drills tunnelling in the basement and the thud of hammers tattooing on the roof. Fine particles of asbestos dust floated through the smoke-filled room. Occasionally, smull lumps of plaster would fall from the ceiling on to the heads of learned science professors, causing them to look up in wonderment at this unsolicited demonstration of the law of gravity. Next to the doctored fruit machine the Probationary Lecturer in Bible Studies was arm-wrestling with the Senior Fellow in Human Relations. One of them accidentally knocked the Regius Professor of Cosmetic Surgery who shifted his arm-chair nearer to the television, put another two coins in the slot, and settled down to watch the final round of *Hernia Can Be Fun*. Nearby, a white-haired woman in a black evening dress was rocking a pin-table gently to and fro while murmuring encouragement to the balls in a foreign tongue. Suddenly, shouts of laughter and rage rose from a far corner of the room where someone's carefully constructed pyramid of empty lager glasses had fallen or been knocked to the floor.

Baxi hurried across with a dustpan and brush to sweep up the broken glass. He had on a short white jacket and a white bow-tie held in place by elastic. On his way back to the bar he was hailed by a bald man in a ginger wig.

'Waiter, another pint of mead and another Bloody Mary. And don't drown it in Worcester Sauce this time.'

'You have to watch that little bugger with the change,'

warned his companion, the Reader in Soil Technology, while Baxi was still in earshot.

The man in the ginger wig brushed asbestos dust from his grey beard. 'Haven't I seen him before somewhere? I recognize those shifty eyes.'

'He used to work in the university car-wash. Before that he ran the candy store in the Dental Centre. He's been a student here for some time.'

Baxi returned bearing the drinks on a round tin tray that he balanced flamboyantly on the tips of his fingers. He swabbed the table with a cloth, emptied the ashtrays, and set the glasses down on clean Chase Manhattan beermats.

'Very kind of you, Sir,' he said, pocketing the meagre tip. Stingy cunt, he thought; serves you right there's no vodka in your Bloody Mary. He went from table to table collecting dirty glasses and eating scraps of damp Scotch egg. Behind one of the vinyl settees the Junior Lecturer in Conveyancing was lying slumped across the comatose body of the Senior Lecturer in Conveyancing. Baxi dragged them as a single entity to a place where they wouldn't get trodden on, noticing as he did so that someone had been sick over the Breathalyzer. He fetched a bucket and cloth and washed it down before resuming his place behind the bar.

From this vantage point he kept an observant eye on the heavy drinkers. Without being seen he made frequent entries on a sheet of graph paper he kept concealed beneath the counter. He had already filled up a dozen similar sheets and was well on his way to accumulating sufficient data to complete his term project for Behavioural Psychology 301. This was provisionally entitled 'Alcoholics in Academe: A Comparative Study of Drunkenness in the Arts and Sciences'. His preliminary findings indicated quite clearly that drunken scientists tended to buckle slowly at the knees as a prelude to collapsing forward on their faces; whereas drunken men and women on the Arts side were prone to rock unsteadily on their heels before toppling backwards on their heads. The next stage of his research was designed to

54

control for statistical differences between beer and spirits drinkers.

There was a sudden commotion behind the jukebox. The Dean of Divinity had overturned his wheelchair while demonstrating a balancing trick on one wheel. When the hubbub had died down, Baxi made another entry under Arts in the Real Ale column. He then made a number of quick computations to test his impressionistic belief that drunkenness in the Applied Sciences was increasing at a faster rate than in the Theoretical Sciences. The evidence certainly pointed to such a trend, though it could have been wholly due to the singleminded efforts of Professor Grogan, Head of Catering Studies.

Baxi continued working on his project between the various calls on his services. He felt quite pleased with its progress; he might even have a chance of winning the Vice-Chancellor's prize for the most original student essay on the life and character of the university. In rare moments of idleness he wondered how he would spend the prize money. Some of it would go on a pair of waterproof shoes and some secondhand underwear. Maybe he'd spend half of it on music; he could have his zither re-strung and buy his Dad a proper saxophone case in place of that tatty old golf bag. He fingered the tufts of brown hair that had begun to grow on his recently-cropped head. Unaccountably, the tufts grew more profusely on one side than the other, suggesting a controlled horticultural experiment with two different fertilizers.

'Baxi,' called a familiar voice from the far end of the room. 'When you've done preening yourself, fetch me a pint of bitter and a whisky chaser before I die of thirst.'

'Right away, Professor Grogan.'

Shortly after midnight he rolled down the metal grille and switched off the Liberace tape. He rinsed out the dirty glasses, vacuumed the floor, locked all the doors and handed in the keys to the campus security police together with the obligatory quarts of stout. Lights were going out in the Hayek hall of residence as he climbed wearily up the eight flights of stairs to Denise's room. Denise was sitting at her desk copying out an essay on Free Trade lent to her by a fourth-year student in exchange for a handful of her underarm shavings. Baxi fell on her bed and closed his eyes.

'You haven't come here just to sleep, have you?' Denise said.

Baxi grunted unintelligibly.

'I thought we were going to fuck,' Denise reminded him.

Baxi arranged himself in the foetal position, hands clamped between his knees. 'I haven't been to the bank yet,' he managed to say. 'I'm going first thing in the morning, after my paper round.'

'Bank? What's the bank got to do with it? I've never charged you for it yet.' Maybe I should start, she thought; I might get a bit more action.

'The University Sperm Bank, Denise. I can't afford to chuck it away, they're paying in dollars now.'

Two floors below, Colin Lumsden was balancing on a chair in the middle of the room. He was endeavouring at the same time to slip a noose over his head. The noose was fashioned from a pair of braces bought for him by his fiancée the very day before she had decided to become his ex-fiancée. They had arrived, gift-wrapped, with a message, 'To Colin, my precious everlasting love,' scribbled on the back of the price tag.

How could she have been so callous? he asked himself once more. Without a word of warning she'd simply run off with one of the building workers who'd given her a wolf-whistle from the scaffolding. She'd even had the nerve to send him a bill for her skin ointment, blaming her impetigo on his rubber sheet. No one had shown him any sympathy or understanding, least of all his mother. 'Don't say I didn't warn you,' she'd exulted. 'You had no business getting engaged to a Sagittarian at this conjuncture. No wonder you've started bedwetting again.' Since his examination fiasco she had refused to speak to him, except to remind him of her wasted outlay on his education. She was furious because she had already won planning permission for an extension to her booth to accommodate a salon in Socio-Economic Forecasting. She reckoned that that was where the future lay.

He tightened the noose around his neck and fastened the other end of the braces to the metal light-fixture, using a granny knot. He gave a couple of sharp tugs to ensure it would take his weight. This time he didn't want any slip-ups. Three days earlier he had drunk half a bottle of ouzo and a full bottle of tequila, exactly as the manual recommended, but had then fallen fast asleep before putting his head inside the plastic bag.

He gave a final glance around the room. All his belongings were packed away in cardboard cartons, except for his pyjamas which were rolled in a damp ball in the waste bin. Propped ostentatiously on the radiator was a sealed envelope containing his last will and testament. This had gone through several drafts before he had settled on the final distribution of his textbooks, his Bing Crosby records and his kidneys.

'Goodbye, crappy old world!' he cried. 'And good riddance!' He kicked the chair aside. The noose tightened around his neck, causing unanticipated pain. His short body revolved first one way, then the other. He found himself being lowered gently down on the end of his elastic braces. As his feet touched the floor he caught sight of himself in the wardrobe mirror: an undersize person with a normal-size head that was now connected to the ceiling by a twisted pair of Young Executive Suspenders.

'Sod it,' he choked, struggling to loosen the painful noose. The suicide manual was lying open on the floor by a box of his personal effects. 'Bloody rubbish!' he yelled, as he swung a foot at it and missed.

Presently he felt hungry. Despite the lateness of the hour he went out and bought faggots, peas and mash from the Medical Centre automat. He ate them in the telephone booth while trying to ring his mother. He had twice tried ringing her earlier in the day to say his last farewell, but on both occasions all the Porthcawl lines were busy because of the World Trade Fair. This time he got through at the second attempt.

'Madame La Casablanca,' cooed a voice.

'Hello, Mummy, it's me.'

'Who?'

'Colin. Your son.'

There was a devastating pause. 'I no longer have a son.'

Lumsden rubbed at the pink weal around his neck. 'Don't be like that, Mummy,' he implored. 'I need to tell you something. It's urgent.'

'Do you wish to tell me that you have now passed Futurology 201? That is the only matter of urgency we have to deal with.'

Lumsden screwed his eyes shut. 'No,' he confessed, 'I haven't felt like studying. You see, I've got this illustrated manual . . .'

'I am not interested in your manual, illustrated or otherwise. I am interested in knowing only that you have resumed your studies.' Her voice took on the sombre tone in which she informed her clients of impending misfortune. 'You are a deep disappointment to your father.'

'Daddy?' Lumsden rarely thought of the gaunt, asthmatic man who had dropped dead while helping him blow out the candles on his birthday cake.

'He was in touch with me last night,' said Madame La Casablanca. 'You are causing him deep unrest. The table shook uncontrollably.'

Lumsden caught sight of his pained face in the small mirror. Did he always look that ugly? The pips went. 'Mummy, listen to me!' he cried. He scrabbled in his pocket for coins but had used them all in the automat. 'This is our last conversation,' he shouted into the dead mouthpiece. That's so typical of her, he thought, as he trudged back across the campus through the night drizzle; she always insists on having the final word.

58

9

Pale winter sunlight filtered through the dormer window, casting slanted beams across the walls and the tiny kneehole desk. On the desk was an open dossier and a reconditioned tape-recorder. Hedda Hagstrom twiddled with a knob and repeated the question.

'When did you start having these dreams?'

Margery Hambro squeezed her podgy fingers one by one, as though counting off the days, weeks or months. 'Not long after I got married. Duggie says it's because I don't eat enough roughage.' She sniffed discordantly, causing the red lights on the tape-recorder to flutter and bounce.

'And you say you often get the feeling your husband despises you, looks down on you. What exactly does he do to make you feel that?'

'In my dreams, you mean?'

'In your waking state, Mrs Hambro.'

Margery pushed the heel of her left shoe off with the toe of her right and scratched her foot on the sisal matting. Her initial nervousness had passed and she was beginning to relax. Just talking to someone was already making her feel better. 'Oh, it's just little things really. Nothing very much.'

'Such as?' Hedda Hagstrom persisted. She was holding her silver propelling pencil like a hypodermic syringe.

Margery felt slightly foolish having to give examples; she was probably making a fuss about nothing. 'Well, like always sitting in the back seat of the car whenever I drive him anywhere. Or getting me to use the tradesman's entrance instead of the front door. Silly little things like that.'

While Margery spoke, Hedda Hagstrom constantly nodded at her in encouragement, like a television reporter interviewing a shop steward. 'Anything else? It's all in the strictest confidence, of course.'

Margery shifted her thighs on the slatted chair. Next time, she decided, she would bring her own cushion. 'Yes, there is one thing. What really gets my goat is when he calls me Sonia.'

Hedda Hagstrom turned the pages of the dossier. 'Sonia? Was that his first wife?'

'No, he calls his first wife Eileen. I don't know what her real name was.'

'But why does he call her Eileen?'

'Because that was the name of George Orwell's first wife. And Sonia was the name of his second.'

Hedda Hagstrom's eyes glazed over with incomprehension. 'What?'

'Duggie's one of them Orwell freaks you read about,' Margery explained. 'He worships his memory. He spends all his time collecting stuff about him.' She wasn't allowed in the outhouse but she'd peeped through the window once or twice at all the junk laid out on the shelves like in a museum. The whole place needed a good dusting. 'He's gone up to Sotheby's today,' she revealed, 'to bid for a Burmese policeman's truncheon.'

Hedda Hagstrom ceased nodding her head and shook it in disbelief. So that's what he gets up to; no wonder he's always sending apologies for absence to the Illiteracy Subcommittee. Wait till the Vice-Chancellor hears about this.

'That's the main reason why he married me,' Margery went on. 'He said he was following in George Orwell's footsteps by dropping into the lower classes. He said he was too old to go down a coal mine or fight in a revolution, so he proposed to me instead while I was doing the front step. He said I was the lowest-class person he knew.' She smiled shyly. 'I was ever so chuffed. It's not every charlady who gets the chance to marry an educated professor, even one as old as Duggie.'

It seemed such a long time ago that he'd courted her with

60

bunches of cut flowers and chocolate brazils. He used to explain to her the difference between Oppidans and Collegers, and read bits aloud from *Animal Farm* while she cleaned the cooker. Those were the good times, she thought wistfully, especially the week they'd spent on honeymoon picking hops in Kent. 'He liked teaching me about things then,' she continued. 'He used to show me how to warm his claret for him and how to eat grapes with a knife and how to sit with my knees together when visitors called. It's really all down to Duggie that I don't drop my aitches no more or sing when I'm pegging out the clothes.' She stopped and looked abashed, conscious that she'd been jabbering on.

Hedda Hagstrom was busy making notes on a jumbo pad. Margery gazed admiringly at her fine features and platinum blonde hair tied in a single plait with a black velvet bow on the end. Lucky devil, she thought; fancy being clever and beautiful. She must be very content with life.

The morning sunlight had faded from the room. Heavy clouds moved above the skylight and presently snowflakes began to fall on it and melt. The temperature was required to drop another two degrees Fahrenheit before the heating came on. Margery gave a little start as the tape-recorder clunked.

'Good,' Hedda Hagstrom said. 'We're making progress.' She ejected the tape, labelled it, and inserted a new one. Her finger hovered above the record button. 'Margery? Is it all right if I call you Margery?'

'It's better than Sonia.'

'Margery, could we go back to something you mentioned at the very beginning?' She flicked through her notes. 'Here it is. You said you had a habit of baby-snatching. It might have a bearing on the case.'

Margery waved her hand in disavowal. 'Not baby-snatching. Pram snatching.'

Hedda Hagstrom smiled benignly. 'If that's the expression you prefer. It amounts to the same thing.' Foolish woman, she thought.

61

'I've never gone off with a pram with a baby in it,' Margery said defensively. 'Though one I took from outside Woolworth's once did have a toy golliwog in.'

Hedda Hagstrom stared at her across the narrow desk. 'How extraordinary. What exactly is the point of stealing empty prams? Empty cars, I could understand. Occupied prams would make some sense . . .'

Margery was beginning to show signs of agitation. She twisted strands of her straw-coloured hair between her fingers and chewed the ends. 'I been taking baby clothes too,' she confessed. 'The chest of drawers is full of them. Duggie's always complaining that there's no room for his thermal underwear.'

'Baby clothes?' This was getting ridiculous. 'But you're not pregnant? Are you?' Hedda Hagstrom consulted her notes, wondering whether she had overlooked some vital piece of information. The woman certainly looked as though she might be pregnant. Could it be that her husband was too mean to buy the necessary things? She scribbled a note on her pad: 'Overspending at Sotheby's?'

'I'm not in the family way,' Margery said in a curiously strangled voice. Her entire body was shaking. 'I never have been. Never, never, never, never, never.' She slapped the desk hard with each utterance.

Hedda Hagstrom drew back in alarm. My God, she thought, the woman's gone off her head. Would she turn violent, like that student in Farm Management who had demanded an instant cure for his agoraphobia? 'Please try and keep calm,' she counselled. She poured a beaker of water from a dusty carafe and pushed it nervously across the table. While Margery was sipping it she retreated to the window. It had stopped snowing but the window was pock-marked with melted flakes. Through the blurred glass she could see a yellow bulldozer pushing along a growing mound of rubble watched by three men in dark suits and gumboots. From somewhere in the direction of the mosque came the jangling clatter of scaffolding being dismantled or assembled. She stood at the window for some

62

time, her hands clasped behind her back, pondering the complexities of her latest case. Why on earth would a childless woman go to such lengths to accumulate prams and babywear? It flew in the face of all common sense. A thought suddenly occurred to her. She traced a symmetrical pattern on the sisal matting with her heel. 'Tell me, Margery,' she said thoughtfully, 'this obsession you have with baby things – is it shared by your husband?'

Margery made a sound at the back of her throat like a fizzy drinks can being opened. 'What, Duggie? Are you kidding? He hates babies. He can't abide children of any age. He says they're like machines that keep going wrong, except you can't send them back to be repaired.'

Hedda Hagstrom's pale blue eyes narrowed with interest. 'Really? I wish you'd told me that before. It puts a new perspective on the case.' Why did she always have to wrench these important facts from her clients, she wondered. It was as though they were deliberately out to test her diagnostic powers. She walked around and around the small room, deep in thought. Suddenly she stopped and turned.

'Have you discussed with your husband the possibility of starting a family?'

'Hundreds of times.'

'And how does he react? Think carefully before you answer, this is very important.'

'He gets all shirty.'

'You mean he gets aggressive? Does he strike you or throw the furniture about?

Margery considered the question. 'Well, the last time I mentioned it he turned his chair to face the wall and ate his dinner off his lap. The time before that he shut himself in the lavatory and refused to come out until Gardeners' Question Time.'

Hedda Hagstrom nodded in self-confirmation. 'Just as I thought. The root of the problem lies not in you but in your husband. He's suffering from what is technically known as a Repressed Paternity Syndrome.'

Margery's hand flew to her throat. 'Is that like cancer?'

'No, no. What it means is that Dugg . . . your husband has a deep-seated longing for a child, possibly a son and heir, though he won't admit it, even to himself. That's why he's fixated on this Orwell person. Don't you see, Margery, he's symbolically adopted Orwell as his son. It's a form of compensation for not having the child of his own that he really wants. Nothing could be clearer.'

Margery frowned in consternation. 'I don't get it. If he wants a kid so badly why does he go up the wall if I even so much as mention it?'

An enigmatic smile played at the corners of Hedda Hagstrom's mouth. 'The human personality is a very complicated mechanism. It's a well-established psychological fact that people profess to hate the very thing they most desire. The more they want it, the louder they deny it.'

Margery allowed this intelligence to sink in. 'Does that mean when Duggie moans at me for saying my prayers aloud in bed it's because he really wants me to?'

'Possibly.' Hedda Hagstrom hunched her shoulders defensively. 'I'm not suggesting that everyone always says the opposite of what they mean. I don't, for example. I always say exactly what I mean.'

'But how can I tell, then, if someone's speaking the truth or not?'

Hedda Hagstrom gave a laugh like the cry of an exotic bird. 'I'm afraid you can't, Margery. You have to leave that to the experts. Just imagine, if people like you could understand the mysteries of the psyche, there'd be no need for people like me.' She glanced down at the gold Rolex suspended upside down on the lapel of her white coat. Eleven forty-eight already, and she still had three more cases to attend to, including that of the newly-appointed Professor of Jurisprudence who believed he was a werewolf.

'Good. That's all settled then.' She closed Margery's dossier with a flourish. 'My advice is to start a family right away.

Never mind what your husband *says*, it's what he *wants* that
counts. As soon as his problem has been solved you'll find
that yours will clear up too. That's how these things work.'
She opened a drawer in her desk and took out a bundle of
illustrated manuals fastened by a rubber band. 'Take one of
these, it'll show you the most reliable methods of conception.
They've all been tested in my lab on student volunteers.'
From a different drawer she took out a prescription pad and
scribbled what appeared to be a brief description of Knossos
written in Linear B. 'This is for the new fertility drug.
It practically guarantees twins.' She pressed the buzzer to
summon the next case. 'By the way, you'd better start attend-
ing my Emancipation Workshop on Thursday afternoons.
It's specially intended for women like you with husbands like
yours.'

10

A strong north-easterly wind had been blowing across
the campus for several days. It sent tiles flying off the
new roof of Senate House on to the piazza and covered
walkways. It blew away the Dean of Divinity's invalid car
while the Dean was in the middle of a three-point turn.
At night it howled in the scaffolding around the minaret
like the wind in an early horror movie. It rattled windows,
slammed doors, scattered religious tracts and blew cartons
of milk off the high windowsills of the Hayek hall of
residence.

The Vice-Chancellor was forcing his body through the gale
as he stumbled across the heavy clay. He kept both hands
clamped to his white steel hat, partly obscuring the letters
VC painted in vermilion day-glo on the front, back and
sides. 'The Philosophy accounts are still very disappointing,
Hambro,' he bellowed, barely troubling to conceal his lack

of disappointment. 'You're going to be in the red again.'

Hambro scurried along in his wake. He kept falling further and further behind because of his short legs and his preference for circumventing rather than leaping over ditches and frozen puddles. 'We are doing all we possibly can,' he called out to the Vice-Chancellor who was unsuccessfully trying to vault a low concrete wall. 'I've even had young Skillicorn parading up and down the shopping arcade in sandwich boards.'

The Vice-Chancellor's face registered surprise at this unexpected display of enterprise. 'Any results?' He sat astride the wall detaching the seat of his tracksuit trousers from barbed wire.

'He was arrested for knocking down the Christmas decorations.'

The Vice-Chancellor hurried on and then waited impatiently for Hambro to catch up. Just look at him, he thought, tiptoeing along in his galoshes, plucking his trousers up at the knees like some old tart afraid of a bit of mud. What he needs is a good long stint in the university allotments. Hambro arrived mopping his face with the large white linen handkerchief that he habitually wore in his sleeve. His deerstalker hat had been blown off several times and on one occasion he had been forced to stamp on it to catch it. The two men stood together on the same unsteady plank as a huge and mysterious yellow machine trundled across their path.

'I've been doing some hard thinking,' the Vice-Chancellor coughed through the diesel fumes. 'About the problems of Philosophy.'

Hambro looked at him in amazement. 'Really? Hm. Perhaps we could persuade you to give a paper at our seminar next Tuesday? Skillicorn was due to give one, but now that he's in custody . . .'

'I don't mean thinking about it in that sense. I mean from the promotional angle. It seems to me there's one last possibility for you to try.'

66

He waited until Hambro finally said, 'Yes, Vice-Chancellor?'

'A shop.'

The word was blown away by the north-east wind and had to be repeated. Hambro tried it on his own lips. 'Shop.' His bushy eyebrows joined in the middle and moved about like a furry caterpillar crawling across his forehead.

'The university owns a small commercial property in Tozer Place. You could take over the basement. It'll need a lick of paint and some disinfectant. It was where Dr Hagstrom used to breed her rats before the Animal Liberation mob set them free.'

Hambro edged his way gingerly between metal drums with 'Danger' stencilled on the sides beneath a skull and crossbones. 'A shop, in Tozer Place? But surely that's the red-light district?'

The Vice-Chancellor nodded as best he could while gripping his protective headgear like a man suffering an attack of migraine. 'Yes, it's a prime site. You need to be in the thick of things, obviously. It's no good being stuck out in the suburbs, is it?' Silly old prat, he thought, he hasn't got a clue about property values. That little shop was a first-class commercial proposition; or would have been if it weren't such a fire hazard. 'This really is your last chance, Hambro,' he called out as he clambered up a mound of building rubble and slithered down the other side on all fours. 'You've had every opportunity. If you bungle this one it'll be curtains for Philosophy.' And all who sail in her, he added gleefully to himself.

The two men parted company at the fenced-off artificial lake. Hambro turned left at a walkway leading to the library where, trapped between a mobile cement mixer and a violent mechanical digger, he realized with dismay that he had again failed to raise the awkward question of relinquishing his appointment as Dean of Faculties. The Vice-Chancellor turned right and made his way briskly around the perimeter of the lake. Thin ice had formed over three-quarters of the surface, confining the grebe, coot and mallard to one small corner where they circled and bobbed among the bulrushes and submerged bedsteads. None of these living or inanimate objects was observed by the Vice-Chancellor as, with head bent low, he followed the wire fence all the way round to the treacherous steps of Admin II.

Inside his office, he at once changed into satin shorts and matching singlet and began pedalling ferociously on the exercise bicycle. When the timer buzzed he climbed into the rowing machine and willed his arms and legs to bear unendurable pain. Afterwards, he took a cold shower and a sauna in the adjoining room which had, until recently, been his secretary's office.

He now sat at his desk examining his diary and shaking with exhaustion. At eleven o'clock he had a meeting with the Arts Faculty mullahs to discuss their revised proposals for library censorship; at twelve-fifteen he was due to receive a delegation from the Students Under Canvas Action Committee about the loss of accommodation in the recent gales; and at four-thirty he was chairing a forum sponsored by the local Junior Chamber of Commerce on the subject of 'Opportunities for the Small Investor in the Modern University'. Not too bad a day, he thought, as he picked his nose with two fingers.

Presently he summoned his secretary on the intercom. Miss Pollins emerged from the cubbyhole that now served as her office, shielding her eyes from the light. Before she had a chance to cover her knees with her skirt the Vice-Chancellor started dictating.

'Letter to the Department of Anglo-European Literature, University of Texas. Dear Professor Ichikawa, Further to yours of the fourteenth, blah, blah, blah . . . I am delighted to report that the University Senate has now formally consented to the sale of our entire collection of Jane Austen papers, including her unpublished novel on the condition of landless labourers in Thanet, and her recently discovered love sonnets to the Duke of Wellington. I look forward to receiving your banker's draft for the agreed sum (US dollars) in early course. New paragraph.

'It may interest you to know that we shall shortly be auctioning some of our rare historical documents. Among these we include the Treaty of Brest-Litovsk and the wartime diaries of Attila the Hun (27 Vols.). These diaries were fully authenticated by members of our own History department shortly before it was closed down. Please let me know if you would like a copy of our December sales catalogue. We at Consolidated Tractor Fuels are always pleased to . . .'

Miss Pollins coughed discreetly.

'We at this university are always pleased to . . . blah, blah, blah.' He swivelled in his swivel chair and turned his mind to the next item. 'Memo to the Head of Catering Studies, copy to the infirmary. Dear Professor Grogan, Further to the epidemic of amoebic dysentery among your third-year students . . .'

Baxi turned over in his sleep. He was ambling across a sunlit quadrangle with books under his arm and a bottle of Moët et Chandon raised to his lips. The choir was practising in the cloisters. Their purified voices echoed around the ancient stones, rising, rising, up to the gilded spires and the lark-embracing sky. The sun sparkled on the fountains tinkling in the middle of the lawn. He lay on the manicured grass and opened a slim volume of verse. Presently he closed his eyes and thought about lunch. Should he have fresh lobster at that agreeable little trattoria overlooking the river? The waiters always pampered him there. Or should he get the college scout to bring smoked salmon and wild strawberries and a bottle of hock to his rooms? After lunch he would punt upriver and then meet his tutor for a game of croquet. He smoothed his hand across the grass. The sun's honeyed rays caressed his brow and warmed his body though his cream silk shirt.

His alarm clock seemed to explode. He sat up with a jolt and stared into the darkness. It took him a little while to find his matches and light the kerosene lamp. He dressed quickly, lying on his back, and hurried off to scrub out the guard-dog kennels before starting on his paper round.

11

Shortly after breakfast Hambro discovered his wife sitting naked in an empty bath. Her legs were splayed out, dangling over the rim, and the magnifying side of his shaving mirror was propped between her thighs. Before he could ask if the waterpipes were frozen or the bathplug was malfunctioning, she said, 'Look, Duggie, I'm learning all about my body. These are my *labia minora* and these are my *labia majora*.' Her plump fingers pulled at the delicate folds like an Italian housewife attempting tortellini for the first time.

Hambro looked away, frowning in disapproval at this unauthorized use of his shaving mirror. He opened the bathroom cabinet and checked that his cut-throat razor, shaving brush and bowl, and medicated soap were in their proper place. 'Are you likely to be doing . . . that much longer?' he enquired. 'I should quite like to use the bath for its intended function.' He took off his belted dressing gown and hung it behind the door. Despite the electric wall-heater he was shivering inside his flannelette pyjamas.

'We can bath together,' Margery suggested. 'We never done that yet.'

Hambro made a face as though having been offered a bottle of British wine. 'Bathing is a private activity. We are not rugby footballers or Japanese.' Whatever will she think of next, he wondered. Using the same toothbrush? Sharing the same newspaper?

'We ought to bath together,' Margery persisted. 'Dr Hagstrom says so. She says it's the best place to do the exploring.'

'Exploring?'

70

'Exploring each other's bodies. It's all part of my therapy. You can read about it in her booklet.' She pointed to the illustrated manual propped open behind the mixer taps. Hambro glanced at it and retreated quickly to the master bedroom. Why, he asked himself as he fiddled with the double bow on his pyjama cord, had she begun to behave in this extraordinary fashion? The day before yesterday he had told her in the clearest possible language how much he disliked her new snakeskin hat only to discover her, that very same evening, wearing it in bed. Worst of all, she had started asking him highly personal questions. She wanted to know if he was Rhesus negative, and whether there was any history of congenital madness or deformity in his family. Soon, no doubt, she would be demanding to know his salary or the contents of his will. Now, at this very moment, she was sitting in a state of complete undress in an empty bath and reciting Latin in a cockney accent. 'Frankly,' he muttered aloud to his reflection in the wardrobe mirror, 'if this is part of her cure, I much prefer the malady.'

Margery came in while he was fastening his Brasenose sock-suspenders. She was wearing a loose smock in primary colours that on someone else might have looked vaguely exotic. For a moment Hambro had a terrible feeling that she was about to dance around the room. Instead, she handed him a paint manufacturer's colour-chart and said, 'I'm thinking of painting the nursery. What about Caribbean Dawn for the walls and Pimento for the woodwork?'

Hambro laid the chart aside and tucked his shirt inside his underpants. 'Sonia, we have no nursery, nor any need of one,' he said with weary reasonableness.

Margery sidled up to him and took his hand. 'Duggie,' she purred, 'the reason we don't need a nursery is because you don't want us to have a baby. Am I right?'

'That was my line of reasoning. I see no obvious logical flaw in it.'

Margery squeezed his hand very gently in her own. 'How badly don't you want a son and heir?'

71

'I beg your pardon?'

'I mean do you just sort of dislike the thought of it, same as you dislike it when I cry with my mouth full? Or do you really *hate* the thought of it?'

With his free hand Hambro fastened his Brasenose tiepin. 'It is not the thought so much as the actuality that is the object of my revulsion. You know this perfectly well. Why must you keep asking?'

Margery nestled against him. 'I just like to hear you say it. Specially when you get so stroppy.' Thank the Lord he hasn't changed his mind, she thought, as she waved him goodbye from the garden gate. Poor old Duggie, fancy suffering from a frustrated paternity thingummy all these years. No wonder he always looks so miserable.

Hambro was so distracted by the morning's events that it was not until he was paying his fare on the bus to Tozer Place that he realized he had forgotten his galoshes. It was going to be one of those days, he knew, when he stepped off the bus into a puddle.

Tozer Place was the middle bar of an E-shaped cluster of streets that ran between the old chest clinic and the new asbestos factory. Above the streets, in a zig-zag pattern, hung faded bunting in patriotic colours. Most of the original iron lamp-posts had been preserved. Some of these had wire baskets of plastic ivy suspended from the crossbar and from others hung Coronation portraits or official notices urging members of the public to curb their dogs and beware of pickpockets. Neon signs flickered weakly in the mid-morning light. A few solitary men wandered up and down glancing sideways at display boards featuring oiled male torsos, triple-decker hamburgers, and disembodied female breasts. Girls in sequinned tights chatted on the corners in twos and threes or watched their washing revolve in the laundromat.

Hambro hurried past them. He kept his eyes fixed ahead and his hand on his wallet. As on both his previous visits he overshot his destination and had to retrace his steps. Number 18b was a narrow doorway between a Mexican take-away and a vegetarian advice centre. Above the opening was an illuminated glass sign saying B NGKOK PLEAS RE PAL CE. Hambro crossed the threshold and crept down the bare passage. Half-way along his way was barred by a young Maltese or Cypriot sitting by a bead curtain. He seemed to be manicuring his nails with a penknife. 'Twenty-two pounds,' he said lethargically. 'Including one free alcoholic drink.'

Hambro coughed and pointed to the basement stairs at the end of the passageway. 'Philosophy,' he said. 'I am Head of Department.' He showed the man his campus security pass and library ticket. 'We've been through all this before.' The last time he had been obliged to pay and was then refused a refund by the Senate Subcommittee on Wages and Conditions.

The man eyed him warily before initiating a shouted conversation in Maltese or Greek with someone on the other side of the bead curtain. 'Okay,' he said reluctantly, with a circular wave of his penknife.

Hambro picked his way down the stone cellar steps as if each one might be booby-trapped. The time before he had missed his footing while trying to decipher the foreign graffiti. Now, as on both previous visits, he struggled to open the heavy wooden door at the foot of the stairs before working out that it had to be pulled and not pushed.

Skillicorn had finished whitewashing the brick walls and was stripping multiple layers of paint off a kitchen table with an electrical apparatus. The air was heavy with fumes. Tea chests containing books and learned journals and university enrolment forms were stacked haphazardly among abandoned rat cages. In one corner stood a blackboard and easel and a plaster bust of Nietzsche, the ear of which had been successfully, though visibly, restored with superglue.

Skillicorn switched off the paint-stripper. 'Hello, Sir. It's all coming along splendidly.' His boyish face beamed with inexplicable pleasure beneath the flecks of dried whitewash. 'The signwriter's due after lunch. I think you'll approve of the colour scheme.' He wiped his hands on an enrolment form and took a folded sheet of drawing paper from the pocket of his dungarees. The dungarees were short in the leg, making his own legs appear even more giraffe-like. He unfolded the drawing paper and spread it flat on the kitchen table. It showed a sketch of a sign in Gothic lettering saying THE MIND SHOP.

'It looks terrific, don't you think?' Skillicorn enthused.

Hambro grunted non-commitally. 'It is preferable to the coloured light-bulbs favoured by the Vice-Chancellor,' he conceded. He poked about in the dingy basement rooms, peering into cobwebbed alcoves containing nothing but stale rat droppings. Daylight drifted in like smoke through the pavement window directly overhead. Clop clop, clop clop, went the passing feet which could be seen as well as heard through the reinforced glass. Hambro felt a strange melancholy descend upon him at the thought that, from this vantage point, he could see up the ladies' skirts if the glass were a little cleaner and if his eyes were a little stronger and if he still cared what he might see if they were.

Skillicorn's choirboy voice interrupted his thoughts. 'I was wondering, Sir,' he said, as he brushed bits of dried paint from his hair. 'Would it be possible to get washroom and toilet facilities installed? It's a bus-ride to the nearest gents.'

Hambro drew in breath between pursed lips. 'There is no provision for such amenities in our budget. The Vice-Chancellor refuses to sanction expenditure on frills of any kind. It was only by the slenderest of margins that the Senate voted to allow us the use of a blackboard and easel. The decision would almost certainly have gone the other way if the Dean of Divinity had been awake during the final recount.'

Skillicorn took off his dungarees and draped them over the bust of Nietzsche. 'As it happens,' he piped, 'the people upstairs have been very understanding. I've been using their facilities.'

'The Bangkok Pleasure Palace? How very neighbourly.'

Skillicorn's ears flushed a darker shade of pink. 'The trouble is, it's working out a bit expensive.'

'You mean there's a coin-slot on the door?' How typical of the times, thought Hambro.

'Not exactly a coin-slot. You see, you can't simply take a bath or shower. There's a compulsory sauna and massage too. It's twenty-two pounds a time, though you do get one complimentary drink and a ten per cent discount for the Peekaboo.'

The two philosophers continued mulling over the ablutions problem while eating lunch at a nearby hot-dog stall. 'Perhaps we could come to some reciprocal arrangement with the upstairs people,' Hambro suggested. He was trying to direct ketchup from the plastic tomato on to his hot-dog. Each time he squeezed it it sighed and spluttered.

Skillicorn moved discreetly out of the line of fire. 'Yes, we could offer them a cash discount on certain of our courses. Ten per cent seems to be the local rate. Or,' he went on excitedly, 'we could allow their girls access to our books and periodicals. They seem to spend a lot of time sitting around looking bored.'

'Yes,' Hambro agreed. 'Provided they don't read them in the bath.'

They continued discussing the finer points of the proposal as they strolled back to their new premises. The signwriter was already at work at the top of a ladder. He had sketched a chalk outline of the lettering on the fascia and was now painting the first Gothic character. Below him, men in raincoats, marines from the visiting Soviet warship and young women in fishnet stockings were watching with interest and speculating on the nature of the services soon to be available.

'The Mind Shop?' said the proprietor of the vegetarian advice centre to a short-order cook from the steak house. 'I expect it's something to do with drugs. I knew it would happen as soon as they legalized LSD. It's going to spoil the neighbourhood.'

Hambro turned to Skillicorn in astonishment. 'Did you hear that? I should have thought the name was self-explanatory.' He gave a quick smirk of derision. 'You can guess, of course, what the Vice-Chancellor wanted to call it.'

'Plato's Place?'

'Thinkerama.'

They spent most of the afternoon putting up shelves and arranging books according to the Dewey decimal system. Hambro found the physical work exhausting and fell asleep on the bus home. He was shaken awake by the conductress when they reached the terminus and charged an additional sixty pence. He had to wait forty-five minutes for the bus back.

His wife was just hanging up the phone in the hall as he opened the front door. 'That was my dad,' she informed him. 'He wants to come and stay with us for a bit. I said you wouldn't mind.'

Hambro went straight through to the living-room without removing his coat and slumped in his perforated armchair. 'Your father? I thought he was in Pentonville. He hasn't escaped again?'

Margery sniffed indignantly. ''Course he hasn't escaped. He's on parole. In any case, it wasn't Pentonville, it was Reading.'

Hambro's bushy eyebrows locked in puzzlement, as though he was attempting to master the instructions on the back of a packet of fuse-wire. 'Then it must have been Pentonville just prior to Reading?'

'No it was not. It was Durham before Reading. My dad's never been in rotten Pentonville,' she added crossly. 'I wish you wouldn't keep talking as though he had.'

12

A spray of fine misty rain was falling over Hampstead. The heath was deserted except for a pensioner walking his three-legged dog and an elderly lady jogger taking tiny strides across the wet slopes. The dog yapped at her heels as she crossed the asphalt path and headed for the gates leading out of the heath into Parliament Hill. She turned left at Hampstead Heath Station and trotted into South End Green, paying no attention to the dapper little man in galoshes who was balancing on the steps of the ornate Victorian drinking fountain. The man was holding a pair of field glasses trained on the building opposite. This was a tall, redbrick building divided into flats above a double-fronted shop. There were no faces at any of the windows nor any sign of movement inside.

The window that was of particular interest to Hambro had a grey blanket nailed or pinned across the lower half and old newspapers stuffed in the gaps around the frame. He wiped rain off the field glasses, sharpened the focus, and tried to read the date on the newspaper. All he could make out was a football score: Liverpool 0 Yeovil 5. The flaked green paint on the window-frames looked as though it had not been touched since Orwell's day. This was the room he had lived in in the mid-1930s, above the famous bookshop. From the high window he would have been able to see across the heath and to gaze down at the drinking fountain upon whose steps Hambro was now precariously perched. Imagine, he thought, it was in that very room that *Keep the Aspidistra Flying* had been conceived and largely written! His eyes misted over with emotion. For a moment he fancied he could hear the clack, clack, clack of that ceaseless typewriter above the roar of the London buses . . .

Presently he crossed the road into Pond Street and stood transfixed outside the corner shop, easily the most celebrated bookshop in the history of English letters. The door was ajar and Hambro allowed his fingers to caress the blistered paint beneath the brass handle. A small flake fell away under his touch. He retrieved it intact off the pavement and wrapped it protectively in his white linen handkerchief like a forensic expert at the scene of a crime. In his eagerness he inadvertently stepped forward on to the rubber mat at the entrance to the shop, causing a bell inside to ring.

A shop assistant materialized from somewhere in the interior gloom. 'You'll have to be quick,' she said. 'It's early closing.'

Hambro hid his handkerchief behind his back like a schoolboy caught smoking in the lavatory. 'Yes, I'm looking for a book,' he said, flustered. 'A secondhand copy of ah, um, Fowler's *Modern English Usage*. It's a present for my wife.'

The girl looked at him unblinkingly. 'Fowler's what? This is a chemist's.'

Hambro stared around him in confusion at the shelves of nasal decongestant, facial hair removers, and denture fixatives. There was not a secondhand book to be seen. 'I'll take a bottle of shampoo,' he said in desperation.

'What kind?'

'Kind?'

'Dry, greasy, or flyaway?'

He ran an exploratory hand over his shining dome fringed with grey down. 'Do you perhaps have one for dandruff? More correctly, against dandruff?'

The girl handed him a dark green bottle shaped like an hour-glass. He thought he recognized it from a current television commercial featuring two hirsute rivals, one of whom married the pretty blonde. 'Actually, a small bottle will suffice.'

'That is a small bottle. One pound seventy pee.'

Hambro looked at the girl over the top of his spectacles. 'No, this is a large bottle. The word large appears unambiguously on the label.'

The girl gave a sigh as if, at that moment, the pointlessness of the entire human enterprise had dramatically been revealed to her. 'It comes in three sizes, large, mammoth, and family. The large one is the small one. One pound seventy pee.'

Hambro pocketed his change along with his handkerchief. On the way out he turned for a final look at the hallowed walls, just as the girl switched off the lights.

78

He returned on the early afternoon coach from Victoria and took a taxi from the bus station to the Mind Shop.

'The what shop?' asked the taxi driver, consulting his little black book.

'The Bangkok Pleasure Palace will do.'

Skillicorn was outside pinning hand-painted posters on a revolving display board. Swinging above his head, from the first-floor premises, was an inflated life-size rubber doll. He unrolled a poster and fastened it to the board. It read:

PHILOSOPHICAL PROBLEMS SOLVED WHILE-U-WAIT
AN APPOINTMENT IS NOT ALWAYS NECESSARY

A sudden gust of wind lifted the rubber doll to a horizontal position and simultaneously swung the display round to reveal a second message:

MORAL UNCERTAINTIES? ETHICAL DILEMMAS?
COME TO THE MIND SHOP — AVOID THE METAPHYSICAL COWBOYS

Skillicorn stood back to judge the effect of his handiwork. He had to dip his head quickly as the rubber doll swung towards him feet first as though it knew what it was doing. 'Ah, there you are, Sir,' he said, as Hambro approached holding a dark green bottle shaped like an hour-glass. 'The leaflets arrived this morning.' He passed his Head of Department a sheet of recycled paper printed on both sides in smudgy ink. 'I'm afraid it's full of mistakes. They've misspelled "deontological" and they've quoted the wrong fee for the evening class on Existentialism for the Handyman.'

He tore the wrapping off a bundle of leaflets and divided them in two. 'Shouldn't we be making a start, Sir? I rather thought you'd be here lunchtime, as we'd arranged.' There was the faintest trace of reproach in his voice.

Hambro made an apologetic face. 'I had a matter of some importance to attend to in London. In the Hampstead area to be precise.' He gave the shampoo bottle a little shake, as

79

the instructions on the back recommended. 'It was something I've been meaning to do for a very long time.'

They each took a bundle of leaflets and began handing them out on opposite sides of the street. Hambro paraded listlessly up and down repeating in a dismal monotone, 'All you wanted to know about Hegelianism but were afraid to ask.' Now and then he paused and felt in his coat pocket to make certain that his handkerchief was still in it. In one brief moment of panic he felt compelled to take it out and reassure himself of the safety of its contents as well as to remind himself of his life's ultimate purpose.

On the other side of the street Skillicorn was engaged in argument with a man in a butcher's apron. Hambro watched his junior lecturer flapping his long arms and jerking his knees in excitement as he expounded his views of the fact/value distinction before a gathering crowd. Was I as keen as that at his age? he asked himself as he thrust a leaflet into the hands of a passing belly dancer. His thoughts went back to those early days at Oxford and Princeton; he had certainly written monographs and learned articles and attended conferences in foreign places at somebody else's expense. He could even vaguely remember discussing the Negation of the Negation with his wife during one of their nature walks in the New Forest. Wasn't that the occasion on which she had first heard celestial voices? Or was that in the thunderstorm on the Norfolk Broads? No, it couldn't have been Norfolk, that was when she was still going through her Menshevik phase . . .

He was startled into the present by a knuckled hand tapping on his shoulder. He turned to see a towering man dressed in a bright blue suit with spangles. 'Okay, squire,' the man said. 'Sign me up for Tuesdays at three.' He stabbed his leaflet with a ringed finger, causing his bracelets to jangle.

Hambro tried not to manifest surprise. 'By all means. A very discerning choice, if I may say so.' He handed the man an enrolment form. 'Have you by any chance read the

Critique of Pure Reason? You'll find it useful background material.'

As if by way of response, the man produced a thick roll of banknotes secured by a rubber band. 'How much?' He peeled off two in readiness.

Hambro recoiled. 'Fees are payable to the university registry.' He drew the student's attention to the small print at the foot of the enrolment form. 'Please remember to bring your own notebook, pen and ruler. Gowns, of course, are no longer compulsory.'

Within the space of an hour he enrolled a dozen more prospective students for the course on Tuesdays at three. 'There's a remarkable revival of interest in Kantianism,' he observed to Skillicorn as they later stood in line for lunch at the pie-and-eel stall. 'Do you think it's anything to do with Bulkowski's latest monograph?' Perhaps I should have read it, after all, he thought.

Skillicorn ran his finger down the closely printed leaflet. 'Tuesdays 3 p.m.,' he read aloud. 'The Mysteries of Kant Unveiled.' His normally open face closed into a frown. 'Those blasted printers,' he squeaked in complaint. 'Look how they've spelled Kant.'

13

Margery Hambro took the thermometer from her mouth, shook it in the way the nurses always did in the hospital soap operas, and held it to the light. Her heart pumped with excitement when she read the temperature – 98.9. That was her ovulation peak according to the daily chart she kept hidden inside her pillowcase with the chocolate brazils. She formed a mental picture of a tiny egg nestling inside her, waiting for the kiss of life from one of Duggie's wriggling tadpoles. She rushed downstairs and telephoned a taxi.

Ten minutes later she was speeding up the hill towards the university. Hurry, hurry, she urged the driver silently, before my temperature starts to drop. As she examined the boils on the back of the driver's neck she wondered when would be the best time to reveal to her husband that he was about to become a proud father. Should she break the good news as soon as she was pregnant, or wait until it started to show? Duggie probably wouldn't notice any difference, so she could even wait until the actual birth and present it to him as a nice surprise. First, though, she had to conceive. It was a lot more difficult than she'd realized. She was beginning to think there might be something wrong, either with Dr Hagstrom's manual or with Duggie's little winkle. Duggie's was definitely different from the ones in the illustrations; none of them had that funny bump on the end like a tinned loganberry.

The taxi pulled up outside a building constructed of concrete blocks and surrounded on all four sides by scaffolding as though it were being packaged for transportation to a foreign buyer. Margery barged through a door marked 'Philosophy and Horticulture' and ran upstairs to her husband's office.

The annotated copy of *Language, Truth and Logic* fell from Hambro's hands as the door was flung open with sudden force. He swung round in his chair expecting to see masked men wielding Armalites or Kalashnikovs.

'Quick, Duggie,' Margery cried. 'That feeling's come over me again.' She was simultaneously unbuttoning her blouse and kicking off her shoes.

Hambro pressed a hand to his heart. He could feel it galloping around beneath his waistcoat, out of all control. He took a bottle of pills from the drawer and swallowed two without water.

'Don't just sit there, Duggie, I've got a taxi waiting.'

Hambro's eyes were closed and he was taking slow deep breaths. As soon as he was able to he said, 'Sonia, I am in the middle of a tutorial.'

Margery turned and noticed for the first time a young

woman in a turquoise *chadhor* sitting almost out of sight behind the steel filing cabinet. 'I'm sorry, Miss, I never seen you.' Her skirt had fallen round her ankles and she was having difficulty stepping out of it. 'Could you come back in ten minutes? I need my husband urgently.'

The lower half of the young woman's face was veiled. Her small pink eyes flickered and turned towards her tutor.

'All right, Miss McLaughlin,' Hambro said. 'Perhaps we had better take a break.' He made a comprehensive gesture, inviting her understanding and commiseration. 'I'll be working down at the Shop till five. We could pick up the threads again at five-thirty.'

The young woman gathered up her things and put them in a shoulder bag. 'I'm afraid that won't be possible,' she said with exaggerated dignity. 'From five until seven I have instruction in the Koran with the Arts Faculty mullah.' On the way out she turned in the doorway, dipped her head, and made a sign with her hand. '*Salaam aleikum,*' she said in a Liverpool accent.

Margery quickly locked the door and arranged the chair cushions on the floor. 'Hurry up, Duggie, it's perishing in here.' Just in time she stopped herself from mentioning the effect it was having on her body temperature.

Hambro knew from recent bitter experience that compliance would be the least troublesome of the notional alternatives open to him. 'Why do you have these carnal urges at such inconvenient times?' he grumbled. On a previous occasion she had dragged him out of the Senate House in the middle of a crucial debate on indexing the chalk allowance. Could she now be taking aphrodisiacs as part of her calorie-controlled diet? He folded his thermal underpants in four and placed them in the out-tray.

Margery was thumbing frantically through her illustrated manual. They had already worked their way through the elementary methods and were now making slow progress towards the more advanced sections of the programme. 'We'd better try Flamingo,' she decided. Monkeypuzzle had been a flop, and Corkscrew was unsuitable for confined spaces. Sooner or later, she thought, one of them's bound to work.

Hambro began groaning aloud in physical and moral pain as his wife pulled his limbs about on the floor-cushions. 'Sonia, I cannot possibly hold my leg in that ridiculous position. My lumbar vertebrae have never been the same since Starfish Two.'

Margery hushed him. She raised his leg and propped it on a pile of bound volumes of the *Proceedings of the Aristotelian Society*. 'There, now stop grizzling.'

She had spoken to him in that manner far too often of late, Hambro reflected, as his leg was raised higher by the addition of Bulkowski's collected essays to the pile. The other evening she had actually rebuked him for talking during the climax to her favourite television melodrama. He had merely been pointing out the logical fallacies in the heroine's deathbed revelations as and when they occurred. If she continued to behave in this manner he really would have to ask her to cease all further contact with Dr Hagstrom. In any case, he was growing tired of cold meat and pickles for dinner every Thursday.

The telephone rang. Lying partially twisted on his side in the Flamingo position he could only just reach the handset. 'Philosophy,' he gasped, as his wife's full weight descended on his solar plexus.

'I want my money back, you lousy twister,' shouted an unknown voice.

'Do you have the right extension? This is a shared line with Horticul . . .'

'This mail order rubbish you sent me. *The Blue Book* by whatsisname, Winkelstein or someone . . .'

'Wittgenstein, actually.'

'What's bloody blue about it I want to know? There's not a single bloody picture in it. Even the bloody story's a load of bloody garbage.'

'It requires more than one reading.'

84

'Highly stimulating and provocative it said in your bloody hand-out. I never even got a bloody hard-on.'

The receiver slipped from Hambro's grasp as Margery suddenly began bouncing up and down on him like a zealous sales assistant demonstrating a water bed. He could still hear the voice complaining bitterly above his head as the receiver swung to and fro on the end of its cord.

'. . . Trades Descriptions Act . . . legal proceedings . . . Office of Fair Trading . . .'

Hambro craned his neck and managed to call into the passing mouthpiece, 'Perhaps you should start with *The Brown Book.*'

'Be quiet, Duggie.' Margery pressed her hand over his open mouth. 'Try and concentrate on what you're doing. The taxi's costing a fortune.'

Hambro's eyes closed in despondency. Something, somewhere, had gone badly wrong with his grip upon the world. It had never been part of his life's plan to sell philosophy from door to door, or to serve behind the counter of a basement shop, or to wear the brand name of a petfood across the back of his MA gown. Nor did he wish to be lying on his office floor with *Language, Truth and Logic* wedged in the small of his back and his cleaning woman bumping up and down on his front. As if that weren't enough a complete stranger was now shouting abuse at him down the telephone. Not even Orwell had borne such tribulations.

Presently it was all over. He gripped the middle handle of the filing cabinet and hauled himself painfully to his feet. As he did so the workmen seated on the scaffolding outside the window broke into spontaneous applause and raised their steel hats in salutation.

Lent

14

Heavy snow fell on the first day of Lent term. It settled on the frozen snow that had fallen over the deserted campus on Christmas Eve and Boxing Day. Winds coming off the sea blew it into deep drifts on the roof of Senate House and against the north face of Admin II. Later, men in bright orange overalls shovelled it off the access roads and stacked it in grey piles along the walkways. On the main piazza snowball fights broke out between conflicting Muslim factions, each one of which claimed moral victory. Milk froze in the cartons on the high windowsills of the Hayek hall of residence.

Hambro stood at the window of the university library watching snow being blown about in all directions, like the snowstorm in a glass paperweight. He breathed on the tips of his fingers and pressed his knees against the cold radiator as though to generate warmth by the power of suggestion. The long reading desks were occupied by students and by lecturers too junior to qualify for rented offices. Most of the readers wore overcoats, scarves and gloves, and several had hot water bottles on their laps. Now and then someone would get up to stamp his feet on the concrete floor or to rub feeling and colour back into his face. Next to the bare New Acquisitions shelves was a cardboard barometer showing the sum of money saved since the introduction of the winter fuel economies.

Hambro decided to work at home. He caught the afternoon bus to the Esplanade, via the gipsy encampment and the hostel for surrogate mothers. He walked along the quay, past the marina and the submerged pier. The sea and the sky became one, the colour of workhouse laundry. He kept in the lee of the old harbour wall and made his way to the corn exchange. The narrow streets which had recently been packed with Christmas shoppers were now even more crowded with people hunting for bargains in the January sales. Despite the snow and the slight hill, Hambro decided to walk the half mile home. He was panting when he arrived and had to steady himself for a moment or two against the Edwardian hallstand. As he entered the sitting-room he was aware of a sudden movement from the corner of his eye. He turned in alarm to see a wiry man in a seaman's jersey advancing towards him. Instinctively, he raised his arm to ward off the blow.

'Hello, Douglas, my old son,' the man said.

'Mr Shanker.' Hambro felt first relief, then pain, as his father-in-law's powerful hand gripped his own much softer one. 'We were expecting you for Christmas. Did the Parole Board reconsider their decision?'

Mr Shanker clicked his tongue. 'No, no, something cropped up at the last minute, I had to change me plans.' He went to the bay window and surveyed the suburban street from behind the net curtains. The only moving things were a midwife having trouble with her scooter and a TV detector van cruising slowly up and down.

'You're not in any trouble with the, ah, authorities?' Hambro asked tentatively. He was still mindful of the embarrassing scene with the Fraud Squad at the wedding reception.

'Me, Douglas?' Mr Shanker smiled. He had a small mouth crammed with large overlapping teeth that always reminded Hambro of collapsing headstones in a derelict churchyard.

'I ask only because my position at the university is a somewhat delicate one at present. Any extra-mural collisions with the law could well . . .'

'Now don't go fretting yourself, Douglas,' Mr Shanker purred. 'I'm not in no trouble with the law. Me and the filth are like that.' He looped his middle finger over his forefinger. 'That's why I need to steer clear of the Elephant for a bit. Know what I mean?'

Hambro felt sufficiently reassured to pour two large glasses of malt whisky from the decanter instead of two small glasses of blended from the Sainsbury's bottle. His father-in-law circled the sitting-room, glass in hand, inspecting the bookshelves and flicking through the learned journals that Hambro still took on subscription but no longer bothered to read.

'Fascinating little number, philosophy,' Mr Shanker declared. 'I've always been dead keen on it.'

Which is more than I could truly say, thought Hambro.

'I got properly hooked on it when I was in Reading. They've got a cracking little library in the Oscar Wilde wing.' He swirled his glass, imbibed the aroma, and took a medicinal sip. 'In my last year there I won the Governor's essay prize.'

'Congratulations. What was the topic, moral justifications for punishment?'

'A Solution to the Prisoner's Dilemma.'

The two men chatted on about Frege, Quine and Bulkowski, oblivious to the fading light. It had stopped snowing. Commuters and bargain-hunters were returning home; their cars passed by the window in a steady stream, spraying arcs of slush over the occasional lone pedestrian. Without rising from his chair, Hambro reached for the switch on the reading lamp. Almost before the light came on Mr Shanker had darted over to the window and closed the damask curtains.

'Careful, Douglas,' he warned. 'Anyone could have been passing.' He peeped out between the curtains. 'You got a thing or two to learn about security.' Even as he spoke there was a sound of a door being opened at the rear of the house. He put a finger to his lips and switched off the light.

'It's only your daughter returning home,' Hambro pointed out. 'On Thursdays she attends Dr Hagstrom's emancipation seminar, after she's done the ironing.'

'You sure?' Mr Shanker whispered in the dark. 'The noise came from round the back.'

'She uses the tradesmen's entrance.'

Mr Shanker waited until he recognized Margery's voice trilling in the kitchen before switching the light back on and resuming his seat. 'This quack she's seeing? What's he called, Dr Hag . . . what?'

'. . . strom. It's a she.'

Mr Shanker's mobile face became pensive. He turned the whisky glass first one way, then the other, between his supple fingers. 'Is it about her anorexia? Last time I saw her she looked like Gandhi.' He laughed at the back of his throat, giving off a sound like one Jackson Pollock being scraped across the surface of another. 'The screws asked if I was going to use her to pick the locks with.'

Hambro topped up the glasses with generous measures. 'Her anorexia has been spectacularly cured. You would now be most unlikely to confuse her with the Mahatma.' The Buddha, perhaps, he muttered under his breath. A worrying thought suddenly struck him. 'Just a moment. If you haven't yet seen her, who let you in?'

Mr Shanker's overcrowded teeth came on display. 'I let myself in. The attic window was unlocked.' He leaned forward and tapped his son-in-law on the knee. 'You see what I mean about being lax on security? Just think about it, Douglas. I might have been a burglar.'

They continued chatting for a while about the wintery weather, the Australian wine scandal, and the abdication crisis. Presently Mr Shanker drained his glass and rose to his feet. 'I better go and see the girl, I've got a little something for her.' He took from his pocket a silver filigree bracelet that would only just have slipped over his own slender wrist. 'It's a very tasty piece,' he confided. 'Part of a larger set. She mustn't wear it outside for a bit.'

When he set eyes upon his daughter he decided to leave it in his pocket. She was breaking eggs into a basin with one hand and whisking them with the other. When she turned and saw it wasn't her husband she let out a cry of delight.

'Hello, Princess,' her father said, enclosing her in a bear hug. 'Sorry I couldn't make it for Christmas. There was a spot of bother down the Elephant.'

Margery put the kettle on for tea. 'You didn't miss much,'

she said with feeling. 'It was the worst Christmas I ever had in my whole life, including that time when you, Mum, Granddad, and Uncle Evelyn were all inside.' She set out two Coronation mugs and a plate of homemade ginger biscuits. Mr Shanker sat at the table and listened sympathetically to his daughter's troubles.

'First of all, Duggie forgot to buy me a Christmas present. Getting nothing at all was even worse than getting Fowler's *Modern English Usage*. I was livid, especially as I'd gone to all the trouble of knitting him a nice pair of bedsocks and matching hot-water-bottle cover. So he goes out on Christmas morning to try and buy me something, and the only shop he can find open is that little Paki grocer's under the railway bridge. He comes back half an hour later with a jar of vindaloo paste and a packet of poppadums wrapped up in a brown paper bag. I ask you, what kind of Christmas box is that? He knows very well spicy foods don't agree with me.'

She poured her father's tea, added four spoonfuls of sugar, stirred it for him, and continued.

'Then on Boxing Day the telly goes on the blink. Duggie takes the back off it to try and mend it with a spanner, and blows out all the fuses. So there I am, sitting all alone in the dark, missing the Dirk Oesterbroek Christmas Show and the omnibus edition of *Hernia Can Be Fun* while Duggie's fiddling about with candles in his garden shed. Don't talk to me about Christmas.'

She poured batter mix into a pan of smoking fat and adjusted the flame. Seconds later she loosened the pancake with a spatula and flipped it over. Her father watched her as she busied herself with sugar and sliced lemons. She's got very big round the middle, he thought; no one else in the family had ever run to fat. 'Princess?' he asked casually. 'You're not in the club, are you?'

She turned on him with unexpected wrath. 'No I am *not*. That's one thing I definitely am not.'

'All right, all right,' her father said, raising both hands in a show of unconditional surrender. 'I was only asking.'

93

'You know whose fault it is that I'm not?' She shook her spatula at the door leading to the sitting-room, where Hambro was still ensconced. 'His. He's the one to blame. If it wasn't for him, you'd have been a grandfather soon.'

Mr Shanker wiped batter mix off his sleeve with the corner of the tablecloth. 'Be fair, Princess,' he said mildly. 'You can never be sure about these things. Your Auntie Beatrice always used to blame your Uncle Evelyn for being barren, until he put your granny up the spout.'

Margery shook the frying pan and banged it on the stove. 'I know for a fact it's Duggie's fault,' she cried bitterly. 'That was the worst thing of all that happened over Christmas. Do you know what he went and did, the rotten bugger?'

Mr Shanker sucked his back teeth in contemplation. 'He hasn't become a Justice of the Peace?'

'Much worse than that. He had himself vasectomized. He sneaked out on New Year's Eve and had it done in the Corporation's mobile van. He said he was just popping out for a packet of pipe-cleaners.' Strands of damp hair had fallen over her eyes and she pushed them back with her forearm. Tiny drops of perspiration shone on her upper lip. 'I'll never forgive him for that. It's typical of him, saying he didn't want children and really meaning it all the time.' Her soft mouth hardened at the edges. 'Anyway, two can play at being selfish. I'm not bothering no more to warm his claret in the airing cupboard. And why should I polish his rotten aspidistra? It's ruining my best duster.' She set out two plates, two forks and a pot of damson jam she had won in the Methodist Christmas raffle. 'Come on, Dad, tuck in.' She pushed towards him an ovenproof dish containing a pile of sugared pancakes. '*He's* not having none. Sod him.'

As she ate and listened to her father's gossip Margery became more relaxed and equable. She was intrigued to learn that one of her cousins had been adopted as the Liberal candidate for a safe Greenpeace seat, and that another had married a Greek shipowner. 'Least, that's what he said he was. Turns out that he's got this little fishing boat in Lowes-

94

toft. Young Doreen works her fingers to the bone filleting cod.'

Margery put her head back and laughed with her mouth full. 'Oh, Dad,' she sighed happily, 'it's going to be so good having you to stay. I haven't laughed like that for ages.' She dried her eyes with her knuckle. 'In fact I haven't had a good laugh since Duggie slipped on the ice outside the fever hospital and was nearly run over by an ambulance.'

15

After the snow came torrential rain and fierce gales blowing from the east. Flood warnings were posted in the harbour and were quickly followed by floods and then by newspaper pictures of elderly people wading stoically through their front parlours carrying their pets to safety. On the university campus, high above the town, the rains lashed against the advertising hoardings around the minaret, and there was an unconfirmed report that the Vice-Chancellor had been blown off the north face of Admin II while climbing it for charity.

Baxi hunched his shoulders inside his waterlogged jacket and made his way to the Students' Union. He kept to the duckboards but water was already seeping through the soles of his shoes despite his recent attempt to repair them with the hard covers of *The Wealth of Nations*. Gangs of workmen dressed in orange rubber capes were digging new holes in front of the Computer Centre and filling in old holes at the rear of the Catering School. The wet air shook with the sounds of their shovels and ribald laughter.

The entrance to the Students' Union was crowded with people standing about as though practising fire drill. Baxi elbowed his way through and jumped into the paternoster, brushing water off his head with both hands. He got off at level five and went into the recreation and reading room.

This contained nothing but long rows of games machines, flashing and bleeping electronically. He went systematically along the rows feeling inside the returned-coin slots. He retrieved two one pound coins, a bent Swiss franc, and a tap washer. He put the tap washer in the drinks dispenser and succeeded at the fourth attempt in getting half a paper cupful of tea or coffee.

Later he joined the queue in the cafeteria. He put on his tray a roast beef and a horseradish sandwich, a slice of Dutch apple tart, a dish of semolina, a packet of salted peanuts, a roll and butter, and a large glass of chocolate malt.

'After you, gentlemen,' he said to the foreign students behind him in the queue. They thanked him in broken English as they filed past one by one, pushing their trays towards the hot meals counter. Baxi followed slowly, wolfing down all but one of the items on his loaded tray.

'Semolina, is that all?' said the girl behind the till.

Baxi patted his stomach. 'I've only just eaten,' he confessed.

He sat for a while in the television lounge, drying his feet on the curtain. Channel Four was screening a hitherto banned exposé of corruption and deceit in the Boy Scouts movement, which was followed by a human documentary in which retired milkmen reminisced at length about the golden age of doorstep deliveries. As soon as Baxi's curiosity on this topic was sated he took the paternoster down to the main concourse.

In the centre of the concourse trestle tables had been set up for the distribution of non-political literature and the sale of alternative food and hand-made earrings. Students of assorted nationalities stood about in small groups chatting earnestly about the news from home and the rate of exchange against the dollar, or spitting into the multicoloured fountain that rose and fell in a series of cascades beneath the high glass dome. Baxi strolled up and down, hands in pockets, his defective shoes squelching on the simulated flagstones.

'Dope? Hash? Coke?' he enquired, addressing the generality rather than anyone in particular. 'Uppers? Downers? Glue?'

He went across to a group of robed African students who were talking excitedly about the unexpected fall in the Dow-Jones Index. 'Moroccan Marvel?' He pressed a finger to one nostril and sniffed with the other. 'Only the best, direct from the local Drugs Squad.'

The dark curly heads shook in unison.

'Afghan Acid? The Red Army's favourite.'

Again the heads shook.

'Video nasties? Tickets for Royal Ascot? Examination papers?'

At the mention of this last item there was a sudden flurry of interest. 'Which exam?' asked two people at once.

Baxi opened and closed his jacket to allow a tantalizing glimpse of the contents of his inside pocket. 'I've got Remedial Accountancy, Paranormal Sciences (Part One), and Supply-Side Economics.'

'What about Hotel and Casino Management?' asked a man with tribal scars on his cheeks.

Baxi made a popping sound with compressed lips. 'I can get it for you easily enough, but it'll cost. That departmental secretary's a right little crook.'

A muffled conversation ensued, followed by the passing of folded banknotes in Baxi's direction. 'Nice doing business with you, gentlemen.' He bowed from the waist and moved back into the crowd. 'Work permits? Literacy certificates? BBC shares?'

Before reporting for duty in the Senior Common Room he called in at the Sperm Bank.

'You again?' said the Canadian nurse, rolling her eyes. 'This is your third time today.'

Baxi took the familiar buff card and filled in the details. 'I've got an active social conscience.'

The nurse handed him a squat glass bottle with a screw top. She smiled archly. 'I don't suppose you need the magazines?'

He sat in the cubicle for a few minutes reading the herpes

97

warning and counting his money. Erratic breathing sounds came from the adjacent cubicle, as of someone with pneumoconiosis doing press-ups. There was a smell of undiluted pine disinfectant.

Presently he took from one of his pockets a small manila envelope and slit it open with his thumbnail. He held it over the bottle and squeezed out several large blobs of cafeteria semolina. He screwed the lid back on the bottle and ate the remains of the semolina direct from the envelope, head tilted back, as if swallowing oysters. He returned to the reception desk adjusting his clothing ostentatiously.

'Speedy Gonzales,' observed the nurse. She stuck a label on the bottle and put it in a freezer cabinet in a drawer marked:

IQ 120–130: CAUCASOID: MUSICAL.

Baxi counted the dollar bills and folded them away. 'I'll be dropping in for another deposit first thing in the morning,' he declared. 'If I can summon up the energy.'

He arrived three minutes late at the Senior Common Room to find a crowd of disgruntled members hammering on the metal grille. 'Where've you been, Baxi?' roared Professor Grogan, Head of Catering Studies. He climbed over the Dean of Divinity's wheelchair and shouldered aside the Instructor in Martial Arts to get to the bar. Still complaining volubly, he carried off a pint of Belgian lager in each hand and a double Scotch held beneath his chin.

Baxi spent the next twenty minutes frantically pouring drinks to the accompaniment of abuse. It was past six-thirty before he found time to plug in the electronic fruit machine, empty the coin-box on the Breathalyzer, and put on the Mantovani tape. Gradually, the evening settled into its usual pattern. The Law lecturers occupied a table to themselves playing pontoon, the lecturers in Warehouse Management challenged the Professors of Soil Technology to an arm-wrestling competition on the chess table, and the Visiting Fellow in Biblical Studies monopolized the pinball machine. By ten o'clock Baxi had filled up two more sides of graph paper. His term project was coming along quite well, despite the constant interruptions. Dr Hagstrom had said that if it scored an alpha mark she might consider taking him on as a research assistant. He quite fancied the idea of working in a lab in a long white coat, even if it was only a part-time job counting the number of times the white rats bit the black rats. You had to start at the bottom, even in Experimental Psychology. He put his pen aside at the sound of a familiar cry. 'Coming at once, Professor Grogan,' he replied.

He closed the bar shortly after midnight. After clearing up the broken glasses he took a sheet from his order pad and scribbled a brief note to his parents on the back of it.

Dear Mother and Father,

Sorry I didn't write last week. I've been very busy with my studies. I know you think education is a waste of time, but there's more going on at the university than you'd ever guess. I've discovered some amazing things doing my project, but I can't tell you about them in writing.

Sorry to hear about the problems you've been having in the new council flat. No wonder they let you have it rent free. I'm enclosing enough money to pay for the exorcism. If it doesn't work let me know your new address.

Your loving son.

P.S. I read that the Baker Street underpass is closed for repairs. Where are you playing now?

He posted the letter in the box outside the Hayek hall of residence. Denise's light was still burning. He wondered if she would have any French cigarettes or stale bread. He trudged up the eight flights and paused outside her door. A voice he recognized was alternately calling out commands and whimpering for forgiveness. There followed slapping sounds interspersed with cries of anguish. Baxi crept away, belatedly remembering Denise's late tutorial with Mr Poulter-Mogg on the Spanish Inquisition.

16

Beneath a powdering of freshly fallen snow Tozer Place looked much as it usually did on garbage day. Dustbins and plastic sacks lined the kerb in an almost unbroken phalanx from the Mexican take-away to the Peeperama. A privateer rubbish truck was grinding and shuddering and whining its way along. It was accompanied by six dustmen in green uniforms who looked as if they might all be members of the same dangerously inbred family. They left behind them a meandering trail of eggshells and fishbones and a substance that resembled military porridge.

Hambro navigated his way through the debris with fastidious care. He lifted his dainty feet unnecessarily high over offending objects, like a city dweller practising the steps of a rural dance. Despite his best efforts he arrived at the Mind Shop with inexplicable pinkish blobs on the toes of his best galoshes. He hurried down the basement steps relieved that, on this occasion, no one had accosted him to ask the time or the way to the nearest funeral parlour. Such encounters had already cost him his wallet, his university security pass, and his Brasenose cufflinks. He pushed briefly at the heavy wooden door before remembering to pull it.

Skillicorn was standing on a chair and hammering on the ceiling with the plaster bust of Nietzsche. 'Will you please try to make less noise,' he yelled. 'I'm trying to conduct a seminar.'

The shrieks, groans and grunts overhead continued unabated. They were accompanied by a curious squelching and splashing, as if grapes were being trodden in a zinc tank by emotionally disturbed peasants. Skillicorn gave a final despairing thump on the ceiling with Nietzsche's badly cracked head before jumping off the chair. 'All right, Mrs Phipps,' he said, 'please carry on as best you can.'

A woman wearing butterfly spectacles and tangerine make-up rose from the table and stood facing the rest of the class. To Hambro's bewilderment she held up first nine fingers, then five, and began gesticulating with her hands, face and body in silent mime. He stepped quickly aside as she came trundling backwards in his direction, stamping her feet and crying, 'Whoo whoo, whoo whoo.'

'Train!' cried a member of the class over her embroidery.

'Shunting!' cried another.

The woman ceased stamping and whoo-ing and pointed to the floor.

'Lines!'

'Rails?'

'Track!'

The woman nodded a vigorous affirmative. She paused for a moment to think, held up more fingers, and commenced peeling an imaginary fruit or vegetable.

'Apples!'

'Swedes!'

'Potatoes!'

The woman pointed encouragement at the originator of this last suggestion and made the sign for the shortened form.

'Spuds?'

'Taters?'

The woman smiled in relief and clapped her hands before resuming her place at the seminar table.

A man with unevenly spaced bumps on his forehead turned to his neighbour in puzzlement. 'Track?' he queried. 'Taters? I don't get it.'

'Tractatus,' explained his neighbour above the applause.

Skillicorn defended his pedagogic methods to Hambro while they were queuing for lunch at the sausage-on-a-stick counter. 'It's just to familiarize them with the texts,' he said, jerking his arms and knees ataxically. 'Last week I had them playing pass the parcel with *Being and Nothingness.*'

17

The stars were strung out across the dark velvet of the sky like a display of trinkets in a cut-price jewellers. Heavy frost covered the neat suburban landscape. It glittered on the front lawns and deserted pavements and on the roofs and bonnets of illegally parked cars. Somewhere in the far distance a heavy goods truck was straining up a hill.

Mr Shanker stood at his bedroom window waiting for the clouds to come. They were supposed to arrive from the south-west followed by a warm front giving way to scattered showers and the promise of further rain or snow. Just look at that diabolical moon, he thought. He checked his watch and drummed his fingers impatiently on the windowsill. He was wearing dark flannel trousers tucked into his socks, a navy blue seaman's jersey, and the grey balaclava helmet he had started knitting in Wormwood Scrubs and finished in Reading. Strapped around his waist was a leather pouch containing a pencil torch, a wad of scented plasticine, and a thin strip of metal pointed at one end and rounded at the other.

After half an hour he crept downstairs and paused on the first-floor landing. Through the open door of the master bedroom he heard Hambro cry out in his troubled sleep. It was something about shooting a runaway elephant. He's not such a bad old codger, Mr Shanker thought. Pity he's not hitting it off too well with the Princess. It wasn't all that surprising, though, given his peculiar social background and his very dodgy ideas about Leibnitz. Still, she had promised to cherish as well as obey, so there was no call for her to make those faces behind his back.

He shut the front door softly behind him and stood in the shadow of the front porch watching patches of wispy cloud pass across the face of the moon. As he was unlatching the garden gate one of the local foxes trotted past carrying scraps of Kentucky Fried Chicken in its jaws. Mr Shanker went in the opposite direction. He walked at a natural pace, keeping close in to the side so that his shoulder brushed against the white-laced privet and rhododendron bushes.

The houses became more imposing as the slight gradient developed into the foot of a hill. He stopped at a beech tree on the corner and observed the large detached house opposite. In the window was a poster advertising a bring-and-buy sale in St Aloysius Church that was held last Saturday. He crossed the road and went stealthily round the side of the house and into the back garden. There was no sight or sound of movement within, nor would there be for another six days according to his recently acquired and inexpensive friend, the local paper boy. He slipped on his leather gloves, tightened his belt, spat over his shoulder for luck, and clasped both hands around the drainpipe.

Less than a mile away, where the fast track of the westbound line passed through a cutting, Colin Lumsden was lying face down on a railway sleeper. His shins were resting on one rail and his neck was propped at an awkward angle on the other. A thin sprinkling of frost glinted in his hair. Now and then he raised his head and twisted it from side to side in order to ease the stiffness. He wondered if it was a mistake to be wearing a scarf.

After a while he decided to change his position. He turned over on his back and gazed up at the Plough and parts of the Milky Way. It was an improvement on staring at the ground, he decided. He found that when he closed his left eye the moon was directly above the signal box; when he closed his right, it was over the Keep Out warning. How did it do that, he wondered. If he'd done science instead of Social and Economic Forecasting he might have learned the answer. Now he would never know.

He looked once more at the dial on his luminous watch.

It was 03:10. Where the devil was the 02:42? The trains were supposed to run on time now that they'd been denationalized. By moving his head a little he could see the lights of Central Pier Station, and beyond them the sodium lamps along the motorway. What this country needs, he thought, is a properly integrated transport system.

Footsteps sounded on the gravel. A linesman appeared carrying a lunchbox in one hand and a red lamp in the other. 'What's your game, then?' he said. He shone his lamp on Lumsden's supine body. 'You got a ticket?'

'I'm not travelling. I'm waiting for the 02:42. Is it always this late?'

'You can't use rail facilities without a ticket. Anyway, there's no 02:42 on a weekday.'

Lumsden sat up. 'There certainly is. Look.' He handed the linesman a timetable with one departure time double-underlined in red biro. 'It should have left Central Pier Station fifty-five minutes ago.'

The linesman examined it by the light of his lamp. 'This is the autumn timetable. You want the winter one.'

Lumsden gave a small cry of despair. 'Oh, Christ. When's the next down train then?'

'Not till 05:18 on a weekday.'

'What? 05:18? What kind of train service is that? I'm practically freezing to death.' Lumsden got to his feet and massaged his neck and his knee-joints. I could try road transport, he thought. He hobbled off in the direction of the motorway.

'We run a more frequent service in the spring,' the linesman called after him. 'The new timetable comes out in March.'

Lumsden cupped his hands around his mouth to make a megaphone. 'Keep it. I shan't be needing it,' he shouted back in triumph.

He walked along the track to Central Pier Station. The platforms were deserted except for dozens of stray cats and someone slumped on a pile of mailbags. He crossed the line to investigate, but it was only the Head of Catering. On an impulse he went into a telephone booth, but found that he had the wrong coins. He dialled the operator. 'I'd like to make a reverse-charge call.' He gave his mother's number and his name. The cold damp of the stone floor seemed to enter his body through his feet and rise higher and higher as he waited. Through the glass he could just make out an advertisement for holidays in the sun and a metal sign saying, 'Alight here for the Winter Gardens, Waxworks and University.' He recalled the day, more than two years ago, when he had first seen that sign. He had arrived with a trunk and a collapsible bicycle and a heart full of hope at the prospect of higher education. It had been a crisp autumn day and the platform was strewn with fallen leaves. He had walked to the far end of the platform, scuffing the leaves, breathing in the invigorating sea air, and whirling his arms like a windmill. When he returned to his luggage he found that someone had stolen his bicycle.

The telephone suddenly exploded with sound, as though a wayward tennis star had smashed his racquet over the umpire's microphone. 'I'm sorry, caller,' the operator said. 'The subscriber refuses to accept the charge.'

'That's ridiculous,' Lumsden wailed. 'Did you tell her who it was?'

'The subscriber says she knows nobody of that name.'

Lumsden shook the receiver as if to bring it to its senses. 'Mummy,' he cried. 'It's me, Colin. I'm ringing to say goodbye. Hello? Mummy? Hello? Hello? Hello? Hello . . .?'

18

Margery Hambro walked round the block for the fifth consecutive time. She paused frequently to stare at the window displays in ironmongers and building societies and secondhand furniture shops. Dusk was falling and lights were coming on in and around the harbour. Queues for suburban buses were beginning to form outside Boots the Chemist and the Bureau de Change. For the fifth time Margery inspected the display of contact-lens cleaning solutions, swing-bin liners, and antiseptic mouthwash before noting the exchange rate of sterling against drachma, yen, forint, peso, ruble, escudo and dinar. Her feet were starting to ache inside her fur-lined suede bootees. It was still only ten minutes to five by the Esplanade clock.

She went down the harbour steps and slowly made her way to the glass apartment block in the exclusive quarter of the seafront. After a short wait she pressed the top bell in the row of twelve. Almost at once a voice crackled through the speaker.

'Yes?'

'Hello, it's me. Margery.'

'Who?'

'Margery Hambro. I hope I'm not too early.'

There was a meaningful silence. 'Didn't we say five o'clock? I make it four minutes to.'

Margery sighed into the circular metal grille. 'I been round the block five times. Shall I go round again?'

The silence was a little longer this time, as though the question was receiving the fullest consideration. 'No, that would make you late,' Hedda Hagstrom decided. 'Please do come right up.'

Margery took the express lift to the top floor and peeped through the spyhole of Hedda Hagstrom's reinforced door. A miniature blue eye stared back at her and then the door was opened on a chain. Hedda Hagstrom was wearing a black leotard with a white sash loosely knotted around her waist. Her thick platinum blonde hair was coiled in a single serpentine plait on top of her head without visible means of support. Her mouth formed a welcoming smile as she pointed at Margery's suede bootees. 'Shall I relieve you of those?' She carried them off at arm's length and dropped them in a pedal-bin. 'Do make yourself at home, Margery.' She pointed to one specific white leather chair in the row of three facing the panoramic window. The chairs were in exact linear and spatial alignment with each other and the window.

Margery padded across the room in her stockinged feet trying not to put all her weight on the fluffy white carpet. 'Nice view,' she observed, squeezing herself carefully into the designated chair. 'You'd be able to see our place from here if it weren't for the Corporation mosque.' She chatted on nervously about the shocking price of dairy products and the latest moves in the abdication crisis. It was the first time she had ever visited her counsellor at home and she was not quite sure of the proper rules. Should she have brought some flowers or a box of chocolate brazils? Duggie could have advised her if they'd been on speaking terms; her dad might have known, too, but he was always asleep in the daytime.

'It's been so cold,' she continued. 'The bedroom's like an iceberg. I could hardly move me jaws to say me prayers.'

Hedda Hagstrom was smiling like an air hostess on a charter flight to Spain. 'The weather has been bad,' she agreed. 'Is that why you've been absent from the Thursday seminars?'

Margery's cheeks reddened. 'I did mean to come last week, but I got all behind with the shopping. The wheel came off my basket when I was running for the bus.'

Hedda Hagstrom gave her a look of disappointment tinged with mild reproval. 'If you recall, Margery, the object of the exercise is to free yourself from shopping and domestic chores. These are for your husband to do. We covered all that in the first two workshops.'

Margery's eyes widened in appeal for some understanding of the special nature of her case. 'I've tried that, but it doesn't seem to work. Duggie's useless around the house. He keeps mistaking the tumble-drier for the dishwasher. You should see what he did to my best dinner service. And he's no better at shopping, neither. The last time I asked him to get a tin of stewed steak from the corner shop he came back with Pedigree Chum.'

Hedda Hagstrom listened in silence. She betrayed none of the displeasure she felt at the violation of her syllabus, other than in the tightening of muscles in her jaw and the drumming of her fingers on the Benares coffee table. Some people, she acknowledged, were simply born to suffer; Margery quite possibly was one of those women who positively thrived on subordination. Why would she have married the man in the first place if not out of a profound sense of her own worthlessness? Why, too, would she insist on bringing her quilting to the emancipation seminar if not to demonstrate to her potentially enlightened self that her degraded self was still firmly in control? Hm. There was promising material here for her address to the Helsinki symposium on Ms Jekyll and Mrs Hyde.

She unknotted and re-knotted her white sash until the two ends were of precisely the same length. 'Well, Margery,' she said brightly, as if to begin rather than continue a conversation, 'anything positive to report on the maternity front? You have been keeping to the programme?'

Margery rubbed one stockinged foot apprehensively over the other. This was the moment she'd been dreading. Every time she was asked for a progress report she had no progress to report. No one had ever told her to her face, but she had the definite feeling that everyone in the workshop regarded her as the classroom dunce. All the other women seemed to be doing marvellously; one of them had just left her husband and five kids to become a ventriloquist, another had chucked away her twin-set and pearls and bought herself an airman's uniform, and three others had set up home together in a loft. She always seemed to be the odd one out. She couldn't even spell 'chauvinism' properly, let alone understand all that stuff about clitoral and vaginal thingummybobs. Anyway, it was all right for them, they weren't married to Duggie.

'Well, Margery?' Hedda Hagstrom prompted.

Margery was unable to look her counsellor in the eye. She seemed even more scary than ever in that black leotard and her hair twisted around her head like a snake. Wouldn't it be lovely to have a body like that. She wished now she'd stuck to her pomegranate diet. 'I'm afraid it's bad news,' she said in a halting voice. 'But it's not really my fault. Duggie went and did the dirty on me.'

'You mean he destroyed the manual? I did warn you of that possibility.'

'No. He hid it a few times, but I always managed to find it again.'

'What then?'

'He had himself doctored.'

Hedda Hagstrom blinked uncomprehendingly. 'But he already has a PhD.'

'No, I mean the same as you do with cats. He found out that I was off the pill and that I'd given his rubber sheaths to the St Aloysius jumble sale. That's when he had it done.' Margery gave a full account of her husband's shopping expedition for pipe-cleaners that had served as a cover for his surreptitious visit to the Corporation's mobile van. 'They even gave him a certificate to prove it. He keeps it in a frame on his bedside table, next to the photo of his wife.'

Hedda Hagstrom listened with mounting fascination. How extraordinary, she thought. And how *very* interesting.

'It seems as if he didn't want a son and heir after all,' Margery opined. 'Despite saying how much he hated children. Trust him to be contrary.'

Hedda Hagstrom was deep in thought. She stood by the panoramic window gazing down at the moving figures below. Shop assistants and office workers were scurrying along the damp pavements to join the lengthening bus queues. Along the Esplanade groups of elderly day trippers were returning from their inspection of the submerged pier, the climax to their guided tour of the town and its principal monuments of historical and cultural interest. Further along, around the marina, workmen were taking down the illuminations which had earlier been switched on by one of Dirk Oesterbroek's studio assistants due to the last-minute absence of Dirk Oesterbroek himself. Music from the steam-organ in the children's carousel could only just be heard through the double glazing. Still looking down at the activity below, Hedda Hagstrom said, 'This is one of the most extreme cases of Repressed Paternity Syndrome I've come across for some time. Your husband must be quite desperate to have performed such a symbolic act.' Even in the Brize Norton case, she thought, the patient never went quite that far. She pulled a cord at the side of the window and a full-length black-and-white curtain swished across.

'You don't still think he wants a kid?' Margery's voice squeaked in incredulity. 'Despite what he done to himself?'

'Not *despite* what he done . . . did. *Because* of it. And I don't think it, I know it.' Hedda Hagstrom seated herself on the black leather pouffe by the hi-fi and hugged her knees, almost lovingly. 'Don't you see, Margery? It was a cry for help from a deeply frustrated man. He could hardly have made his craving for a child any plainer.'

Margery's mind was racing to try and catch up with her counsellor's. 'I don't get it. How can he have children now that he's had his winkle blocked up, or whatever it is they do?'

A revelational smile started at the corners of Hedda Hagstrom's mouth and spread by slow degrees across the rest of her face. 'He can't give you one himself, Margery, but somebody else can give you one on his behalf. That's what he's trying to tell you. By going to the mobile van he was in effect saying, "Look, I'm too old and decrepit to father my own healthy offspring. Please, please, please find a younger, more virile substitute to perform the service for me." In the Brize Norton case, the local cricket team came to the rescue.' She smoothed her hands down the underside of her long, elegant legs. She kept her feet together to ensure that the white carpet could not be seen between them from any angle.

'Do you have a lover, Margery?' she said, as though

110

enquiring if she had an endowment mortgage or a valid passport.

Margery let out a spluttering laugh. 'Me? Are you kidding?' She wiped tiny flecks of spittle off the Benares table with her sleeve.

'You really ought to provide yourself with one,' advised her counsellor. 'Do you know how to go about it?'

'Put an ad in the local paper?' Margery guessed. The only time she had advertised in the classified columns was to sell a rusty mangle that Duggie had paid a fortune for in the mistaken belief that it had once belonged to Orwell's landlady in Kentish Town.

'I'd recommend you try the university. You really want someone comparable to your husband in IQ, somatype and socio-cultural background. I could give you a computer print-out of suitable candidates. It's as well to do these things scientifically.' She stood up in a manner that made clear that the counselling session was at an end. She fetched Margery's suede bootees from the pedal-bin and waited while she put them on standing on the doormat. 'A friendly word of advice,' she said, in a huskier voice than usual. 'You're going to have to do something about your appearance. Buy some proper clothes. Visit a decent hairdresser. Try and have your teeth fixed.' She touched Margery lightly on the arm in a gesture of encouragement. 'Don't look so worried, I'm sure your husband can afford it. After all, he'll be the main beneficiary.'

As soon as Margery had gone Hedda Hagstrom took a fierce shower, rubbed herself with aromatic oils, wrapped herself in a white cashmere bathrobe and settled down to work in her study. She switched on the microcomputer and fed a floppy disk in the disk-drive. On a prompt from the monitor she then typed LOGOXPIP KHOMCENT SMARTYBOOTS. A table of statistical data appeared on the screen which she examined with intense concentration. This was her most ambitious research project to date: a large-scale survey, amply funded by the Khomeini Centre,

111

designed to show that Muslim converts were more successful at university than their infidel counterparts. According to her working hypothesis, Muslim students would score higher marks because prostrating themselves in prayer five times a day stimulated the supply of blood to the brain. She now carried out a statistical comparison of examination results of Muslim and infidel students matched by sex, father's occupation, height, weight, hair colour and chest measurement. As the figures flashed up on the screen she could hardly believe the evidence of her eyes: there seemed to be no significant differences between the two groups. Muslims did slightly better in Accountancy and Fisheries Science, but this was offset by the infidels' performance in Acupuncture and Chiropody. In all other subjects, whether Arts or Sciences, practical or applied, their average scores were identical.

Hedda Hagstrom drummed her fingers on the keyboard in exasperation. What could possibly have gone wrong? There could be only one rational explanation for such a freak result: those incompetent research assistants must have entered the figures in the computer incorrectly. Two of them were known Methodists; it was probably a mistake employing people like that on such a sensitive project. She knew from prior experience that there was only one way to overcome a problem of this nature. She ran the figures again, column by column, this time altering all those which seemed intuitively wrong. In less than an hour she had succeeded in ironing out all the errors which the research assistants had very likely made. The academic superiority of Muslim converts was now palpably established, as anticipated by her theoretical model and by her research sponsors. She switched off the computer, pressed her fingers to her eyes, stretched her arms above her head and stifled a yawn. As always, she felt both exhilarated and exhausted after a demanding session labouring at the far frontiers of knowledge.

19

The sun was shining from a blue, almost Mediterranean sky as Hambro emerged from the portico of Wigan Station and into the cosmopolitan bustle of Market Place. Following his street map, he crossed into King Street, turned left at the Mercedes-Benz showrooms, and waited in line for the 603 bus to Ince. He felt a guilty twinge of disappointment at the noticeable absence of barefoot children and shrivelled men in cloth caps and clogs.

The wide-bodied bus came almost at once. He sat on the lower deck beneath a sign in two languages urging passengers to buy shares in the bus company. They sped along the Manchester Road past narrow streets of tastefully renovated terrace houses and patches of landscaped greenery laid out with flower beds and shrubs in terracotta pots. Hambro could barely contain his excitement at the thought that He would have walked these very streets, passed these self-same ornamental lamp-posts, crossed the road at the same pedestrian underpass they were now driving over, the chill northern wind sawing through His flimsy but well-cut jacket to the vulnerable chest beneath.

To the bemusement of other passengers, Hambro took out his Polaroid camera and began pointing and clicking it at pillar boxes and corner shops and old men talking in doorways.

'Fox Tavern,' the driver called out for the second time. 'This is your nearest stop, Sir.'

Hambro found himself outside a mock-Tudor pub festooned with coloured lanterns. It was four o'clock in the afternoon but the car park was full. Music and laughter rang out from within as the clientele took full advantage of the local licensing reforms. Hambro consulted his street map and

113

followed the bend in the road past the hypermarket and equestrian school. Rather to his puzzlement, the names of the streets did not exactly correspond to the names on his map. Even the layout of the streets looked worryingly different.

After twenty minutes of fruitless searching he decided to ask. He approached a short line of people waiting to use the Chase Manhattan cash dispensers. 'Could somebody kindly tell me,' he piped, 'where I might find the tripe shop? I think you know the one I mean.'

A collective growl rose from the queue. 'Clear off. Go back to where you came from,' shouted a middle-aged man in designer jeans.

'Muckraker!' cried a pregnant teenager with a small baby dangling from her neck in a canvas sling. A newly ordained woman priest pointed her cross at him and made a sign of absolution, and somebody else flung a half-smoked Havana at his feet.

Hambro backed away in alarm. Abuse was still ringing in his ears as he hurried down the pedestrian underpass to the other side of the road. He stood in the doorway of a Belgian patisserie and once more consulted his map and notebook. Before he had managed to locate his present position on the map he was approached by a woman in a sealskin coat and matching sealskin hat.

'I saw what happened,' she said sympathetically. 'Take no notice of them. Some people here are very touchy about the tripe shop.'

'Really?'

'They can turn very nasty sometimes. A professor chap from London got stoned by the mob last year.'

'How very odd. I should have thought Wigan would be extremely proud of its association with . . .'

The woman dipped her head. 'I know where it is,' she revealed. 'The actual tripe shop, as used to be.'

'You do?' Hambro gave a small skip of delight, almost colliding with a customer carrying an armful of baguettes.

114

'It's just round the corner, I'll show you.' She led him past the fresh pasta shop and the Habitat showroom and into a side turning of refurbished terrace houses. Each front door had been painted a different colour and most had names fashioned in wrought-iron instead of numbers. Half-way along the street they came to a small shop with an illuminated sign saying Acapulco Solarium.

'This is it,' said the woman, with a flourish.

Hambro went to the middle of the road to get a comprehensive view. 'You're quite sure? According to recent scholarship, Darlington Street was identified as the site.'

The sealskin hat shook from side to side. 'No, there were a tripe shop in Darlington Street, but it's not the one you want. This is definitely the one that Whatsit stayed in before war.'

Hambro fidgeted uncertainly with his tattered street map. 'It is true the experts are still divided on the issue. You probably saw the acrimonious exchange in last week's *TLS*.'

The woman pushed open the shop door. 'Beryl,' she called. 'Here's another one.'

A younger woman appeared from behind a partition of rubber plants and creepers. She wore a smart grey housecoat with a black and red logo embroidered on the breast pocket.

Hambro introduced himself and briefly explained his life's purpose. 'It's scandalous that the authorities haven't put up a commemorative plaque.' He pointed to a suitable spot for it above the illustrated panel of Acapulco by night.

'I suppose you want to see his old room?' said the proprietor. She looked him up and down like a second-hand car dealer being asked to make an offer on a vintage model.

'I can't tell you how much that would mean to me.' Hambro put one foot inside the solarium and erstwhile tripe shop.

'I usually ask a fee. For the inconvenience and wear and tear.'

Hambro produced his wallet without hesitation. 'By all means.' He took out two ten pound notes and handed them to her.

115

She looked him straight in the eye. 'The fee is fifty pounds.'

Hambro handed her another three notes and followed her eagerly through the shop and up a thickly carpeted stairway. She opened a door on the first floor landing and stood aside to let him in. Hambro was overcome with emotion as he crossed the threshold. He steadied himself against the door-jamb as he gazed around in veneration at the Sanderson's wall coverings, hi-tech table and chairs, and corduroy bean bags. When he was able to speak he said, 'His bed would have been just there. He slept by the right-hand wall, in the bed nearest the door. The horsehair armchair would have been about here, and the dreadful sideboard would have been over there . . .' He pointed to each of the places in turn, describing the exact layout of the room as it had been so graphically recorded by its famous occupant. He closed his eyes and smelled the carefully documented smells.

'Are you feeling all right?' asked the present owner of the room. 'You look a bit peculiar.'

Hambro sucked air in through his nose like a health fanatic on a mountain top. 'I have never felt better in my life.' He reloaded his camera and began taking photographs of the fitted carpet, Liberty's curtains, and slimline radiators. The proprietor smoothed the sides of her grey housecoat. 'There used to be a lot of old junk in here,' she said casually. 'I don't suppose you'd be interested in that sort of thing?'

Hambro's finger froze on the button. 'You mean you actually have the original . . . artefacts?' He felt he would have to sit down.

'We found it in the attic when we were doing the insulation. It's nearly all been sold now. Two nice gentlemen from California bought most of it.'

Hambro's face was like that of a small boy whose strawberry ice-cream has just fallen out of its cornet. 'Not *all* of it, surely?' he pleaded.

The proprietor flicked at a speck of imaginary dust on the chaise-longue. 'There might be the odd item left. I could go and check if you like?' She went out and did not return until several hours later, by Hambro's emotional clock.

'There's this,' she announced. She proffered a porcelain chamber pot with a hairline crack running from the handle to the base. 'It needs a bit of a polish.'

Hambro's fingers trembled as he took it from her. He held it to the light, turning it at every angle, like an antique dealer dating a Ming vase. 'It's magnificent. It's most probably the one that belonged to Mr Brooker, your predecessor by several removes.' He hooked his thumb over the rim. 'This is how he used to carry it when it was full.' He walked a few paces with it, by way of illustration. 'It's a miracle it has survived.'

'You'd like to purchase it, then?'

'Most assuredly.'

The proprietor took out a red notebook and flicked through the pages. 'Here we are, item eighty-three. A hundred and sixty-five pounds, inclusive of VAT.'

Hambro almost dropped it. 'Isn't that rather expensive?'

The woman sniffed. 'Not to our American buyers. Of course, if you'd rather leave it . . .' She made as though to take it from him, but he turned quickly away, hugging it protectively to his chest with both arms. 'I'll write you a cheque at once.'

She wrapped it in tissue paper and coloured string, complete with a small loop for carrying it by. 'I'm glad you decided to buy it,' she confided as she showed him out. 'I don't like to see our national heritage being shipped abroad.'

20

It was fairly quiet in Tozer Place for a Friday afternoon. One or two of the local girls sauntered up and down swinging their handbags by the straps and somehow managing to convey how little they had on beneath their long Astrakhan coats. A cluster of Swedish sailors from the visiting nuclear submarine stood on the corner trying to decide between the falafel take-away and the Stripperama. Three dwarfs in black-and-white minstrel make-up were doing a soft-shoe shuffle on the pavement, watched by an equal number of policemen. A clergyman on a bicycle was ringing his bell and calling hello to total strangers.

'It's been a pretty disastrous week, Sir,' Skillicorn admitted. His normally cheerful face hung down in several places. 'Only two people turned up for my lecture on Machiavelli for the Small Businessman. And one of them thought it was something to do with pasta manufacture.' He pushed irritably at the inflated rubber doll whose feet were persistently nudging the back of his neck. One of the posters on the revolving notice-board had been torn by day trippers and he was endeavouring to repair it with Sellotape. It read: LUNCHTIME SPECIAL: SCHOPENHAUER IN THE SHOPPING HOUR.

Hambro gave his junior lecturer a consoling pat on the arm. 'Try not to take it personally. The history of western philosophy is a story of ups and downs. We are just going through a bit of a trough.'

Skillicorn brightened a little as he pulled crumpled strips of sticky tape off his fingers and thumbs. 'At least we're not doing too badly on some of the ancillary sales. The Phenomenology sweatshirts are selling like hot cakes.'

An ambulance went by. All heads turned to stare, as though the urgent clanging of its bell did not convey sufficient information to the senses. The three dwarfs immediately ceased their soft-shoe shuffle and one of the girls in Astrakhan coats stubbed out her cigarette and fingered her rosary. Hambro watched it until it turned the corner. It was the third ambulance he had seen that day, though the other two were merely making their routine call to Catering Studies. He felt the ache of mortality like a phantom limb.

Mr Shanker appeared at his elbow from nowhere. 'Hello, Douglas, old son. Fancy seeing a man like you in a place like

118

this.' His mobile features became hyperactive. 'Not to worry, mum's the word.' He put a finger against his nose and winked conspiratorially.

Hambro directed his father-in-law's attention to the painted Gothic sign above the doorway. 'As you can observe, I am here in a teaching capacity, not in the pursuit of pleasure.' He thought it prudent not to enquire into Mr Shanker's own motives for being in Tozer Place.

'The Mind Shop, eh,' Mr Shanker said. 'Classy bit of signwriting. Like a funeral parlour.' He cleared his nasal passages with an implosive snort, but refrained from spitting. 'What's it all about then, Douglas? You flogging the subject retail now?' He listened with close attention to Hambro's edited account of the intellectual origins of The Mind Shop and to the brief history of its fluctuating fortunes.

'Things are in the doldrums right now,' Hambro concluded, 'but we're hoping trade will pick up in the tourist season. Skillicorn's putting on a series of special lectures for works' outings and coach parties. He's calling it "Hi De Heidegger".'

Mr Shanker sucked thoughtfully on his cavernous back teeth. 'Okay if I take a butcher's?' He peered into the doorway.

Hambro led him along the passage towards the basement steps, experiencing only mild surprise when his father-in-law exchanged warm greetings with the surly young Cypriot or Maltese who still sat on duty at the bead curtain.

'Nice lad, Spiro,' Mr Shanker averred, as he pulled open the door at the bottom of the steps which Hambro was trying to push open. 'Strong as an ox he is, but none too bright up top. He played Desdemona to my Othello in the Wormwood Scrubs Shakespeare Festival. He did very well till the final act when the silly bleeder tried to throttle *me*.' He prowled around the seminar room looking at the journals and students' notebooks and abandoned knitting patterns. Now and then he drove his thumbnail into one of the exposed beams or rapped on the wall with his knuckles as if to communicate with someone incarcerated on the other side. He had on a loose-fitting suit with padded shoulders, the material of which underwent subtle changes of colour according to the light.

'I'm amazed that business isn't booming, Douglas,' he said, with an air of genuine puzzlement. 'With a site like this you should be minting it.'

'So you keep saying. You are beginning to sound like the Vice-Chancellor.'

Mr Shanker ran his eye over the accounts ledger for the first half of Lent term. Something seemed to be troubling him. He jerked his bony chin towards the ceiling. 'That lad of yours upstairs? The one with the artificial limbs.'

'Skillicorn.'

'You sure he hasn't got his fingers in the till?'

Hambro let out a tiny squawk of indignation. 'Skillicorn? Embezzling? Certainly not. He was recently cleared of all charges of misappropriating the chalk allowance.'

Mr Shanker looked sceptical. 'I should keep an eye on him if I was you. No one could be as innocent as he looks.'

Hambro felt his neck grow hot at this unwarranted slur on his junior lecturer's integrity. The Vice-Chancellor had said exactly the same thing during the disciplinary hearings. 'Skillicorn comes of a very sound family,' he pointed out. 'His father was Scumbo Skillicorn, he used to fag for me at Eton, and later became a Minister without Portfolio in the minority government. He might have become one of our finest political orators if it hadn't been for his cleft palate. And, what is more, Skillicorn's mother was a close friend of my wife. They used to open the batting together for Gloucestershire.'

Mr Shanker shrugged his shoulders as if to acknowledge a possible error of judgment. 'Okay Douglas, if you say so. All I'm saying is, you have to be careful in an area like this – it attracts some very dodgy customers.' He took up the accounts ledger once more and flicked through the pages. Hambro left him to it while he went to telephone the Royal

120

Eric Blair Society; he had heard an alarming rumour that his election as Honorary President was to be contested. He returned grim-faced ten minutes later to find Mr Shanker still engrossed in the accounts.

'Tell you what, Douglas,' he said, stroking the open ledger with his palm. 'I could probably put a bit of trade your way, if you're interested like.'

Hambro stared at him over the top of his glasses.

'I've made a few contacts with the local entrepreneurs. There's nothing like the old personal touch to make the wheels of commerce go round. Know what I mean?'

'Hm,' Hambro said doubtingly. 'Would they have philosophical interests?'

Mr Shanker showed most of his overlapping teeth. 'I shouldn't be a bit surprised, they've got interests in nearly everything.' He took up a stick of chalk that was secured to the easel by a strand of wire and made some rapid calculations on the blackboard beneath Skillicorn's blindfold drawing of Diogenes not quite sitting in his tub. 'We can talk about my percentage later.'

As evening fell the two men walked together to the bus stop. Tozer Place was beginning to come to life. Rock music blared from the dark interior of an army surplus boutique and coloured laser beams flickered on and off display boards advertising fizzy drinks and adult movies. A woman in a tartan shawl had set up a small table in a doorway and was demonstrating the three-card trick to a party of foreign schoolteachers on a cultural exchange. The evening air was heavy with the aroma of hot fat, roasted chestnuts, and leaded petrol fumes.

'Never mind the bus,' Mr Shanker said before they got to the stop. 'We'll take a cab.' He waved at a line of green taxis parked almost opposite. The driver at the head of the line folded away his newspaper and pulled across in a tight U-turn. 'Where to, guvnor?'

'Hello, Vernon, my old son,' Mr Shanker beamed. 'Nice to see you out and about again.'

'Hello, Mr Shanker.' The driver jumped out, opened the rear door, and waited until his two passengers were comfortably installed before he shut the door without slamming it. Soon they were travelling at maximum permissible speed along the arterial road, through the prizewinning tunnel, and on to the suburban freeway.

Mr Shanker turned to his companion as they sped past the middle management housing development. 'What's come over the Princess lately? She's been acting very peculiar.'

Hambro's bushy eyebrows rose and fell. 'Princess?'

'Margery,' Mr Shanker explained.

'Margery?'

'My daughter. Your missus. Your second missus.'

'Ah. Yes.' Hambro examined the liver spots on the backs of his hands. Was it his imagination, or were they spreading?

'Last week she was a blonde,' Mr Shanker said. 'Now she's a kind of redhead. And I swear she's been shaving her legs with my razor.'

Hambro grunted in sympathy. 'I believe it is to do with her rejuvenation programme. She has turned up the hems of her skirts and is learning to smoke. She has also taken out a weekly subscription to *Ms Methodist*.'

Mr Shanker clacked his tongue disapprovingly. 'I don't like it, Douglas. She was never like this in the Elephant. She had a right go at me the other day because of her wonky teeth. She reckons it's all down to me. I can't help me genetics, can I?'

They passed the gipsy encampment and turned off before the Designated Picnic Zone into a road bordered on either side by stunted conifers. The sodium lamps burned orange against the darkening sky.

'And where does she get to every evening?' Mr Shanker demanded. 'There's never any dinner cooked. I'm sick of living off chicken pot noodle.'

Hambro checked the days off on his fingers. 'As far as I am aware, on Mondays, Wednesdays and Thursdays she goes disco dancing in the Salvation Army hut, and on Tuesdays and Saturdays she takes comportment lessons in the university library. I am not sure of her movements on Fridays and Sundays.'

Mr Shanker sniffed disparagingly. 'Chicken pot noodle, I ask you. There's no way we'd have put up with that muck in Reading or the Scrubs.'

The taxi swung into a side turning and came to a smooth stop outside the only house in the street in total darkness. Hambro took out his wallet to pay the driver.

'No, no, no,' Mr Shanker protested. 'You put that away.'

Hambro hesitated before taking out a ten pound note. 'It's very kind of you to offer, but I can hardly let you pay, given your . . . circumstances.'

Mr Shanker took the note, folded it in two, and pushed it in Hambro's top pocket. 'Don't be silly, Douglas. Vernon's not the sort to ask for money, are you, Vernon?'

The driver shook his head without turning round. He got out and opened both the rear doors.

'How very generous of him,' Hambro remarked as he tried to open the front door with his office key.

'He's a very generous lad, our Vernon. And a very good wheels man, too – one of the fastest in the business. I'd recommend him strongly if you ever need to get away in a hurry. Know what I mean?'

21

While her father and her husband were pouring boiling water into plastic tubs of chicken pot noodle, Margery Hambro was sitting restlessly in the bar of the Senior Common Room. For the past ten minutes she had been trying to attract the attention of the man slumped on the settee opposite. She kept crossing and uncrossing her legs and flapping her short but voluminous candy-striped skirt like a waitress shaking cake crumbs off a tablecloth. Already she was beginning to itch from the elastic on her French knickers and the metal clasps on her scarlet suspender belt.

The stranger opposite now appeared to be smiling crookedly at someone sitting in the empty seat beside her. She smiled back and shifted a little to the left to be in the direct line of his vision. Gradually his eyes closed and the pint glass in his hand tilted at an acute angle. Margery noticed for the first time that he was wearing only one sock.

'Can I get you something else, Miss?' Baxi hovered over her. He was holding a round tin tray on which a number of silver coins were suggestively displayed.

'Another pina colada, please.' Margery felt her tongue stumble over the unfamiliar syllables. It was her third drink of the evening on a comparatively empty stomach.

Baxi looked at her quizzically as he took her empty glass. 'Excuse me asking, Miss, but are you Arts or Sciences?' If she's Arts, he thought, she's going to bugger up my correlations.

'Chalk it up to Professor Hambro,' Margery giggled. She had the curious sensation that it was someone else talking inside her body. It was a nicer feeling than she usually felt. When Baxi returned with her pina colada she asked without inhibition who the man sitting opposite was.

'That's Professor Grogan, Head of Catering Studies. He won't be with us after next term. He's being seconded to the Institute of Germ Warfare.'

Margery watched in disappointment as the Head of Catering Studies slid forward on the settee and toppled harmlessly to the floor. Finding herself a lover was proving a lot more difficult than Dr Hagstrom had led her to believe. She had spent all the previous evening in the lounge bar of the Dog and Duck without once being spoken to by the visiting Tanzanian marines. The night before that she had spent four hours jumping up and down in the Salvation Army disco until her breasts were black and blue and the sweatpads under her armpits had disintegrated.

124

She gulped her drink and surveyed the handful of men still conscious or unaccompanied. Two were balancing pint glasses on their foreheads, one was kicking the jukebox, and one was reading the pull-out supplement of *Illustrated Plumbing*. She thought she recognized the latter from a Faculty party she'd once attended to commemorate the twinning arrangement with Consolidated Tractor Fuels. Unless her memory was playing tricks, he was the chap who'd mistaken her for the cloakroom attendant. She had held on to his hat and overcoat for half the evening before finding somewhere to hang them. To make things worse, Duggie had left on his own, forgetting she was with him. Lucky the Vice-Chancellor had given her a lift down as far as the firing range on the back of his moped.

She now walked unsteadily across the bar and sat next to the man who wasn't really a total stranger. 'Hi,' she trilled. 'Remember me?'

The Reader in Drainage Technology looked down at her legs and then raised his gaze in slow appraisal of the rest of her. He turned back to his pull-out supplement.

'I'm Margery. Mrs Professor Hambro.' She decided on the direct approach recommended by her counsellor. It couldn't be any worse than the indirect approach she'd been using so far. She put her hand on his knee. 'I fancy you,' she cooed. She widened her eyes, unaware of the panda-like effect created by her smudged mascara.

The man stared down at the chubby hand resting on his knee. Oh my God, Margery thought. Supposing he's a . . . one of *them*. They say the university's full of them. She snatched her hand away and wiped it on the seat.

'All right then,' said the Reader in Drainage Technology. 'I'll finish my drink first.'

Margery felt elated. Her first conquest seemed exactly the right type: dark wavy hair, pencil moustache, clean fingernails, and quite young compared to Duggie. Pity about the hare lip. She took a compact from her handbag and dabbed a fresh application of crimson on her cheeks. She

125

smiled at the mirror and wiped lipstick off her teeth. Despite the four pina coladas, elation was beginning to give way to apprehension. This would be the very first time she had ever kissed a man other than Duggie. Would it be just the same, she wondered? Duggie always took out his lower dentures, stuck his tongue out, and kept both eyes screwed shut like a child taking cough mixture.

'Come on then,' said her conquest. He drained his beer glass and left the exact money on the table in a puddle of cider. When he stood up he was unexpectedly tall. He clasped Margery's hand in his own and led her briskly across the bar and through a door bearing a plastic figure in top hat and tails. Inside, the Junior and Senior Lecturers in Conveyancing were each standing astride a porcelain basin and singing the same Scottish ballad. The Vice-Chancellor was drying his hair under the hand-blower while conducting a shouted conversation with the Dean of Divinity, whose feet could be seen beneath the extra-wide door of the invalid cubicle.

It was a funny place to bring her, Margery thought, as she found herself being ushered into a WC with a defective lock. Her companion at once put both hands inside her clothes and began pulling them about like a bargain hunter in the January sales.

'You're too short,' he said. 'Up you get.' Without further warning he lifted her bodily on to the lavatory pan, facing the wall. Almost instinctively, she gripped the cistern with one hand and the top of the hardboard partition with the other. There was no lid on the seat and her foot kept slipping into the pan. It was only with difficulty that she managed to swallow her fertility pill.

'Please keep still,' he said. His huge hands were pulling at her elastic and straps. Suddenly, to her astonishment, she felt him entering her in completely the wrong place. She had the strange sensation of being inflated with a powerful bicycle pump. This can't be right, she thought; there was nothing about this in the manual. 'Excuse me,' she said, straining to see over her shoulder exactly what was happening below.

126

'I think you've made a mistake.' These university people, she thought; they're not half as clever as they like to make out. Even Duggie, for all his faults, had never made a blunder like that. The worst he'd ever done was to touch her private place before remembering to take off his gardening gloves. 'Mister,' she called out. 'Could you just stop a minute?' He was now breathing fiercely, sucking in air through his nose and blowing it out of his mouth. He let out a dry croak followed by a long shuddering gasp. Margery felt herself rapidly deflating. Before she had a chance to step down he picked up the lavatory brush, dipped it in the pan, and twirled the wet bristle prophylactically between her legs. 'All done,' he said, offering her a length of toilet roll.

Margery relaxed her grip on the cistern. As she stared down at the ginger wig of the Professor of Chiropody seated in the next cubicle she felt that she would at least have something positive to report to Dr Hagstrom's seminar.

22

'Come along, Spiro, business before pleasure.' Mr Shanker was addressing the burly young man who normally sat on duty at the bead curtain, cleaning his nails with a penknife, but who was now sitting in the seminar room of The Mind Shop reading a girls' comic and laughing aloud. He looked up and frowned with the effort of making a sudden re-entry into the grown-up world around him. Still frowning he got to his feet and brushed the chalk dust off his Elvis Presley shirt. 'No, Spiro, leave the comic.' Mr Shanker eased it by degrees from the young man's reluctant fists. 'We don't want to give our clientele the wrong impression, do we now?' He took his trilby hat off the plaster bust of Nietzsche and set it at a jaunty angle on his own head. He checked the contents of his briefcase, snapped it shut, tightened the knot in his

Liberal Party tie, and went sedately up the basement steps into the vitreous February sunlight of Tozer Place. Spiro lumbered after him. His neck was wider in circumference than his head, and his elongated arms hung well away from his sides as though in deliberate parody of early man.

As they made their way to their first appointment Mr Shanker reminded him once again of the nature of their enterprise and his own limited but vital part in it. He spoke slowly and deliberately, repeating difficult words, until he was sure that Spiro had grasped the point that what was required of him today was, in all essentials, the same as had been required of him yesterday and the day before. 'Well done, son,' he said, giving him a pat on his sequinned shoulder. Such a nice lad, he thought; what a crying shame he missed out on his fair share of the old grey matter. No wonder he was always in trouble with the law; just think of the way he bungled the Grosvenor Square job. Everything had been going strictly according to plan until Spiro stopped a Flying Squad car to ask the quickest way to Heathrow. It might not have been so bad if the silly bleeder hadn't still been wearing his stocking mask.

The two men now entered a shop with an inconspicuous sign above the door prohibiting admittance to under-eighteens. Shelves of magazines in sealed plastic covers stretched the length of one wall. On the opposite wall were rows of empty video cases illustrated with pictures of partly dressed girls wrestling underwater or wielding atomic weaponry. In the centre of the shop stood a number of tall glass cabinets containing marital aids for use with battery or mains and each carrying a twelve-month guarantee.

Mr Shanker gave these only a perfunctory glance as he touched his trilby hat and addressed himself to a man in dark glasses sitting on a high stool behind the counter.

'Morning, Sir,' he chirped. 'I'm calling on behalf of SAP.'

The man removed his dark glasses to reveal a pair of small mistrustful eyes. 'Sap?'

Mr Shanker repeated the acronym. 'Sponsor A Philoso-

128

pher. I'm your local regional organizer.' He tapped his Samsonite briefcase.

The proprietor locked the cash register and put the key in his pocket. 'You're too late. I'm already sponsoring someone for the Geriatric Fun Run.'

Mr Shanker smiled and touched the fashionably small knot in his tie. 'No, Sir, this is quite different from your usual kind of sponsorship. We give something in return.'

The man's small eyes almost disappeared. 'Give what?'

Mr Shanker opened his briefcase, took out his documentation, and laid it on the counter. 'Each month we ask you to sponsor the philosopher of your own choosing. You can select a different thinker each month, if that's your fancy, or you can stick by the same one for the whole academic year. It's entirely up to you. We cater for practically any school of thought you care to mention.' He spread a selection of postcard reproductions of eminent philosophers across the counter as though to demonstrate a party trick. 'In return we supply you with a picture of the great man of your choice. You'll find it adds a bit of tone to the place.'

The proprietor carefully replaced his dark glasses, using both hands. 'Sod off,' he said. 'And take this rubbish with you.' He flicked dismissively at a black-and-white postcard of Thomas Aquinas looking grumpy.

Mr Shanker retrieved it off the floor and gave it a little polish with the end of his tie. 'That's a very harsh judgment, Sir, if you don't mind me saying. I'd agree with you that some of the epistemological assumptions of Thomism are a bit on the dodgy side, but you couldn't really call it rubbish. Take his *Summa Theologiae* as a case in point . . .'

'Look, Bonzo, I told you to sling your bloody hook.' The proprietor jerked his thumb towards the door. 'I don't want none of your philosophy, I'm doing all right without it.'

Mr Shanker snapped his fingers, as if in annoyance with himself. 'Silly me. There's one thing I totally forgot to mention. As a sponsor you get the full benefit of our protection service.'

129

'Just piss off, I don't need protection.'

Mr Shanker shook his head sadly. 'Oh, I think you do, Sir. This can be a very rough area. That's why we offer our sponsors the services of the Philosophical Front.'

'The filly what?'

'It's our paramilitary wing,' Mr Shanker explained with a trace of pride. 'We take care of your concrete as well as your abstract needs.' He gave a low, almost soundless whistle. Spiro looked up from the adult magazines whose titles he was endeavouring to read by moving his finger along the words. At another signal from Mr Shanker the human embodiment of the Philosophical Front slouched across to the tallest of the glass cabinets, encircled his arms around it, and raised it two feet off the floor. The electronic marital aids cascaded forward.

'For Christ sake go easy,' yelled the proprietor. He raised both hands in the air. 'That stuff's not paid for yet.'

'You see what I mean, Sir,' Mr Shanker sighed. 'About this being a rough area? You're very vulnerable, what with all this expensive gear and inflammatory literature. Know what I mean?'

The proprietor unlocked the cash register. 'Okay, okay. How much?' he said grimly.

Mr Shanker gave another whistle and Spiro lowered the cabinet to the floor with a bump. 'Nothing to pay today, Sir. Here's one of our standing order forms. Half a grand would be about right for an establishment like this. Make it payable to The Mind Shop.' He handed the new sponsor a printed form and a leaflet outlining the main and auxiliary services available to subscribers. 'All you need to do today is decide which philosopher to sponsor for the month of February. Select any one off this printed list.'

The proprietor held the list close to his dark glasses. 'Confucius,' he said morosely.

Mr Shanker sucked air in through the gaps between his teeth. 'Sorry, Sir, he's already spoken for by the Chinese laundry.'

'Kierkegaard then.'

'He's out too. The Danish bacon shop have beat you to it.'

Finally he selected Descartes.

'A very wise choice,' Mr Shanker declared. He fished out a picture of the Parisian sage with a bubble coming out of his mouth saying *Cogito ergo sum.* 'He'll look a treat on the wall over there, next to the French ticklers.'

The air pollution warning was sounding as the two local representatives of Sponsor A Philosopher crossed the street and entered the premises of Akropolis Travel.

''Morning, Mr Kelefthiades,' Mr Shanker beamed, touching his trilby hat. 'I've just popped in for a little chat about Socrates.'

23

The Vice-Chancellor fidgeted nervously with his glass paper-weight as he faced the three young men standing shoulder to shoulder in front of his desk. Two of them wore the now standard dark brown double-breasted suit and white shirt buttoned to the neck without a tie. The third wore a grey *burnous* and a black and white *keffiyeh*. Each had an embryonic beard that was not yet distinguishable from a recent shave with a blunt blade. They stared at the Vice-Chancellor with unconcealed contempt.

'Although I can understand your conduct,' he lied, 'it's another matter to say I condone it.' He took up a sheet of foolscap paper and read from it. 'Seventeen bottles of malt whisky, eleven bottles of gin, twelve flagons of Bulgarian Chablis, three demi-johns of Chianti, two cases of doctored Austrian Riesling, six crates of Budweiser, and a firkin of real ale. All literally poured down the drain.' His tone was one of shock rather than anger, as though he had discovered the Dean of Divinity to be an undercover Rastafarian. 'The Senior Common Room is a complete wreck. The damage runs into thousands of pounds. Due to an administrative oversight the only items covered by insurance were the Breathalyzer and Professor Grogan's pewter tankard. And even they may be excluded from Acts of God and Civil Commotion.'

The student in the *keffiyeh* made a sweeping gesture with his arm, inadvertently striking the saddle of the Vice-Chancellor's exercise bicycle. 'Compensation will be paid in full for all damage done to the Senior Common Room,' he intoned in a nasal Liverpool accent. 'But not for the alcohol. That is the Imam's ruling.'

'But the alcohol was by far the most expensive item,' protested the Vice-Chancellor meekly. It looks like another increase in student fees, he thought.

'That's not our problem,' said the man in the *keffiyeh*. 'The campus has now been declared dry.'

The vein in the Vice-Chancellor's neck stood out like a squeeze of blue toothpaste. 'Who by? By whom?'

'By us, the Merseyside Shi'ites. We're the ruling faction on the campus now.'

The Vice-Chancellor sank back in his swivel chair. He felt as though the blood was rapidly draining from his body through the soles of his feet. There were times when he felt it was a serious error of judgment to have left the cosy and orderly world of industry for the competitive stresses and strains of higher education. If he'd stayed where he was he would by now have been in line for the Thames Valley Regional Office, with a reconditioned company Metro, a pension, and a free medical check-up every five years. Perhaps if he made a success of running the university, CTF might take him back? The very least they could do was give him a trial run as a probationary sales assistant in the Ulster office . . .

He drew himself up straight, put on his let's-all-be-reasonable face, and mopped it with his handkerchief. 'Look,

132

chaps, I can see things from your point of view, please try and see them from mine. It's a well known fact that you can't run a modern university without alcohol. Have you any idea what happens to academics when they're deprived of regular quantities of drink? They tried it at the LSE, and you know what happened there.'

The taller and more menacing of the men in dark brown suits now stepped forward and seemed about to spit on the carpet tiles. 'From now on they'll have to get used to it. Anyone caught drinking on campus will be punished on the main piazza. That is the Imam's ruling.' He jabbed his finger in the air to emphasize every word.

The Vice-Chancellor listened in dismay. If only the university didn't rely so heavily on Khomeini Centre funds he'd soon show these little shits who was boss around here. Without the Centre's generosity there would be no Hayek hall of residence, no Acupuncture School, no bulletproof windows in Senate House, no snooker scholarships. With material support on that scale, and the promise of more to come, you had to allow their followers a certain amount of say. In any case, with a bit of luck this whole religious craze would fade away in a year or two, the same as all the earlier fads like sock-sniffing and necrophilia.

'Look, I know you chaps mean well,' he whined. 'But could you try and keep your more fanati . . . more enthusiastic converts under control? I honestly don't think they ought to go around smashing the place up for religious reasons. Now don't get me wrong, I'm not saying they don't sincerely believe in what they're doing, but even so . . .' He recalled how he'd felt that evening when he'd been summoned to the Senior Common Room to witness the chaos for himself; the TV set gutted, the jukebox in ruins, magazines torn to shreds, the floor awash with beer, wines and spirits, and Professor Grogan down on all fours sucking the carpet.

'No injury was done to persons, only property,' said the man in the *keffiyeh*. 'Our people aren't violent, unless they're provoked.'

The Vice-Chancellor made a half-hearted gesture of quali-
fication. 'It's not *strictly* true to say that no one was injured.
Poor Baxi suffered quite a few knocks. He might have been
drowned in the artificial lake if one of the guard dogs hadn't
pulled him out.' Thank God it was only Baxi, he thought.

The student who had not yet spoken now did so. 'Baxi was
obstructing us in the course of our duty,' he said in the
familiar nasal accent. 'He claimed we were jeopardizing his
research.' His thin lips parted in an equally thin smile around
the notional beard. 'I think we've solved his research problem
for him. He can start all over again now, comparing orange
juice and tomato juice drinkers.' His two companions nodded
in mirthful agreement.

The senior member of the trio then produced two folded
sheets of paper from inside his *burnous* and laid them on
the glass-topped desk. 'This is a list of our demands,' he
explained. 'We expect most of them to be implemented
by the end of Lent term, though we're prepared to be reason-
able and give you until Trinity term to put the more far-
reaching ones into effect, such as the partitioning of the
campus.'

The Vice-Chancellor looked up into the man's blazing
eyes. 'The what?'

'We're not prepared to go on sharing facilities with infidels.
Their close proximity is offensive to us. In future, they will
occupy the back rows of lecture theatres and be admitted to
the refectory only after the Faithful have eaten. They must
also keep to their own corner of the library, between Calli-
graphy and French Polishing. Finally, they'll be allowed to
use the snooker tables only when our players have been
summoned to prayers. The Faculty mullahs will be on hand
to ensure full compliance with these rules.' He gathered up
his *burnous*, turned, and strode to the door followed by his
two companions. All three then paused in the doorway,
raised their fists and chanted something in unison, causing
Miss Pollins to lock herself in her cubbyhole.

The Vice-Chancellor climbed into his rowing machine but

134

felt too dispirited to row. He was still mulling over the sixteen minor and seven major demands that had just been presented to him. Perhaps he shouldn't think of them as demands so much as strongly worded proposals for his due consideration. They could have been a lot worse; after all, the people most affected by them were only students. He could at least be thankful that they hadn't demanded his own conversion, or that of his senior staff. What would he do if they did? he asked himself. Hm. Would a change of faith be such a drastic step in this day and age? Plenty of eminent people were going over to them of their own free will, including the Home Secretary, the Poet Laureate, the entire Ryder Cup team and the Warden of All Souls. There was even a rumour that Dirk Oesterbroek was thinking of converting. If people like that were willing to make the switch there must be something in it. It was certainly worth considering. Besides, who'd be any the wiser if he had the occasional bacon sandwich or glass of Cyprus sherry?

Later that day he strapped on his crash-helmet and drove across the campus on his moped. Fresh snow had fallen and was already turning to slush on the duckboards. Seagulls were circling above the artificial lake. One by one they swooped down for bits of bread intended for the grebe, coot and mallard. A Viennese waltz was playing over the loudspeakers of Radio Free Campus. The Vice-Chancellor caught snatches of the tune above the splutter of his engine and began humming it in a freely improvised way. He noted with satisfaction that the scaffolding around the Arts block was finally being dismantled, but was puzzled to see that the crack in the wall between Horticulture and Philosophy was now even wider than ever. As he was passing the Sperm Bank he was forced to swerve sharply on the ice to avoid a head-on collision with an invalid car being driven recklessly on the wrong side of the road. The Dean of Divinity smiled and waved at him as they passed within inches of each other.

Traffic on the arterial road was slowing to a crawl. The Vice-Chancellor manoeuvred his vehicle in and out between the heavy goods trucks and northbound coaches, parping his horn and making elaborate hand signals. He turned off at the asparagus farm and less than ten minutes later was in open country. Without needing to consult the road map more than once he came to an unmetalled road and bumped along it for three miles until reaching the edge of a disused quarry. The wheels of the moped slithered and skidded in the frozen ruts as he coaxed it up a gentle gradient to a clump of deciduous saplings. Snow had fallen more heavily here. It was piled excessively high on the slender young branches as though coachloads of maladjusted children had been allowed to run loose with foam extinguishers. Each time the wind blew it raised a fine white spray.

He propped his machine against the trees and followed a footpath up the bare slope to a seemingly abandoned workmen's hut. He was panting hard. Each breath gave out a cloud of vapour bigger than the one before. He leaned against the hut waiting for his pulse rate to return to normal. In the distance a goods train gave a melancholy hoot and then it was eerily quiet except for the wind banging against the tin roof. He looked at his watch and waited. Ten minutes later he checked his diary.

Presently he heard footsteps crunching on the frozen path. A woman in a long winter coat with fur trimmings appeared from behind the trees. She was carrying a wicker shopping basket crooked in one arm. She waited until she was almost close enough to touch him before speaking.

'Good day to you, Sir. It is very clement weather for such a time of year.' Her cheeks were purple with cold and a small drip on the end of her nose was growing noticeably bigger. 'I am stranger here. Can you tell me please the way to nearest posting box?'

The Vice-Chancellor looked at her eyes as though to check their colour, number and alignment. He spoke with subnormal clarity, leaving a space between each word. 'There is a posting box in the village store, adjacent to the smithy. It is less than a furlong from here.'

The woman's face gave a flicker of acknowledgement and the drip fell from the end of her nose. 'Do you have some thing for me to post?' she asked.

The Vice-Chancellor handed her a bulky brown envelope sealed with tape. He glanced over his shoulder before whispering, 'Our Professor of Laser Technology reckons your boffins will be over the moon with this little lot. Something to do with submarine detection – it's all mumbo jumbo to me.'

The woman smiled enigmatically and slipped the envelope in her wicker basket beneath an assortment of instant pudding mixes. 'They were very satisfied with earlier deliveries, I think you know it.' She moved a packet of banana whip closer to a packet of kiwi fruit blancmange.

'Yes, we're all very grateful,' the Vice-Chancellor said. 'The . . . um . . . proceeds went to endow a second Chair of Bible Studies.' He held out his hand and said in a loud voice, 'Anyway, must be off. Jolly nice bumping into you like this. Give my regards to Mr Popplewell and all the family. Have a good day.' He strode off briskly in the wrong direction, down the path into the disused quarry. He kept glancing from side to side and casually stopping for no apparent reason, like a man walking a dog which he had somehow forgotten to bring.

24

Baxi hobbled up the steps of Experimental Psychology leaning on a metal crutch. His left arm was in a sling and a small square of grubby sticking plaster was peeling away from his forehead at two corners. Just below his crown, surrounded by long uncombed hair, was a circular bald patch on which a gummy blue substance had been applied a little too thickly. He took the steps one at a time, bringing his left foot up against his right as in certain types of ballroom dance. The top step was being scrubbed and he had to lift each leg painfully over the kneeling figure of the Emeritus Professor of Greek. He knocked on Hedda Hagstrom's office door and waited for the red light to flash on before going in.

'Sit,' she said, almost tempting Baxi to give a tiny yap of obedience or wag an imaginary tail. 'No, not there. Over by the specimen cabinet.'

He limped melodramatically to the other side of the room and sat on a low bench beside a glass tank containing a pickled cerebellum. It gave off a smell that reminded him of his recent stay in hospital. Next to the glass tank was a cage in which white mice with red numbers painted on their backs were pushing tiny levers in exchange for salted peanuts. Baxi watched them enviously.

'I may as well come straight to the point,' Hedda Hagstrom said. She was sitting at her desk, framed between a video recorder and a pile of manuscripts. 'I've marked your term project, *Alcoholics in Academe*. I'm afraid it's a clear fail.' She picked up the dog-eared manuscript in order to let it fall from her fingers. 'The data are totally insufficient to support your main hypothesis. You haven't properly controlled for other key variables, such as religion, home ownership, and mating patterns. And you make hardly any reference to other important studies in the same field, such as my own monograph on vodka consumption and the left-wing vote. It's widely regarded as a classic.'

Baxi pressed the tip of his metal crutch against the sole of his shoe. The hard cover of *The Wealth of Nations* had worn through in two separate places, revealing two holes in his purple sock of exactly the same shape. 'I couldn't get hold of your vodka monograph, it's missing from the library. But I did refer to all your other books and articles, published and unpublished, including the transcripts of your broadcasts on Radio Free Campus, book reviews in the Sunday papers and your letters to the local paper complaining about the seagull droppings on your panoramic window.'

138

Hedda Hagstrom appeared unimpressed. She interlocked her fingers to form an arch and circled one thumb slowly around the other. 'The fact of the matter is, the topic you chose to investigate is a highly complex one. It needed a lot more work than you put into it. The results are all so . . . inconclusive.'

The shadows under Baxi's eyes seemed to darken. 'I know it's not properly finished, but what could I do? The campus was declared dry before I'd got all the facts. What was I supposed to do, invent them?'

'All right, Mr Baxi, don't adopt that tone with me.'

Baxi felt his pride slide down his throat as his voice now rose and fell in open supplication. 'Surely it's worth a pass for effort or originality? Or even for the diagrams of Professor Grogan? I can't afford to repeat the term, I'm already up to my eyes in debt with medical expenses.' His hand went of its own accord to the circular bald patch below his crown. Five days in the university infirmary had cost him more than he had earned in wages and tips for the entire term. He had tried to get the Merseyside Shi'ites to foot the bill and pay him something for damages as well, but apparently infidels didn't qualify for compensation. All they offered him was a secondhand prayer mat and a tourist map of Mecca.

'I'm sorry to hear that you've had some personal problems,' Hedda Hagstrom said evenly. 'But they can't be allowed to cloud the issue. I have a professional duty to judge your work on purely academic criteria. This is, after all, a place of higher learning, not a welfare agency. I'm sure you appreciate that.'

Baxi plucked at his arm-sling. He no longer needed to wear it but had hoped to play on her sympathy. Play on her what? he now asked himself. 'So that's it, then?' he said. 'Four years in this dump for a BSc Failed.'

Hedda Hagstrom shrugged. 'So it seems.' She reached for a term paper by another of her fourth-year students and turned to the bibliography at the back. All her own publications were fully and correctly listed. She gave it a provisional alpha mark and put it aside. 'It's unfortunate perhaps, but not everyone is cut out to succeed in experimental psychology.'

Baxi sat in silent contemplation of the dismal prospect now before him. Who's going to give me a job with my qualifications, he wondered. No one apart from the Foreign Office or the Treasury. At least his mother and father would be pleased; they still renewed his street-hawker's licence every year and still advertised themselves as the Baker Street Underpass Trio. Since the exorcism had gone wrong they'd even been sleeping at their place of work. Oh well, he might as well join them; it would be less cramped than his present quarters. With a show of agony he hauled himself to his feet and limped across to the door thumping his metal crutch like Long John Silver.

Hedda Hagstrom was already busy correcting the proofs for her forthcoming monograph on male hysteria. Without glancing up she said, 'Mr Baxi, I'm prepared to give you one more chance. If, that is, you are still interested in continuing with your studies here.'

Baxi felt relief and gratitude spread through all parts of his bruised body as he leaned it against the door. He had read somewhere in one of his psychology books that prisoners who were regularly beaten by camp guards came to experience a kind of love for their tormentors whenever they showed them the smallest sign of mercy. For the first time he thought he had an inkling of how they felt.

'An opportunity has arisen that would allow you to redeem yourself. I need some assistance with one of my experiments.'

Baxi's relief suddenly evaporated. 'Oh no, I'm not being wired up for Dutch lessons again.' The mere sight of a ball of Edam or a row of tulips was enough to bring him out in a cold sweat.

Hedda Hagstrom made a small gesture of reassurance. 'The language-teaching programme has been temporarily discontinued, pending the outcome of the coroner's report.'

She went on correcting page proofs while she talked. 'You won't, of course, be aware of the fact, but I am at present engaged on a long-term project designed to teach a group of chimpanzees to play Monopoly. One of them has had a mental breakdown and I'd like you to take its place. You need four players for a proper game.'

Baxi picked thoughtfully at one of the loose corners of sticking plaster on his forehead. 'Why not just get another one?' he asked innocently.

Hedda Hagstrom's eyes flicked up as if to detect signs of sarcasm. 'Have you any idea of the cost of a chimpanzee at current prices? They are extremely valuable creatures. Quite apart from the expense, there's the additional problem of getting them past the Animal Liberation pickets. We had to smuggle the last one in dressed in the Vice-Chancellor's academic robes.'

Baxi absent-mindedly transferred his crutch from his good hand to his bad and pointed it like a sten-gun. 'It may sound like a daft question, but why are you teaching a bunch of monkeys to play Monopoly?' Could it be some sort of trick? Once she'd got him in a cage she might pump him full of hormones to make him grow a tail. He wouldn't put it past her.

Hedda Hagstrom seemed to sense his secret fears. She put down her silver pencil and aligned it with the edge of her blotting pad. 'That's a perfectly fair question, I see no reason why you shouldn't know. It's actually part of a larger project sponsored by the Employers' Federation. They want me to prove that even the lower species have natural capitalistic tendencies.' She went on to explain a little more about the background to the study and about her scientific techniques for measuring property accumulation among the primates. 'As for the game itself, I'd want you to be banker. We use bananas and fruit gums as money. You'll soon get the hang of it, the animals did.' She reached for a batch of typewritten letters in her in-tray. 'Perhaps you would like to think it over while I sign these notices of dismissal?'

Baxi ran a hand through his long lank hair. His half-yearly crop had had to be postponed because of his medical bills. 'I don't seem to have a lot of choice,' he muttered.

'Good. I'm sure you've made the right decision. Report to the Cyril Burt wing at eight o'clock sharp tomorrow morning. And Mr Baxi?'

'Mm?'

'Bring a rubber apron and a face towel. The animals are inclined to get over-excited when the stakes are running high.'

When he had gone she returned to his term project on *Alcoholics in Academe*. The correlations really were very weak as they stood. It was an amateurish piece of work, although the illustrations were quite well done. It took her half an hour to re-calculate the figures so that they supported the main and subsidiary hypotheses. In addition to making one or two grammatical corrections and stylistic changes she crossed out Baxi's name on the front page and substituted her own. She summoned her secretary on the intercom.

'Yes, Dr Hagstrom?' he said, standing almost to attention.

'Retype this for me.' She tossed him the still dog-eared, but otherwise improved, manuscript. 'And run off fifty copies. It's my paper for the Zurich Symposium of Abnormal Psychologists.'

When he had left she unlocked the bottom drawer of her desk and took out a wooden figurine eight inches long mounted on a brass pedestal. This was an exact replica of the Nobel Prize for Experimental Psychology. It had been carved for her by an old man in the gipsy camp from photographs and drawings generously supplied by the Swedish Academy of Sciences. She turned it possessively in her hands, caressing the smooth mahogany curves, smelling the fragrant resin, fingering the plaque on the pedestal engraved with her name and academic honours. Soon she felt the familiar excitement come over her. She undid the top two buttons of her white coat and pressed the figurine to her bosom. She

142

closed her eyes, allowing the ecstasy to take complete control . . .

The telephone rang. She snatched up the receiver. 'Stockholm?' she cried in exultation. 'I accept! I accept!'

'It's Baxi here. I've been thinking about the Monopoly. If I make a profit for the bank can I trade my bananas in for dollars?'

25

Colin Lumsden forced open the frostbound window of his room on the fourth floor of the Hayek hall of residence and stared out into the starless night. Through the gap between the half-completed Khomeini Centre and the Edwardian wing of Admin II he could see the harbour lights and, beyond them, the erratic neon sign of the Psycho Motel flashing on the by-pass. He recalled that he had once reserved a room in the motel for his mother which she had vacated shortly before dawn because of a premonition, leaving him to pay the bill.

He raised one foot onto the windowsill. He could hear the east wind humming in the telegraph wires and around the minaret. He wished there could be an electrical thunderstorm or an earthquake or some other natural calamity to mark his departure from this world. A carton of low fat milk and a solid slab of sunflower margarine were frozen to the windowsill. Although he had no further use for either, his strong dislike of waste led him to prise them loose and put them on the lukewarm radiator where they might be found by someone in need. He steadied his left foot on the sill and rolled down the sleeves of his shirt against the cold. Then, as if to catch himself unawares, he brought his right foot up and swung it forward and out in a single kicking movement. 'Goodbye everybody,' he cried out as he fell head first into the blackness.

Margery Hambro turned up the collar of her ocelot coat as she waddled across the campus to catch the last bus home. Beneath her coat she wore a black leotard with a white sash knotted around the waist. Her mainly blonde hair was twisted into a plait that was coming undone at the end despite the little black velvet bow. She felt cold and dejected after a fruitless evening spent sipping tomato juice in a deserted Senior Common Room. Not a soul had spoken to her all evening except a fierce young man with a beard who told her she was sitting on the wrong side of the room. What was the good, she wondered, of knowing and naming her parts if nobody else showed any interest in them. She passed beneath the shadow of the mosque and crossed to the hall of residence. She was half walking, half running, causing her buttocks to wriggle beneath the ocelot coat like two ferrets in a poacher's sack.

When she turned the corner she was surprised to see a figure crawling out backwards from the base of a pyramid of snow which bulldozers had piled there earlier in the day. He stood up, brushed snow from his hair, and tapped his trouser pockets. 'Now I've lost all my coins,' he complained aloud to himself. 'I need them for the payphone.'

Margery took out her torch to help him look for them. Throughout the search he kept up an endless stream of invective. 'That useless bloody manual. I've tried every method in it, and none of them are any good. That's twelve pound fifty down the drain. It's a bloody rip-off.' He sat down in the snow and began to cry. He held his head in both hands as if to support its weight. Margery stood over him, wondering what to do. The last bus was standing at the stop revving its engine; she might just catch it if she ran hard and yodelled to the driver.

She knelt at Lumsden's side and tried to comfort him. 'There, there,' she purred. She put an arm around his shoulder and rocked him vigorously to and fro. When she

144

was able to coax him to his feet she was a little surprised by his shortness. She led him into the hall of residence and up the stairs. He held on to her with both hands, resting his head on her shoulder. Margery made this possible by stooping forward and bending a little at the knees.

'Dr Hagstrom's going to be furious,' he burbled. 'She'll take it as a personal criticism of her methods.' An icy wind was gusting through his room. It billowed the curtains and fluttered the pages of the now discredited manual lying on the floor. Margery closed the window and then sat him on the bed, removed his wet shoes and socks, and draped a blanket over his shoulders. She chipped a lump of frozen milk from the carton and plugged the kettle in for tea.

'There's only one teabag left,' Lumsden whimpered. 'I've been running down supplies.' Inside the blanket he seemed to Margery smaller and more vulnerable than ever, although his feet were those of a fully grown man. She sat by his side and held a chipped enamel mug under his chin while he took tiny sips from it like a defeated hunger striker. Flecks of snow were still clinging to his hair. As they melted they trickled down his unhappy face and fell into his tea. Margery dabbed tenderly at his cheeks with the corner of the candlewick bedspread. He's got a nice little face, she thought. He reminded her of her cousin Desmond before his operation.

After a while he began to perk up and then grew talkative. He told her all about his clairvoyant mother and his miserable childhood on the caravan site in Porthcawl. 'The big boys used to pick on me. They used to make me forecast Derby winners and beat me up when I got it wrong. They even set light to my ouija board.' At Margery's suggestion he later changed into his flameproof nightshirt and got into bed. She pulled the covers up to his chin and tucked the blankets in tightly on both sides in the hospital fashion.

'You're not going yet, are you?' he asked in panic. 'I'm afraid of the dark and my nightlight needs a new bulb.'

Margery dispelled his fears by taking off her coat and

145

suede bootees. She took his hand and listened sympathetically while he told her of his recurring difficulties in establishing telephone contact with his mother and about the ingratitude and perfidy of his onetime fiancée. 'She sent me a postcard the other day to say how glad she was to be engaged to a man taller than herself who never wets the bed. She even had the nerve to ask me to send back the Young Executive Suspenders she'd bought me. Not that I want them any more. Even they let me down when I needed them. Nothing ever goes right for me . . .' His words dissolved into a choking sob.

'Please don't cry,' Margery pleaded. 'You'll only start me off.' Tears at once welled up in her eyes as she called to mind her own misfortunes. 'Nothing's going right for me either.' She fell alongside him on the bedcovers and for several minutes they cried together, though not quite in synchrony, taking it in turns to snort into the candlewick bedspread. Eventually, the student in the next room banged on the wall with a solid object.

'Belt up, Lumsden,' they heard him shout through the plasterboard. 'What are you doing in there, you little pervert, having it off with a pig?'

Lumsden sat up in bed. 'Shut your face, MacDougal,' he yelled at the wall. 'You can't talk about noise, I'm sick to death of your electronic bagpipes.'

'I'll report you to the mullahs. You know what they think about pork.'

'It's not a pig, you thick Scotchman. It's a girl, or rather a woman.'

'Well she sounds like a pig.'

'I'm warning you, just you keep her out of it.'

Margery put a finger to her lips and mouthed a silent appeal for Lumsden not to pursue the argument any further on her account. At the same time she felt deeply thrilled at his readiness to spring to her defence. No one had ever done as much before, least of all her husband. Once when a racing cyclist had practically knocked her flat on a zebra crossing

146

Duggie had apologized to the man for her carelessness and offered to pay the cost of a new front wheel.

She plumped the pillow and got Lumsden settled down once more. The label on his nightshirt was sticking up at the neck, revealing the washing instructions and the fact that it was the largest in the children's size. Margery tucked it out of sight. 'You're ever so nice,' she heard herself say.

'So are you.' Lumsden squeezed her hand. 'I can't usually talk to people the way I've been talking to you. They never seem to listen to me.'

'I know what you mean.'

Synthesized bagpipe music started up in the next room. In the room above someone seemed to be trying to nail a moving object or creature to the floor, and from the room below came the sound of the midnight pips. Seconds later all the lights went out.

'You're freezing,' Lumsden said. He pressed the back of Margery's hand to his cheek.

'Telling me.'

'It's lovely and warm in here.'

Margery peeled off her black leotard and scrambled in beside him. His short lean body was unexpectedly hot against her own. She felt his hands going over every part of her body with a kind of urgency as though he was looking for something in particular. When they kissed she was surprised by the force of his tongue and the sharpness of his toenails. He now gripped handfuls of her waist and buried his face deep between her breasts. 'My darling,' he said in a muffled voice.

'Oh, my lover,' Margery sighed. 'At last.'

They held on to each other in the narrow bed like two shipwrecked sailors clinging to the same piece of flotsam.

That night Margery dreamt she was on a tropical isle. She was lazing by a blue lagoon threading frangipani and bougainvillea through her golden tresses. The sun shimmered through the coconut fronds. She waded into the warm lagoon and floated on her back, her eyes closed against the brilliant sky. Suddenly the translucent water turned icy cold. She

147

tried to swim to the bank but found that her legs were held fast by weeds. The more she kicked to free herself the more entangled she became. She awoke with a start to a smell of ammonia and her lover's wet sheets knotted around her ankles.

26

'I really am most grateful for everything you've done.' Hambro closed the sales ledger with a satisfying slap. 'Philosophy has broken all previous records for Lent term, or any other term. You have virtually turned it into a boom industry.'

Mr Shanker smiled modestly. 'It's been my pleasure, Douglas. Like I say, I've always had a soft spot for the old subject. It deserves to prosper in this materialistic age.' He shook demerara sugar on the froth of his cappuccino and watched it slowly sink. At the next table a customer was complaining loudly about the discovery of fingernail clippings in the parmesan.

'I gather from Skillicorn that we are almost certain to win the Arts Faculty shield. If we win it three times in a row we can keep it.' Hambro felt genuinely pleased at the dramatic upturn in his department's fortunes, notwithstanding the fact that it had occurred largely in his absence. Since his father-in-law had become actively involved in the promotion of philosophy he had been able to devote much more time to his extramural interest. In addition to building a small annexe in the garden to house the Burmese collection, he had travelled the length and breadth of the country canvassing support for his candidature in the forthcoming election for the Honorary Presidency of the Royal Eric Blair Society. His main source of support seemed to be in the dormitory towns and the hill-farming communities in the West Country, with pockets of support in the South Wales bible belt. His rival, on the other hand, was clearly doing well in the inner-city tenement blocks and among disgruntled members of the retired military. The result was bound to be close and might well be decided by the Overseas and Commonwealth vote.

'As I see it, Douglas,' Mr Shanker was saying, 'this is only the beginning. There'd be no stopping philosophy in a place like this, if you went about it properly.'

'So you keep insisting.' Hambro wiped an arc of condensation off the window of the trattoria and peered across the street at The Mind Shop as though to discern for himself its unrealized potential. Skillicorn was standing outside dressed in an old-fashioned frock-coat and top hat to publicize his study group on *Das Kapital*. In the ill-fitting costume his arms and legs appeared more than ever to be completely independent entities.

'Don't mind me saying, Douglas,' Mr Shanker went on, 'but the thing is, you're not exploiting the shop to its full capacity. You need to expand its activities, branch out in new directions, make better use of all the local talent. Know what I mean?'

Hambro picked at an ancient strip of lasagne verdi embedded almost invisibly in the green tablecloth. 'I don't really think that I do.'

Mr Shanker spoke without the least trace of exasperation or condescension, as though he were explaining slopping-out procedures to a first-time offender. 'Well, the first thing you need to think about is joining forces with one of the other local businesses. Pool your resources, so to speak. It's what we entrepreneurs call vertical integration.' He scraped his glass cup on his glass saucer and took a dainty sip. 'The business upstairs would be ideal. Believe you me, you'd make a winning team. You see, Douglas, in a place like this philosophical interests are bound to be a bit different from what they'd be in Oxford or the Scrubs. Stands to reason. It's all a question of adapting to your environment.'

Hambro struggled to hold on to the core idea. 'You mean enter into partnership with the Bangkok Pleasure Palace?'

149

He looked across at the inflated rubber doll that was swinging in close proximity to Skillicorn's top hat as if seeking to nudge it off. 'Do we have sufficient in common?'

'Enough but not too much. There's no point in duplicating services.' Mr Shanker leaned across the table and gave a confidential wink. 'As a matter of actual fact I've already had a chat with their guvnor about a merger. He wasn't too keen on the idea at first, but the Philosophical Front finally got him to see the sense of it.' Rousseau was dead right, he thought; some people really do have to be forced to be free.

Hambro stared into his empty expresso cup as if to find some sign or message among the muddy dregs. 'It seems an improbable union to me, I must confess. On the other hand, your judgment in these matters has proved to be impeccable. You really do seem to have a gift for putting philosophy across. In earlier and better days you would have made a first-rate college tutor.'

The customer at the next table who had earlier complained about the presence of fingernail clippings in the parmesan was now complaining about the absence of mozzarella on the pizza capricciosa. Mr Shanker plucked a toothpick from the cruet, wedged it between his canine and incisor, and left it there. 'As I see it,' he said, returning to his theme, 'it's all wrong to keep philosophy sealed off down there in its own little basement. It shouldn't be cut off like that from all the goings-on in the world outside. It ought to be involved in the life of the community.' He pointed at Skillicorn who was now having some difficulty preventing the local children from swinging on his coat-tails. 'Take old Marx, now. He had the right idea. He said that base and superstructure weren't really two separate and independent things. They were closely connected with each other, fed off one another, like. After all, Douglas, that's what your dialectic's all about – the unity of opposites.' He fell silent while he worked the toothpick in and out between his huge molars. It was a mistake to have had the osso buco, he now realized, as he probed and sucked at the stringy detritus. Still, it made a

150

change from chicken pot noodle. 'Course, we'll have to change the name of the place,' he announced without preamble. 'We need to let our clientele know that thesis and antithesis have merged into a synthesis.'

Hambro closed his eyes in a show of pain. 'Not the Bangkok Philosophy Parlour?'

Mr Shanker put back his head and laughed. It sounded like a starting pistol going off in the indoor swimming baths. 'No, Douglas, don't worry, we don't want nothing cheap and nasty.' His quick eyes lit up in sudden inspiration. 'I know. We'll call it The Mind and Body Shop.' He raised his empty coffee cup in salute. 'Here's to the unity of spirit and matter.'

Trinity

27

The first day of Trinity term was marked by squally showers and sunny intervals giving way to longer periods of rain and shorter sunny intervals between. Daffodils were in bloom all along the barbed-wire fence around the artificial lake. Unidentifiable green shoots had also appeared on the university allotments and on the walls and roof of Senate House. Maintenance staff had been busy throughout the Easter vacation. They had enlarged the guard-dog kennels with unwanted shelving from the library and dug drainage ditches and latrines at the northern and southern limits of the tented accommodation. The Victorian wing of Admin II had also been refurbished. The old oak doors had been replaced by fire-resistant laminated panels and the floors and stairs had been treated with a hard-wearing varnish that acted both as a deodorant and a fungicide. Decorators were still at work on the exterior, applying the final coat of ultramarine to the pebbledash. Students hurried beneath the ladders, covering their heads with books or free copies of the *University Advertiser* as they made their way to the registration desk. Some of them were dismayed to discover that their degree course in Supply-side Economics had been discontinued without warning, while others were pleased to learn that the Certificate in Martial Arts had been raised to Diploma status. They queued patiently and quietly on the newly-treated stairs clutching their enrolment forms, university savings stamps and literacy certificates while listening to light orchestral music on Radio Free Campus. The music broke off abruptly in the middle of a piece by Franz Lehar to broadcast a pre-recorded address by the Vice-Chancellor welcoming everyone back for the new term and urging them all to work hard and play hard and to uphold the reputation of the university in the town and not to throw their empty crisp packets in the main piazza.

Hambro was aware of none of these events, basking as he now was in the warm Barcelona sun. He sat in the Café Moka, opposite the Hotel Continental, drinking sangria and watching the crowds go by. Young women in bright summer frocks strolled up and down the Ramblas among the flower-sellers and sweetmeat stalls and heavily armed policemen. A legless man on a trolley was selling tickets for the bullfight and a woman in Andalusian costume was dancing an uncon-vincing flamenco by the entrance to McDonald's. Visiting Chelsea supporters threw English coins to or at her as they stampeded past.

Hambro turned to his airmail edition of *The Times*. Nothing much seemed to be happening at home; the Home Secretary had changed his name to Abdullah, the Channel tunnel had caved in again, everyone was complaining about the new five pound coin. When he turned to the obituary columns he was shocked to see Bulkowski's name at the head of the page. Apparently he had died of a stroke while denouncing the neo-Platonists. Hambro felt a trembling ache as he read the words he had written two years earlier about his former colleague. Had he given the man his full due? Should he perhaps have mentioned Bulkowski's expertise as a rose grower and his prowess on the skateboard? And was it wise to have mentioned that shocking incident in the ski-lift during the Salzburg conference? Full of doubts and misgivings he folded the newspaper away and turned his mind to more agreeable thoughts. He had, he told himself, a great deal to be pleased about. During his stay in Catalonia he had not only succeeded in locating the exact place outside Huesca where Orwell had been shot through the throat, but had also managed to penetrate the five hospitals at Sietamo, Barbastro, Lerida, Tarragona, and the Sanatorium Maurín, where the wound had been treated. He now had in his possession a yogurt pot filled with mud from a garlic field, a spent cartridge case, and five ceramic bedpans. In addition,

156

he had been able to bribe the receptionist at the Hotel Continental to put him in the same room that Orwell had occupied prior to making his lucky escape from the Communist authorities. The bedside lamp had an ancient and slightly singed paper shade which the manager had promised to let him have in exchange for his Polaroid camera. He sucked on his pipe and sipped his sangria in contentment. All in all, it had been a thoroughly worthwhile and productive four weeks' stay, despite the diarrhoea and the sunburn and that silly misunderstanding at the road-block with the Guardia Civil.

He flew home a week later and took a taxi direct from Stanstead International to Tozer Place. 'I want The Mind and Body Shop. I can give you the directions.'

'No need, squire. It'll be my third time there today.'

The little one-way street was busier and noisier than Hambro had remembered it. The taxi crawled along, frequently braking to avoid running down jaywalkers and performing artists. 'Scum. Rubbish,' the driver kept repeating. He sounded his horn at a lady dwarf walking on stilts and then at a fire-eater who at once retaliated by directing his flame at the front tyres. Hambro leaned out of the window and was disconcerted to see an unruly throng milling about outside The Mind and Body Shop. He paid the taxi off and edged his way through the crowd. By standing on tiptoe he was just able to see the top half of Skillicorn's body. His junior lecturer was flailing the air with his long arms as though trying to beat off a swarm of bees.

'Gentlemen, gentlemen,' he cried above the clamour. 'Will you please listen. The Hegel seminar is completely sold out. Tickets for the four o'clock repeat will be on sale in thirty minutes. Try and show some restraint.'

The crowd continued to jostle and bump. A hatless Guards officer began using barrack-room language and a man with mutton-chop whiskers struck out at the inflated rubber doll with his shooting stick. 'Spiro?' Skillicorn called out in desperation. 'Where's Spiro? Someone get the Philosophical

157

Front. It's typical, they're never here when you need them.'
He ducked expertly as the lower half of a double-decker
cheeseburger flew towards him, followed almost at once by
the upper half.

Presently Spiro lumbered into view clutching the same
girls' comic he had been reading all term. He was dressed in
beige flannel slacks and a beige tee shirt decorated across
the chest with the Mind and Body Shop motif of a pair of
pointed breasts wearing a pair of horn-rimmed spectacles.
Obeying Skillicorn's repeated appeals to use only the mini-
mum of force he quickly managed to disperse the crowd, so
enabling bona fide students and the Head of Department to
enter the premises.

'Quite a demand for Hegel,' Hambro observed. 'Curious
how intellectual fashions change.'

'It's like this every day,' Skillicorn said. 'Especially for the
topless seminar on *Sittlichkeit.*' He inspected the most recent
damage to his jacket. One of the leather elbow patches had
been torn off and two of the three buttons were missing. He
shrugged philosophically and straightened out a poster that
had been crumpled in the mêlée. It read: YOU'VE TRIED
THINKING LATERALLY – NOW DO IT HORIZONTALLY.

'I'd better show you round the joint,' he said. 'It's changed
out of all recognition since you last saw it.'

Hambro noticed that his junior lecturer no longer addressed him as 'Sir' and that his accent and some of his
locutions were a little strange.

'Mr Shanker's really revolutionized the old curriculum.
That bloke's a right genius when it comes to higher education.
Know what I mean?' He led Hambro up a flight of stairs on
which a line of men were waiting two abreast. Someone at
the end shouted a protest against queue-jumping. 'Teaching
staff,' Skillicorn replied, flashing his university pass. As they
reached the first floor Hambro was just in time to see a girl
in a silver wig and thigh boots disappear into a cubicle
followed by two Detective Inspectors from the Vice Squad
unbuttoning their coats.

158

'This is your actual Hermeneutics Department,' Skillicorn announced. He gave a broad sweep of his arm, encompassing two corridors running at right angles to each other and decorated in the same Taj Mahal wallpaper. 'Logical Positivism's on the same floor, just through that door and round the jolly Jack Horner.' He sucked on his back teeth. 'We bought out the Vegetarian Advice Centre and knocked the walls through to make room for our new Exegetics wing. Mr Shanker reckons that by the end of the academic year we'll have taken over half the street for philosophy.' He looked, though did not altogether sound, like a house prefect showing round a school benefactor on Open Day. Still enthusing about curriculum changes and plans for expansion he guided Hambro up another flight of stairs and along a passageway illuminated by coloured lights revolving beneath the glass floor. Hawaiian music twanged from an invisible source. Hambro paused outside a quilted door with a sign above saying 'Private Tuition'. From the other side came the sound of continental butchers flattening veal escalopes in a hurry. 'It's Alderman Piltdown,' Skillicorn confided. 'He's being chastised again for failing to resolve Russell's paradox. He's a dead slow learner, poor old geezer.'

They went down a flight of stairs and up another. Hambro felt geographically lost, but guessed that they must now be on the premises of what had formerly been the Mexican take-away. Perhaps that would account for the unusual odour? He followed Skillicorn along a wide carpeted passage with alcoves on either side. In each alcove, lit by a hidden spotlight, was a bust of an early Greek thinker. As they were passing the smiling face of Epicurus, Hambro tugged at Skillicorn's ragged sleeve. 'Listen. What's the cause of that splashing and gurgling? Is there trouble with the plumbing?'

Skillicorn smiled tolerantly at the forgivable error, as he sometimes did when one of his third-year students ran into difficulties spelling 'Hume'. 'It's Mr Shanker's latest addition to the syllabus – Spinoza in the Jacuzzi. He likes to call it his overflow seminar.'

159

Mr Shanker himself appeared just as the tickets were going on sale for the matinée performance of Kierkegaard-à-GoGo. He was wearing a fawn seersucker suit with wide lapels and a pleated back in the continental mode. In one buttonhole he sported a white carnation and in the other a Liberal Party badge. His calf shoes were in two contrasting shades of maroon and had very pointed toes protected by metal rims. Hambro felt he could easily have passed for a medical insurance salesman or a television chef.

'Hello, Douglas, my old son,' he said predictably. 'How was the Costa del Sol?' He gripped his son-in-law's shoulders in paternal greeting, causing Hambro to flinch at the prospect of being kissed on each of his sunburned cheeks in turn.

'I can assure you that that part of the Iberian peninsula holds not the slightest fascination for me.' The thought of Orwell oiling himself on a crowded beach was one of those images that refused to take shape, like the thought of the Vice-Chancellor playing the cello.

Skillicorn was hopping from one leg to another, waiting for an opportunity to speak. His limbs were going in different directions at once as though he was trying to keep his balance on a rolling log. 'Excuse me, guvnor,' he finally said, addressing Mr Shanker. 'Okay if I scarper now? I'm due up at the main campus at four to give me lecture on Rank.'

'Ranke?' Hambro enquired. 'Who on earth is Ranke?' Another of these young German or American prodigies I should have read, he thought guiltily.

'Rank and file,' Skillicorn explained.

'I beg your pardon?'

Skillicorn eyed him with forbearance. 'Rank and file, Gilbert Ryle.'

'Good lad, that,' Mr Shanker said as Skillicorn bounded away. 'He'll teach anything I ask him to. He's got a real sense of vocation.'

Hambro felt bound to agree. 'You certainly seem to have made a big impression on him. Not least of all linguistically.'

Mr Shanker gave a throaty chuckle. 'He's at the im-

160

pressionable age. I'll soon have him voting Liberal, same as Spiro.'

He chatted amiably for a while about the rise in property values in Tozer Place and the Scandinavian border clashes and the unexpected intervention in the abdication crisis by the Boilermakers' Union. Hambro never ceased to wonder at the range and depth of his father-in-law's knowledge of certain aspects of current affairs, such as fluctuations in the foreign exchange markets and the signing of extradition treaties. He could always quote the rate of yen to deutsch-mark to the nearest two decimal points or name the Defence Minister's latest Russian boyfriend. It gave Hambro pause to reflect that there might, after all, be something to be said for a philosophical training.

'We need to have a serious business natter, Douglas,' he now said. He gripped Hambro's elbow as though to make, or possibly prevent, a citizen's arrest. 'Let's go somewhere quiet, away from the hoi polloi.' He led Hambro along another passage and down some marble steps into an ante-room divided into sections by silk-panelled Chinese screens. He pointed Hambro to a reproduction Hepplewhite and went across to the mahogany drinks cabinet. Gazing at the Laura Ashley fabrics, the silver candelabra and Persian carpets, Hambro found it hard to believe that he was sitting in what was once the seminar room of the original Mind Shop, and prior to that the home and breeding ground of Dr Hagstrom's rats.

'It's our VIP lounge,' Mr Shanker informed him, swirling the ice cubes in his glass. 'We can't have our professional and executive clientele queueing on the stairs with all the yobbos and the plainclothes mob. Credit cards only here.'

Hambro sipped his Chivas Regal. Without leaning forward he could see protruding from behind one of the Chinese screens the footrest of the Dean of Divinity's vacant wheel-chair. Muted laughter came from behind another screen and then a plummy female voice announced, 'Brigadier Jimpson, please. Your tutor is now ready for you in the Jeremy

Bentham suite. I think I ought to warn you, she's very displeased with your essay on the Pain and Pleasure Principle.'

The room fell quiet and Hambro thought he recognized a familiar sound coming from above. He glanced round and up at the pavement window and saw the shadows passing across. Clop, clop, clop, clop, went the leather soles. He found it oddly comforting to know that some things remained stubbornly the same in the face of flux and alteration, things immune from fashion and the cult of progress. As Pareto so memorably said, the essential core of reality was constant and indissoluble, only surface phenomena ever changed. Or was that Feuerbach?

'More expansion, Douglas,' Mr Shanker was insisting. 'That's what we got to think about. This place isn't suitable for all the activities I got in mind. We need better premises – no pun intended, ha, ha.'

Hambro looked into his cut-glass tumbler. 'I gather that you plan to convert the whole of Tozer Place into another Athens. Do you think we can muster the intellectual resources?'

Mr Shanker unsheathed his buckled yellow teeth. 'You leave that side of things to me, old son. I know how to cope. It's all down to my time in Reading.' He tapped his temple with his bony index finger. 'You get a first-class training in the Oscar Wilde wing.'

28

The overheated, windowless room smelled of something sweet and sickly, tinged with the fragrance of lavender disinfectant. A single fluorescent tube flickered and hummed overhead. Above the door, mounted on a platform, was a video camera operated by remote control. Its wide-angle lens was focused on the four creatures squatting in the form of a square on the straw-covered floor.

'Nice one, Herbert Spencer,' Baxi said. 'Double six. You get another throw.' He was addressing the chunkiest and hairiest of the chimpanzees hunched around the Monopoly board. At the side of each player was a pile of bananas and a copy of the rules in three different languages. Baxi waited until Herbert Spencer had moved his piece to Park Lane before passing the dice on to the next player. 'Wake up, Huxley, it's your throw. And stop playing with your privates, you filthy beast.'

Huxley rattled the dice in his hand and threw a five and a three. He handed six of his bananas to Baxi and began piling small wooden blocks on the board.

Baxi groaned. 'What are you doing now, dumbo?' He made a face like a village idiot. 'You can't build hotels on the Gas Company. Use your bloody loaf.' He removed the hotels from the board and handed back the six bananas, one of which Huxley immediately peeled and ate.

He turned to the third player who was plump and gingery and deeply engrossed in Herbert Spencer's armpit. 'Come on, Darwin, pick up the dice. No, no, no, use your *hands*. How many more times? I warn you, if you spit them out once more you'll be disqualified.' He leaned across the Monopoly board and put his face very close to Darwin's. 'You know what'll happen to you if you're disqualified?' he leered. 'It'll be back to breakfast television.'

The game was won by Herbert Spencer, his fourth victory in a row. He carried his winnings to a corner of the room and piled them up in bunches of five. He sat behind them counting them over and over again. Later he built them into a single pyramid and encircled his arms around them possessively, his bright black eyes shining with greed, triumph and fear.

Darwin was sulking in the opposite corner. He had gone bankrupt early in every game and was now testing the dice with his teeth as though suspecting some malpractice. Huxley

163

pranced about the room on all fours gathering handfuls of straw and throwing them at Baxi and making rude gestures at the video camera.

Baxi was reading a paperback novel about lust, corruption and disembowelment in a medieval monastery. It came complete with sketchmaps, a list of principal characters, chapter summaries, footnotes, and English translations of the Latin dialogue. He was interrupted by a sudden shriek from the dimmest corner of the room. He looked up to see Darwin and Huxley seizing bunches of Herbert Spencer's private possessions while their lawful owner tried to beat them off with the Monopoly board. 'All right you lot, pack it in,' Baxi remonstrated. 'Remember who you are. You're supposed to be enlightened capitalists. You've said goodbye to the law of the jungle.'

Later that day he went to see Denise. As he turned into her corridor he literally bumped into her Moral Tutor. 'What are you doing in the girls' quarters, Baxi?' he growled, still buttoning up his waistcoat.

'Same as you I expect.'

Mr Poulter-Mogg drew back his narrow pinstriped shoulders. 'I am here in an academical capacity.'

Baxi winked extravagantly. 'So I see. Your flies are undone.'

Mr Poulter-Mogg's hand flew to his securely fastened zip. 'I shall report your insolence to the Dean.' He pushed his way past and turned at the swing door. 'When did you last take a bath, Baxi?' He held the very tip of his sharp nose between thumb and first finger. 'You smell like a zoo.'

'He's right,' Denise laughed. 'You do pong.' She was running her hands through Baxi's lank hair in search of fleas, nits, lice and other living things. 'Actually, I find it quite sexy,' she confessed. 'Ever since I saw *King Kong* I've wanted to be fucked by a gorilla.' She undid the buttons of his shirt and slid her hand inside. It was torn across the collar as the result of a fracas caused the day before when Huxley refused

164

to recompense Herbert Spencer for landing on his railway station.

'Not now, Denise. I've got business to attend to.' He was scooping up the remains of her cold Lancashire hot pot with a slice of lemon meringue pie. It was the first meal he had eaten for two days that did not consist exclusively of bananas.

'What business?' Denise's heavy lower lip came forward in a pout. 'At that damn Sperm Bank again? I think you prefer doing it with bottles.'

Baxi gave her his solemn assurance that he had no intention of making a further deposit that evening. 'The fact is, I've got this nice little earner in the Philosophy department. I need the money urgently. The Baker Street underpass was flooded out and ruined my parents' bedding.'

Denise picked one of Darwin's fleas off Baxi's scalp and cracked it between her thumbnails. 'A job in the Philosophy department? You? Teaching what?'

Baxi licked the plate clean, front and back. 'Not exactly teaching. Mopping up after the Spinoza seminar. All right if I borrow your wellies?'

29

The first week of May was unseasonally cold but then it grew warm and warmer still, arousing suspicions about the possibility of a false spring. Day trippers from London began to arrive in air-conditioned charabancs. They sat in rows of deckchairs eating imported oysters and went shopping for hand-embroidered bags for keeping clothes-pegs in. On Bank Holiday Monday the Lord Mayor opened an exhibition of vintage typewriters in the corn exchange while the Lady Mayoress launched a fresh appeal for funds to raise the pier off the ocean bed. Half-way through the month schoolchildren from the continent began to arrive off the ferries to study English language, culture and civilization in the Nissen huts at the end of the Esplanade. Accompanied by their teachers, they went on guided tours of places of architectural and historic interest, including the prizewinning tunnel and the university, and afterwards ate packed lunches in a Designated Picnic Zone. It was at this time that the Clifftop Hotel and Brasserie was awarded two rosettes by a national guide in recognition of its fire precautions. Also, amid a storm of controversy, the barmaid at the same hotel was crowned Miss Cheesecake, despite having won the Mister Beefcake title the year before. Each day the sun seemed to shine a little brighter for a little longer.

It was shining brightly now as Margery Hambro and Colin Lumsden strolled arm-in-arm along the marina on their way to Hedda Hagstrom's apartment. Lumsden was dressed in sharply-creased dark green slacks and a light green shirt that was broad at the shoulders and tapered at the waist. His new brogue shoes had two-inch platform soles, enabling him to come up to Margery's chin without having to stand artificially erect or wear a hat. At Margery's prompting he had recently had his hair restyled. It was now clipped short around the ears and brushed forward on top, from crown to forehead, culminating in a rolling quiff above the eyebrows in the fashion pioneered by Dirk Oesterbroek before his accident. Occasionally he had to flick his head back to see things properly above waist height.

They stopped on the quayside for a few minutes to watch a television crew shooting a scene for a major new drama series about maritime problem families. Margery collected the autograph of the key grip and the clapperboard girl in case they turned out to be famous. Later she asked Lumsden to buy her a candy floss.

'Another one?' he said teasingly. 'Naughty girl.' He nuzzled his face into her neck and added another love-bite to the string of slightly faded ones that stretched from one collarbone to the other like a communicable skin disorder. They ambled slowly past the corporation flower beds and the

Esplanade clock tower, gazing into one another's eyes across the rapidly disappearing candy floss. Once or twice they stopped to whisper and embrace in the middle of the busy pavement, or to play their new nose-biting game.

Margery could never recall feeling so happy. The nearest she had ever come to it before, she realized, was on her brief honeymoon under canvas in the Kentish hopfields. But even that had been blemished by all the earwigs and mosquitoes and by Duggie's inability to follow the manufacturer's instructions for converting two single tents into a double one. She found it hard to believe that she'd known Colin for only a matter of weeks; she already felt she knew him better than her own husband. She knew about the way he liked to have his stomach tickled with the loofah when they bathed together, and about his terror of heights, tunnels, spiders, running water, still water, woodlice and nuns. She knew all about his hatred of menthol toothpaste and foreigners, and about his tendency to get upset when the bus conductor asked him if he was a half fare, or when people called him shortarse.

He was easily the kindest and most considerate person she had ever met. He opened doors for her to go through, helped her on and off with her mac, and never read the paper while she was talking to him. He even took her dad breakfast in bed as soon as he shouted down for it. He was marvellous around the house as well; he'd put up new shelves in the kitchen and laid down cushion tiles in the bathroom as well as ripping out all that gloomy oak panelling in the spare room and painting it a lovely shade of Caribbean Dawn. Duggie would hardly recognize the place when he got back from wherever it was that he'd been for the past God knows how many weeks.

Lumsden forced his tongue in her ear outside Boots the Chemist. As he did so she caught sight of the Esplanade clock above his quiff. 'Oh, Col,' she cried, 'look at the time. She hates people being late as much as she hates them being early.' She seized his hand and ran with him through the

167

crowded shopping precinct, down the flagstone steps, and around the harbour wall. She ran by kicking her legs out sideways to prevent her thighs colliding, so that from certain angles she might have been mistaken for a Kirghiz or Kazakh attempting a Ukrainian dance. By taking shorter but much quicker strides Lumsden was able to keep up with her with his arm at full stretch. They arrived at the apartment block as the clock was chiming the hour. At the final stroke of four Margery cried 'Now!' and Lumsden pressed the top button.

Hedda Hagstrom's voice crackled through the intercom. 'Please come right up. You know how to work the lift?' On their way up Margery adjusted Lumsden's hair while he wiped candy floss off her lips and cheeks with the wetted corner of his tapered shirt-tail. When Hedda Hagstrom unlocked and unchained her door they were already waiting in their stockinged feet, their shoes held out before them like the price of admission.

'Good afternoon, Dr Hagstrom,' they chanted in unison. Margery pointed at Lumsden with her pixie boot. 'This is Col,' she explained. 'The one I was telling you about. He's been helping me with my programme.'

Lumsden mumbled something into his chest. He kept his head bowed as though presenting it for inspection to the school nurse. Please, please, don't let her recognize me, he appealed to some unspecified power.

'How nice to see you both. Do come in.' Hedda Hagstrom smiled at them engagingly as she relieved them of their shoes and dropped them in the pedal-bin. She had been in a congenial mood ever since learning, earlier in the day, that her appointment as Dean of Faculties was now virtually assured. According to the Vice-Chancellor, Hambro had ruined his chances by his unexplained absence from an emergency meeting of the Senate Subcommittee on Academic Espionage. It seemed in fact that he hadn't been present anywhere in the university since chairing a meeting early in Trinity term to allocate the snooker scholarships.

168

Even then he had left early because his sunburn was giving him trouble. It was a very strange way to behave, Hedda Hagstrom thought; with his department doing so outstandingly well he would have had a very strong claim to the post. Still, that was his mistake. The desire for power was no substitute for the will to power. She had proved that time and time again in her studies of rat behaviour.

'Do help yourselves,' she said, setting before them a plate containing four water biscuits and two paper napkins. She was wearing a sheath-like Oriental dress with a high collar and a split down one side that ran from thigh to ankle. She sat with her knees pressed together and her hands folded loosely on top of them. Lumsden felt his neck flush every time his eyes were drawn to the long expanse of silk stocking that was just within touch but unequivocally out of his reach. He dipped his head a little lower and risked a full five-second stare from beneath the cover of his quiff.

'So, Margery, how is the programme coming along?' Hedda Hagstrom gave one of her meaningful looks. 'Any progress to report?'

Margery was trying to eat a water biscuit without making crumbs. She took tiny nibbles around the circumference and gnawed her way systematically towards the centre. 'Oh, the programme's fine,' she said defensively, cupping a hand beneath her chin. 'We been through the advanced manual twice, as well as the new supplement, haven't we, Col? Col thinks it's smashing, don't you, Col?'

Lumsden gave a thumbs-up sign using both thumbs. 'It's great,' he confirmed. 'I can do all the recommended methods now without looking at the book at all. Marge tested me last week and I only made two mistakes, and one of those was because she slipped on the soap and caught herself on the bath taps.'

Hedda Hagstrom's smile seemed to coagulate on her lips. She found it deeply distasteful to contemplate the thought of actual people substituting themselves for the computerized illustrations in her scientific manual. What hubris on their

169

part! It was like the university drama club trying to perform *King Lear.* 'I don't really think we need to go into details.' She gave a tiny involuntary shudder. 'Let's confine ourselves to the matter of ends rather than the means. Is there anything to report in *that* regard?' She kept her gaze fixed patiently on Margery as the seconds ticked by.

'She means are you pregnant,' Lumsden whispered.

'Oh, I see.' Margery hurriedly cleared her mouth. 'Well, not really. Not what you'd call pregnant.'

'Are you taking the fertility tablets?'

'Yes, regular as clockwork. I swallow two every night, soon as I've said my prayers, don't I, Col?'

Lumsden concurred but thought it best not to reveal that he had been taking them too in the hope that they might encourage hair to grow on his face and chest.

'I suppose you'd better double the dose,' Hedda Hagstrom said. 'No, better still I might try you on a different brand. It's still in the trial stage, really, and we need to iron out one or two wrinkles. But we've had some quite promising results with the gerbils.' Odd though, she reflected, about that recent crop of Siamese triplets. A shaft of sunlight was beaming directly on her face, turning her hair into a golden halo. She went to the panoramic window to adjust the curtain and stood for a moment looking down at the moving specks below. Some of the specks would be day-trippers searching for the coach station, others would be young mothers pushing pushchairs, or office workers going home to tea. She never ceased to be astonished at their apparent willingness to go on leading lives of such utter dreariness. Day after day, from one academic year to the next, they would go through the same pointless routine without the slightest prospect of acclaim or international recognition. Why on earth did they bother? Even her white mice demanded sugarlumps. She ran her hands down and across her tight-fitting dress, smoothing out non-existent creases. When she turned from the window she saw Lumsden ogling her legs. Why did he keep doing that, she wondered. And where had she seen him before?

170

There was something familiar about that face and that body odour.

It dawned on her fifteen minutes later while he was standing on the Welcome mat waiting for his shoes.

'I've met you before,' she said. 'Now I remember.'

Lumsden felt his diminutive body shrivel up. I've had it now, he thought.

'You came to see me at the beginning of Michaelmas term. It's all coming back to me now.'

With one shoe off and one shoe on, Lumsden felt an overpowering urge to run or hop away.

'You had a fixation on a cat, or was it a dog? Yes, it was a Welsh corgi, if I'm not mistaken.'

Lumsden nodded his head in relief.

'Good, good. And you've overcome that problem now?'

'Yes thank you, Dr Hagstrom. Meeting Marge made all the difference. I prefer her every time.'

They got back home shortly before Mr Shanker. He found them locked in a tight embrace against the Edwardian hallstand.

'Whor,' he gasped, fanning his face with his cashmere fedora. 'This is no weather for philosophy. The shop's like a Turkish bath.' His seersucker suit was badly crumpled and the white carnation in his buttonhole looked as if it had been pressed between the pages of *Principia Mathematica*. 'Young Skillicorn passed out twice. That lad's going to do himself a mischief if he don't cut down on his teaching load.'

The hallstand began to rock under the combined weight of the two bodies pressed against it. Mr Shanker noted that despite his platform soles Lumsden still had to rise on tiptoe to get his tongue fully in Margery's ear. He noted also that Lumsden was wearing one of the six pairs of dark green slacks that he, Mr Shanker, had supplied him with from part of a larger consignment originally destined for a hostel for young offenders. He tapped Lumsden on the shoulder. 'Be a good lad, Colin, nip along and put the kettle on. I'm gasping for a cup of Earl Grey.'

Lumsden withdrew his tongue from Margery's ear and said with it, 'Right away, Mr Shanker. Milk or lemon?'

While Lumsden was busy in the kitchen, Mr Shanker beckoned his daughter into the living-room. He handed her an unstamped picture postcard of the Pompidou Centre under snow. 'This arrived at the shop this morning.'

Margery held it at an angle from her eyes, barely able to decipher the rain-smudged handwriting. It said:

> 6 rue du Pot de Fer,
> Paris Vième.

Completely destitute. Please send two pairs of rubber washing-up gloves (small). Also cockroach powder.

> D.H.

Lumsden came in carrying tea things on a tray. He poured two cups, using the strainer, and handed one to Mr Shanker and one to Margery. Mr Shanker reached for a slice of lemon. 'Aren't you having none, son?'

Lumsden glanced at Margery. 'No,' she said firmly, turning to her father. 'I don't encourage him to take liquids of an evening.'

Hedda Hagstrom's congenial mood was still intact. As soon as Margery and Lumsden had left she opened all the doors and windows and switched on the electric fan. Dressed only in her white bathrobe she spent the rest of the evening working on the final phase of her research project for the Khomeini Centre. This was designed to explain why the swing to Islam had been so much greater in Liverpool than anywhere else in the country. There were now reported to be almost as many mosques in Merseyside as in Jeddah. Most of the pubs had been forced to close because of the lack of custom, and even the few that remained were now refusing to stock pork-scratchings. Bad language was no longer heard in the docks. It was safe to walk in the streets without fear of muggers or Trotskyites.

172

Hedda Hagstrom felt sure that it was all connected, directly or indirectly, with the decline of Liverpool Football Club. The young supporters of this once illustrious soccer team, now languishing at the foot of the Fourth Division, were renowned and feared for their fervour and commitment. But now that the club had failed to win a match for the past three seasons, these same supporters had suffered a deep sense of shame and humiliation. Taunted and mocked, the butt of endless music-hall jokes and television sketches, it was perfectly understandable that these alienated youths should seek solace and regeneration elsewhere. And where better than in the all-encompassing embrace of militant Shi'ism? It was surely no accident that the most popular venue for Friday prayers was around the goalmouth of the Kop.

Hedda Hagstrom's mind and silver pencil raced along in tandem. She knew, as if by some primordial instinct, that she was on the brink of a major intellectual breakthrough. This was the big one, the one she had been waiting for. Max Weber had established his reputation by showing the causal link between Protestantism and capitalism. She would do the same for Islam and Merseyside. Of course, the collapse of the football club was not the only factor at work. She was too experienced in the ways of research to assume that such a complex phenomenon would have but a single cause. Other things were bound to be involved. There was, for example, the well known local predilection for chip butties. And what about the effect of that extraordinary nasal accent . . .

30

The Vice-Chancellor gripped the telephone aerobically. 'That's a very generous gift, Your Excellency,' he gurgled into the mouthpiece. 'Extremely generous. And most unexpected.' About time, too, he thought; the Americans and the Chinese had been much quicker in showing their appreciation for more or less the same information. He took out his pocket calculator and converted the rubles into dollars. 'Yes, with an endowment like that we'll be able to set up one of the finest institutes of genetic engineering in the Free Wor . . . in the West.' He had a vision of the rich and famous queuing at the doors for chromosome transplants and cloning, or whatever it was that those scientific weirdos got up to with their bunsen burners. It could even turn out to be a bigger money-spinner than the Sperm Bank, given the right sort of publicity. There was bound to be a bit of local opposition from people in the town, of course; a bunch of scaremongers was already going around blabbering about Frankenstein monsters escaping and running amok in the low-cost housing estates. What a lot of childish nonsense! Just because it had happened a couple of times in Berkeley, and more recently in Cambridge . . .

'Beg your pardon, Your Excellency? You'd like the institute to be named after who? After whom? Could you speak up, please, this is a very bad line for some reason.' There was a sound as of a mezzo-soprano falling down a mineshaft. 'Lysenko, you say? Yes, by all means, of course. The Lysenko Institute for Genetic Engineering – it's got a nice ring to it. We'd be delighted to name it after one of your cosmonauts.' He scribbled the name on his blotting pad next to the doodle of a dollar sign followed by a seven digit number. He scored a double line beneath the number and then enclosed it in a box and shaded it all around. It was nowhere in the same league as the Khomeini endowment, true enough, but it was a very tidy sum to play with. He could picture the envious faces of the other five Vice-Chancellors when they heard the news. (Or were there only four now that Oxford had merged with Hull?)

'Yes, Your Excellency, yes, yes. I'll keep in contact with your . . . people in the usual way. It's a pleasure doing business with you, Sir. Thanks once again. *Auf Wiedersehen.*'

174

He expanded the doodle on his blotter and then did six press-ups before summoning Miss Pollins. She came in, blinking rapidly, to find him suspended from the wallbars. He started dictating before her eyes had grown accustomed to the sunlight.

'Memo to the Head of Catering Studies. Dear Professor Grogan, further to the outbreak of salmonella poisoning among your third-year students: you are hereby instructed not to sign any further contracts for the story with press, radio or television until next of kin have been informed. Will you also kindly issue a public denial of the damaging rumour, put about by one of our competitors, that the victims are buried in a mass grave on the university asparagus farm.'

He adjusted his grip on the wallbars, raised his legs to a horizontal position, and held them there for the count of two.

'Letter to the Locations Manager, Metro-Goldwyn-Mayer. Dear Madam, I am pleased to inform you that the University Senate has now formally consented to your request for the hire of our campus next Michaelmas term for the filming of *Tarzan in the Urban Jungle*. Students, lecturers, and professors will be on hand to perform as extras, and in crowd scenes, at the daily rates laid down by our Subcommittee on Wages and Conditions. Naturally, we shall be willing to reorganize our lectures and examination timetable to fit in with your shooting schedules. New Paragraph.

'Concerning the matter of accommodation for your technical crews, you will find that they can all be comfortably housed in our Hayek hall of residence. I envisage no difficulty in relocating the present student occupants. Discussions are, in fact, already under way with the local gipsy community for the use of their encamp . . .'

The telephone rang. The Vice-Chancellor dropped off the wallbars and had to launch himself across the room in order to preserve intact his record of answering it before the second ring. The pips sounded and it was several seconds before a

175

distraught voice said, 'It's Skillicorn here, guv. Somefink terrible's happened.'

A dozen possibilities raced through the Vice-Chancellor's mind: the Dean of Divinity arrested for indecent exposure? Another cock-up in Cosmetic Surgery?

'They're raiding The Mind and Body Shop. I'm in the call-box opposite.'

'Raiding it? Who's raiding it? Oh my God, not the VAT inspectors?' The Vice-Chancellor's heart went up and over like a tossed pancake.

'The Merseyside Shi'ites,' Skillicorn wailed. 'It's terrible, there's fousands of them, they're tearing the place to bits. The Philosophical Front doesn't stand a chance.' There was a noise in the background of plate glass being shattered to the accompaniment of screams and drums.

Skillicorn raised his voice above the tumult. 'They're on the top floor now, slinging out all the portraits and plaster busts. I can't bear to watch. Oh no, there goes Isaiah Berlin, and Gilbert Ryle, and Austin. And that was Apple.'

'Apple? The departmental computer? That's going too far.'

'No, guv, Apple and Pear. A. J. Ayer.'

There was another splintering crash, louder than the others. 'That was Strawson,' Skillicorn sobbed. 'They're really putting the boot in the Oxford school.'

The Vice-Chancellor tightened his grip on the receiver. 'Keep calm, man. Pull yourself together. Where's Professor Hambro?'

Skillicorn ducked in a reflex action as *An Essay Concerning Human Understanding* struck the door of the kiosk. 'I couldn't rightly say. I ain't seen him since he delivered the last lot of canes and straps.'

'Canes?' exclaimed the Vice-Chancellor. 'Straps? What the hell's going on in that department? This is a university, not a reform school.'

'They was needed for our symposium on the Location of

176

Pain. Mr Shanker organized it as part of the Tozer Place Festival of the Arts.'

'Mr who? There's no one of that name on the payroll.'

The pandemonium outside the call box grew louder, as nasal chants of *Jihad! Jihad! Jihad!* filled the air. Skillicorn pressed the receiver hard against his right ear and plugged a finger in the left. 'Professor Hambro's father-in-law,' he shouted. 'He's a self-made man in philosophy.'

'His father!' the Vice-Chancellor shouted back in anger. 'He's got no right to hire his blasted relatives on university business. That's nepotism, I won't have it. I'm running a meritocracy here.'

There was a huge muffled bang. A police siren went wheeng, wheeng, wheeng, in the distance, and then everything went completely quiet.

'Skillicorn? Hello? What was that explosion? Are you all right, Skillicorn? Hello? Hello?' The Vice-Chancellor gaped open-mouthed at the telephone as though having been asked to assess its socio-economic and cultural significance for mankind. 'Hambro,' he muttered with grim satisfaction.

31

Hambro was humming the closing bars of Scarlatti's sonata in F major (Kk 6). He dumped his bedroll in the hall and hung up his poncho. When he caught sight of his face in the hallstand mirror he was a little surprised to note the grey stubble on his chin and the cavernous hollows in his cheeks. His blue serge trousers were stained with grease and frayed at the knees and looked as if they could accommodate at least one more person of similar girth. He hung his beret on the same peg as a garment he had never before seen; it was either a short topcoat or a long jacket and had a vaguely official cut, suggesting service with the Water Board or the

177

Department of Weights and Measures. A yellow and green badge on the lapel announced that 'Short is Beautiful'. Hambro pondered only for a moment over the logical status of this assertion before sorting through the pile of letters on the side table. Several of these proved to be final demands for household bills, three of which were supplemented by threatening and abusive letters couched in legal terminology. There was, in addition, an invitation to subscribe to a new kung-fu magazine at a special discount for university staff, a trial-offer sachet of Australian Gewurtztraminer, a circular advising him of the imminent arrival of a female Messiah, a catalogue for outsize maternity wear, and a telegram from the War Office marked 'immediate', addressed to a former owner of the house. At the bottom of the pile was an envelope embossed with the insignia of the Royal Eric Blair Society. He slit it open with his overgrown thumbnail.

Dear Hambro,
I have several times tried to ring you to discuss the crisis facing the Society in the aftermath of your unfortunate election defeat. As you will have gleaned from the national press, the successful candidate, G. Comstock, has now openly declared his backing for the 'Orwell tendency' in their bid to deflect the Society from its purely scholarly and cultural aims. If this unrepresentative faction succeeds in politicizing our movement, we shall certainly lose the royal patronage. We should also most likely forfeit the sponsorship of the Kentish Hop-growers' Federation and the BBC Staff Canteen. It is imperative that we meet at the earliest opportunity to discuss what steps to take to combat this damaging recrudescence of Orwellism within our ranks.
Yours sincerely,
Sir Reginald Cassington-Dodd

Hambro's ravaged face took on a contemplative aspect as he read the letter through a second time. Not long ago he would have known exactly where he stood on this contentious issue. Now, after his recent experiences, he was much less sure. He folded the letter away and called out, 'Sonia, I'm back.'

There was no reply. He was about to announce his return once more when he heard shouts of either live or recorded laughter coming from the sitting-room. He put his head cautiously round the door, like a visitor looking for the bathroom. His wife was reclining on the sofa. At her side knelt a young man holding a felt-tip pen in one hand and several more in his mouth. He took her palm and drew something on it. Hambro edged forward, one foot at a time, as if testing the floor beneath his weight.

'Hello, Duggie,' Margery chirped. 'You're back at last, then? Everyone's been asking for you.' When he drew closer she was shocked by the sight of his shabby clothes and gaunt, unshaven face. What's he been up to, she wondered. He looks as if he's just escaped from Russia. What could have happened to all the food parcels and razor blades her Dad had sent him? Her attention was diverted by a burst of laughter from BBC 1, on which a celebrity dressed in a dinner jacket was giving an impersonation of the Home Secretary's stammer. Seconds later the entertainment gave way to a commercial featuring a Welsh miners' choir crooning a rhyming couplet about investment opportunities in the Rhondda coalfield.

'Why is this young man staining your hand with coloured inks?' Hambro enquired. 'It seems an odd way to behave.' He took off his spectacles, wiped them with his handkerchief, replaced them, and tucked his handkerchief back up his sleeve.

'Colin's teaching me palmistry,' Margery explained. 'He's very informed about things like that. He'll read your bumps for you too if you like, won't you, Col? He's read my Dad's. He reckons that Dad's bump of knowledge is the biggest he's ever seen.' Her attention was again drawn to the television screen where the celebrity was now hobbling up and down in simulation of the Home Secretary's hip deformity.

179

'Marge,' Lumsden mumbled through his felt-tips, 'you haven't introduced us.'

Still transfixed by the antics of the celebrity, Margery said, 'Duggie, Colin. Colin, Duggie. He is a scream.'

Lumsden removed the pens from his mouth. 'How do you do, Professor Hambro. Sorry I can't shake hands.' He held up an ink-stained palm divided into coloured sections.

'Colin's living here now,' Margery declared. 'He's devoting himself full-time to my programme, aren't you, Col?'

Hambro's bushy eyebrows rose and fell one at a time. 'Living here? But surely your father occupies the guest room? Unless, of course, his parole has been . . . curtailed.' He felt a twinge of apprehension that Mr Shanker might have done something to bring the department into disrepute.

'Dad's all right,' Margery assured him. 'He's in the kitchen darning his balaclava. He says he'll be needing it again now.'

'Then where is this young person being accommodated?'

Margery patted Lumsden's quiff with her free hand. 'He's sleeping in our room now. I mean what used to be our room, but is now me and Col's room, if you see what I mean. It's working out very nice.'

Lumsden peered closely at Margery's palm in search of her truncated marriage line. 'She's right, Professor Hambro,' he said. 'It's a big improvement on the hall of residence. The bed's much more comfy. It's the only double bed me and Marge have ever slept in.'

Margery sat bolt upright, causing Lumsden's pen to squiggle a line unknown to palmistry across her thumb. 'It's not the only double bed,' she cried.

'It certainly is,' Lumsden insisted.

'No it's not. What about that time in the Psycho Motel when I nearly swallowed my thermometer?'

'That doesn't count. That was two singles pushed together.'

'No it wasn't.'

'Yes it was, you kept complaining about getting your bumcheeks pinched between the crack.'

'I did not!'

180

'Yes you did!'

'You little fibber!'

Hambro crept away on the balls of his feet before the issue was resolved. He had a hot bath and a medicated shampoo and a shave with a new blade. Not until he was drying himself did he notice the ill-fitting floor tiles and the chipboard shelves containing body gels and underarm sprays. The bedroom had also changed beyond recognition. The wallpaper had been painted salmon pink, though the pattern of falling sycamore leaves was still plainly visible beneath. His sepia photographs of Eton headmasters 1820–1944 had all been removed, as had his vasectomy certificate and the portrait of his wife in her Girl Guides uniform. Nor was there any sign of her mounted shuttlecock – a memento of her victory in the Gloucestershire Ladies Badminton Final. In its place on the bedside table was a Penguin edition of the Koran, and Dr Hagstrom's illustrated manual open at the hated Starfish Two. None of his clothes were in the wardrobe or the chest of drawers. On almost every hanger hung a pair of dark green trousers or curious triangular shirts, and the shoe rack was given over completely to what looked like orthopaedic footwear.

He sat on the unmade bed gathering his thoughts. It was surprising how much had changed during his absence. Nothing, it seemed, could withstand the worldly passion for flux and alteration. Even the Royal Eric Blair Society had become infected by it. He yawned with a cosmic weariness. It was many nights since he had slept in a place meant for sleeping in. He wondered whether it would be appropriate or indeed permissible to have a brief nap in his former bed. There appeared be universal praise for its quality and comfort. He drew back the covers and saw a rubber sheet stretched across the mattress. He hurried downstairs.

Mr Shanker was in the kitchen trying to thread a darning needle with a strand of hairy wool. 'Hello, Douglas. Long time no see.' He pushed a chair forward with his foot. 'You okay? You look as if you done a spot of porridge in a Turkish nick.'

'Porridge? Nick?'

Mr Shanker rendered the sentence into the King's English.

'Oh no, nothing like that,' Hambro assured him. 'I have been living extremely frugally in a lodging house on the Left Bank. It was absolutely . . . wonderful.'

Mr Shanker sucked the strand of wool to a fine point and aimed it at the needle. Wonderful? Blimey, even Tinderbox Turvey never looked like that after twenty-eight days in solitary. He waited until the needle was threaded before saying, 'I suppose you've heard what happened to the shop?'

Hambro looked a little shamefaced beneath the lines and shadows. 'I'm afraid I've been rather out of touch with local events. I used to see a copy of *Le Monde* occasionally, but you know how insular the French are when it comes to matters of culture.'

'Prepare yourself for a shock, Douglas.'

Hambro closed his tired eyes with thumb and index finger. He really needed a decent sleep before having to face a crisis. 'Don't tell me that base and superstructure have finally become one? I knew those old beams would never stand it.'

Mr Shanker shook his head with expressive sadness. 'It's worse than that, old son. Much, much worse.' He bit off a tiny piece of darning wool and flicked it away with the tip of his tongue. 'You was well out of it, believe me. It was worse than Attica.'

Hambro listened with a mixture of guilt, outrage and remorse to his father-in-law's graphic account of the sacking of The Mind and Body Shop and the ignominious rout of the Philosophical Front. He knew that he should have been on hand to prevent it; they would not have dared to flout his authority as Head of Department and Deputy Dean of Faculties. 'And how is poor Skillicorn now?' he asked anxiously. 'Is he likely to recover? He had such a promising career ahead of him, despite his leanings towards crypto-Intuitionism.'

182

'He's right as rain, physically,' Mr Shanker said. 'Apart from a scorched eyebrow when the rubber doll exploded. It's just that he's lost his powers of speech. He can't even talk in rhyming slang. Still, it's not permanent – the shrink reckons he should be okay again in a week or two, provided he doesn't hear no more Liverpool accents.' He fell silent, visibly moved by the personal dimensions of the tragedy. Presently he said, 'It's a crying shame, I really enjoyed working in that shop. It was my first ever taste of unalienated labour. Know what I mean?'

There was a sudden squall of laughter from another room, followed by thunderous footsteps on the stairs. Hambro raised his eyes to the ceiling without moving his head.

'Sounds like they're having another early night,' Mr Shanker observed. He tried on his renovated balaclava helmet. The grey patch below the chin was a little too dark to be invisible, but the needlework was exemplary. 'You've met young Colin, have you?'

'I do believe I have.'

'He's not a bad lad, really. The Princess seems to fancy him. Pity he's becoming one of them.'

'Them?'

'Shites. He's due to be baptized next week up at the university mosque. It's all his mother's doing – he says she went over to them after seeing a vision of the crescent moon over Porthcawl.'

The thudding overhead increased in volume and tempo, causing the Japanese paper lampshade to revolve first one way, then the other.

'By the way, Douglas, that reminds me. You're kipping in the outhouse now. They've already moved your clobber in.' He gave Hambro a look of commiseration and apology with the parts of his face not concealed beneath the balaclava. 'Sorry, old son, I had to help them with the lock.'

32

Hedda Hagstrom picked up a soggy black banana and flung it angrily across the room. It landed with a soft smack at the feet of Herbert Spencer who picked it up, sniffed it, and tossed it back.

'The whole experiment is completely ruined,' she shouted. 'Six weeks' work and thousands of pounds down the drain.' She paced about the room like a caged animal. Darwin and Huxley cowered together in the corner as far from her wrath as possible.

'It was just to break the monotony,' Baxi said defensively. 'Everyone was fed up with playing the same old game, especially with Herbert Spencer winning all the time.'

The unblemished skin on Hedda Hagstrom's face tightened visibly over the fine bone structure beneath. 'It was not merely an innocent variation on the rules of play,' she hissed. 'It was a deliberate subversion of their basic principles.' She pointed to the video camera above the door. 'I've been studying the tapes. They show that you openly encouraged Darwin to requisition all Herbert Spencer's hotels without compensation. You also made everyone pay Capital Gains Tax whenever they passed Go. And, what's more, you taught them all to respect squatters' rights.' She flung her arms in the air in a gesture of incredulity. 'On top of everything, you even connived in Huxley's attempt to escape from Gaol.'

Baxi traced a circle in the damp straw with his redundant walking stick. Bits of straw were intertwined in his shoulder-length hair, the result of Darwin's effort to make him look more presentable. Darwin now shuffled across and put a comforting arm around his waist.

'Worst of all,' continued Hedda Hagstrom shrilly, 'you let them nationalize the railways and the bank. You've totally corrupted them. They're now sharing out their bananas on an egalitarian basis. Even Herbert Spencer's doing it.' Her pale blue eyes became two metallic points. 'You've failed Psychology 301. I'm giving you gamma triple minus, the lowest mark you can get. That means you can't re-take the course unless you agree to become a Friend of the University.'

Baxi contemplated the holes in his shoes. Friends of the University had to endow a Chair or give their organs to the Medical School whenever they were needed. He took off his waterproof apron and handed it to Huxley who liked to use it as a hammock.

'You are a disgrace to Experimental Psychology, Mr Baxi. I never want to see you in or near my lab again. Is that understood?' She snatched the Maoist paper hat off Herbert Spencer's head, screwed it in a ball, and threw it at the Monopoly board. It struck one of the coloured matchboxes which had been painted to represent council flats placed on Mayfair and Park Lane. Matchstick pickets had been placed around the Gas Company and a sign on the Community Chest indicated that it had now been converted into a hardship fund for hotel kitchen staff. Hedda Hagstrom planted her feet on either side of the board as though about to trample on it. 'What am I supposed to tell the Employers' Federation?' she cried out in despair. 'That they've spent a small fortune to be told that even the apes are in favour of the peaceful transition from capitalism to socialism?'

33

The Vice-Chancellor gripped the arms of his swivel chair until his deltoids quivered beneath his sweatshirt. 'But what were you *doing* in Paris all that time?' he demanded. 'You know very well that sabbatical leave has been abolished.'

Hambro shifted his feet on the carpet tiles. He was beginning to regret having declined the invitation to be seated in the low-slung tubular chair. 'I was working as a *plongeur* in a hotel in the *quartier latin*,' he confessed. Merely saying it was enough to trigger off fond memories of blocked drains, sticky omelette pans and kitchen hysteria.

'A plunger? What the devil's a plunger?' The Vice-Chancellor glowered at Hambro across the wide expanse of glass-topped desk. Was it his imagination, or was the horrible old bugger reeking of garlic?

'It's a kind of washer-up. They normally employ Algerians for the task, but I managed to persuade the manager of my *bona fides*.' As well as accepting half the going rate, he recalled.

The Vice-Chancellor's tone grew more acerbic. 'Professor Hambro, you've got no business swanning off to wash dishes in swanky foreign hotels. You could do that here. We've had a serious labour shortage in our own kitchens ever since the salmonella epidemic.'

Hambro examined the backs of his small neat hands. The loose skin was still covered with pink blotches from exposure to rough detergents. 'I'm afraid our own kitchens would not have sufficed. It had to be that particular kitchen in that particular hotel.'

The Vice-Chancellor's normally flaccid mouth became set like gelatine. Rotten little snob, he thought; he thinks he's someone special because he went to Brasenose College, Cambridge, instead of the Pontypridd College of Commerce. He probably even thinks that his MA in Philosophy is superior to my Diploma in Laundry Administration, despite all the evidence to the contrary. That was the really amazing thing about the likes of him and his Old School Tie brigade – they still hadn't woken up to the fact that they were only the corporals now, not the officers in charge. They could never quite believe it when they were blackballed from the Athenaeum or denied safe Conservative seats. And they were forever moaning about the House of Lords being

packed out with scrap-metal merchants and furniture sales-
men. They had even provoked an abdication crisis because
of the King's decision to enrol the Prince of Wales at Gatwick
Poly. He altered his grip on the arms of his chair and tensed
his pectorals. 'The fact of the matter is, Hambro,' he said
coldly, 'you were absent from your place of work in the
middle of a crisis. While you were scraping dishes in some
posh hotel your department was in turmoil. D'you know
what happened? The Archdeacon was forcibly ejected from
the Bishop Berkeley Bubble Bath. And Lady Tottenham
spent all night hiding on the fire escape dressed in nothing
but Alderman Piltdown's Y-fronts. My phone hasn't stopped
ringing.'

Hambro looked genuinely contrite. He coughed into his
handkerchief and tucked it back up his sleeve with one corner
dangling out. 'I do of course accept full moral responsibility.
I am more than willing to meet the entire cost of Skillicorn's
eyebrow transplant as well as of his speech therapy. He is
making steady progress, by the way; when I visited him in
hospital yesterday he was able to recite simple syllogisms.'
He paused and said gravely, 'I repeat, the moral responsibility rests entirely with me. Fortunately, we also know whom
to hold materially and legally responsible. I trust that their
punishment will be suitably Islamic?'

The prominent blue vein in the Vice-Chancellor's neck
began to jitterbug. 'Punishment? Have you gone off your
chump?' He levered himself out of his swivel chair and
went to the window. Immediately ahead the white minaret
shimmered in the sun against a brittle blue sky. Students
were streaming across the piazza on their way to the mosque
for midday prayers. He was reminded that later in the day
he was due to meet the mullahs to discuss their proposals for
a book-burning ceremony outside the library, as well as the
funding of cheap student flights to Mecca.

He flapped a hand at the minaret. 'The Khomeini Centre
is due to be officially opened in three weeks' time – as
you would have known if you hadn't gone AWOL. D'you

honestly think that I would risk the entire financial future of this company by expelling their followers?' He pulled the waistband of his tracksuit trousers away from his stomach and peered into the cavity as though wondering what might be there. 'I'm not going to be accused of religious intolerance. They're entitled to express their beliefs the same as everyone else. Besides,' he added, 'the Tozer Place property was fully insured. We ought to do quite nicely out of it.'

Hambro took a measured breath and drew himself up to attention like an old soldier at a war memorial. He kept his eyes fixed on the basketball net that now occupied the space between the lithograph of Adam Smith and an aerial photograph of Admin II under scaffolding. 'I cannot accept that decision, Vice-Chancellor.' His voice shook in the back of his throat. 'A physical assault on the foundations of western philosophy cannot be condoned on grounds of pecuniary gain. It offends all notions of common . . . decency, as Orwell would have said.'

'Who?'

'Orwell. George Orwell.'

The Vice-Chancellor's mouth fell open. 'The Huddersfield goalkeeper? What's he got to do with it?'

Hambro remained quite immobile, still breathing deeply, his shoulders back, arms against his sides. He heard himself saying the words he had longed to say so many times before, but had only ever uttered in the bath. 'In view of your attitude, Vice-Chancellor, I feel unable to continue as a servant of this university. To be perfectly frank, I have long felt that your support for me and my department has been less than wholehearted. This was evident from the first day of your appointment when you redeployed all my senior staff to set up a windsurfing school. Poor old Frobisher couldn't even swim.' He paused for maximum effect. 'I intend to terminate my contract forthwith. You shall have my letter of resignation first thing in the morning.'

The Vice-Chancellor smiled misshapenly. 'Don't bother, old cock. Your notice of dismissal is already in the post. Call

188

in on Miss Pollins on your way out and leave her your keys, luncheon vouchers, identity disc and jogging permit. And you can take off that university tie – as from twelve noon you're no longer sponsored by Amalgamated Soya. Now you're on your own.'

Before Hambro had shut the door behind him, the Vice-Chancellor was on the telephone to Hedda Hagstrom.

'Congratulations.'

Hedda Hagstrom's heart did a salmon-leap. 'You mean . . .' The accent did not sound very Scandinavian.

'Consider yourself the new Dean of Faculties. The Deputy Dean has just been awarded the order of the boot, ha, ha.'

Hedda Hagstrom quickly recovered from her initial disappointment. 'That's marvellous,' she breathed. 'I'm honoured and delighted.' She made a mental note to order a fresh batch of headed stationery embossed with her new title. She would also have to send a note to the editor of *Who's Who in Abnormal Psychology*.

'Your appointment will have to be rubber-stamped at Tuesday's meeting of Senate. It can go through after the emergency debate on the imbalance between Arts and Science professors in the crowd scenes in *Tarzan in the Urban Jungle*. But I'd like you to get cracking right away on arrangements for the Khomeini Centre opening shindig. Don't spare the expense, we need to make a good impression on these people. I'm cancelling all teaching for the next three weeks so that everyone can help in smartening up the campus. Some of the buildings could do with a lick of paint, and now would be a good time to drag the artificial lake. We don't want any embarrassing discoveries in front of the TV cameras.' He went on talking at length about security precautions for foreign dignitaries, the sale of official programmes, the hiring of the local fife-and-drum band, and the siting of portable lavatories. 'By the way, have you thought about what to wear on the big day? I suppose you ought to get yourself a thingummyjig, a fez, to cover up your face. You know what these Buddhists are like.'

He had a quick health-food lunch sitting on his exercise bicycle and then summoned Miss Pollins.

'Memo to all Heads of Departments re: Academic Espionage. The Campus Security Police have reported a sharp increase in the number of unauthorized personnel apprehended in seminar and lecture rooms. Most of those detained proved to be in the employ of other universities, home and overseas. A senior academic from Frankfurt was recently caught taking detailed notes in a postgraduate seminar on the Theory of Drainage. The week before, a lecturer from the Sorbonne was discovered with a complete tape recording of Professor Grogan's inaugural lecture on Milk Puddings. The utmost vigilance is now called for to prevent any further thefts of knowledge from this university. Any suspicious signs of note-taking in lecture and seminar rooms should be reported immediately to Campus Security. Meanwhile, please ensure that all members of your department deposit their lecture notes in the strong boxes provided free of charge for that purpose.

'Letter to Professor McGinty, DSc, FRS, FBA, OBE. Dear McGinty, Further to your request for a suspension of boilerhouse duties to enable you to accept an honorary degree from Harvard . . .'

34

A netting of fine white cloud hung beneath the sun as though ready to catch it in case it fell. For several days and nights the humid air had been completely motionless. It was now beginning to have the taste and texture of breath exhaled by a party of publicans trapped in a beer cellar. Electrical thunderstorms had been promised by the weatherman, but although they were often heard rumbling in the distance they never broke overhead. It seemed to everyone that the orange-and-blue flag of Amalgamated Soya that hung limply from the mast on Senate House might never flutter again.

All across the campus students were busy picking up toffee-wrappers, cutting grass, polishing windows and painting immovable objects white. Some of the men had loosened their ties and some had also undone the top button of their white shirts. Most of the women wore long grey cotton dresses and black headscarves knotted beneath the chin. As they toiled they sang to the music on Radio Free Campus, usually devotional songs or, every now and then, the university hymn. When the klaxon sounded they gathered in their subject groups for sandwiches of fish paste or coleslaw and cartons of Scottish mineral water. Presently the Arts Faculty ice-cream van appeared playing the Ride of the Valkyries on its musical chimes. A sign on the rear said 'Beware Students'.

Mr Shanker joined the queue for ice-lollies and low-fat vanilla tubs. His jacket was draped cloakwise over his shoulders in the Mediterranean style, and his sneakers had been freshly blancoed. Because of the warmth, he had replaced his cashmere fedora with a straw boater with a red-and-white band. Without obviously eavesdropping he listened with interest to the muted conversations going on around him about library fees and the going rate for examination bribes. It was, he realized, his first visit to a proper university. It all seemed very different from his own *alma mater*. He strolled about the campus sucking his ice-lolly while gathering, assimilating and assessing visual information with an air of apparent nonchalance. Before long he found himself outside a glass and metal structure that was easily identifiable as the library from the pile of books still burning and smouldering on the forecourt. He skipped nimbly up the steps and tried each of the four glass doors in turn before spotting a typewritten card saying 'Closed for Ramadan'. At the foot of the steps was a signpost with wooden fingers, complete with painted fingernails, pointing the way to the Refectory, Sperm Bank, Computer Centre, and Guard-Dog Kennels. He followed the walkway to the Computer Centre

191

and was astonished at the ease with which he was able to stroll past reception with a smile and a wave and enter the very heart of the building. These people have got a lot to learn about security, he thought. It was all going to be much easier than he'd imagined.

After less than half an hour's reconnaissance, and some innocent questioning, he had learned that the Centre housed three powerful IBM mainframe computers, the most valuable being a recent and unexplained gift from the Pentagon. What struck him most forcibly about this latter item was how comfortably it would fit into the back of Tinderbox Turvey's removals van. He made a few rapid calculations on the back of some scrap print-out: three average men, plus Spiro, using two trolleys and a fork-lift truck, should be able to load the whole caboodle in twenty minutes. He paced out the distance from the main computer room to the rear entrance of the building and back again. He then measured the width of the doors and the widest piece of equipment with the aid of his leather belt. While he was double-checking the measurements of the computer, a bearded man appeared trailing a length of print-out like a broken concertina.

'Oh no,' he sighed. 'Don't tell me it's on the blink again. Dr Hagstrom's going to do her nut. She's screaming for the insanity statistics for Merseyside.'

Mr Shanker buckled his leather belt. 'There's nothing wrong with this little beauty,' he declared, giving the purring grey cabinet an affectionate pat. 'She's a lovely girl. She just likes to be treated with a bit of consideration and respect.' He cupped a hand around his mouth and said confidentially, 'Truth is, she's not really happy in a big, impersonal place like this. She deserves a better home. Know what I mean?'

He continued making notes, recording measurements, and drawing sketch-maps of the building. The security man was very helpful; he explained the workings of the alarm system and held the other end of Mr Shanker's belt. As he busied himself with facts and figures, Mr Shanker felt a growing sense of anticipation at the prospect of embarking on a new

192

class of enterprise. A job like this would call for advance planning, organizational skill, technical expertise; it was just the opportunity he needed to move up into the white-collar side of the business. Running a shop was all right, but it was about time he was socially mobile. Otherwise, he might just as well pack up being a Liberal.

He took a quick snack in the automat before resuming his surveillance of the campus. The muezzin was calling the faithful to prayer as he approached the rear of a low, elongated building that looked as if it might be a fall-out shelter for the socially dispensable. Outside, a young man with shoulder-length hair was sitting on an upturned bucket sharpening a knife on a stone.

'Afternoon, son,' Mr Shanker said amiably. He touched his straw boater with one finger. 'And which department of learning is this, may I ask?'

'Catering,' Baxi said. He noted the gold Rolex and the overlapping teeth. I've seen this character before somewhere, he thought.

'The very place I been looking for.' Mr Shanker took from his pocket a newspaper cutting and unfolded it. On one side it showed advertisements for discount holidays in Kampuchea and herbal remedies for baldness and dyslexia. He turned the cutting over and held it up for Baxi to see. 'I've come about the vacancy.'

Baxi's mouth sagged. 'For Deputy Assistant Chef?' Sod it, he thought, I wanted that myself. A little to his own surprise, he had discovered over the past two weeks that he had a natural gift for catering. It might not have the intellectual challenge of experimental psychology, but at least it solved the stomach problem.

Mr Shanker held the cutting nearer. 'Nightwatchman. It says here, "Must be experienced, trustworthy, of British citizenship, and able to wear a size 36 uniform." I'm your man on all four counts.'

Baxi breathed out in relief. 'Oh, that. Yes, it's a cushy little number.' He lopped the end off a wizened carrot and tossed it in a pail. 'You know that it's only temporary – till Dr Osberton-Gore comes out of his coma?'

Mr Shanker smiled, as though at something that he alone would find amusing. 'Temporary is all I need. Two or three weeks should do the trick.' Even less, he thought, if he could manage without Spiro. He glanced into the ill-lit, steamy kitchens. 'Now, Sonny Jim, where can I find the guvnor?'

Baxi waved his knife ambiguously. 'Professor Grogan's not around. He's helping the police with their salmonella enquiries.' He wiped his hands on the seat of his grubby cooks' whites. 'I can get you an application form.' He disappeared inside and returned a few minutes later with a crumpled sheet of paper spattered with dried flecks of mulligatawny soup. As he handed the form to Mr Shanker it suddenly came to him. 'I know. You're the bloke who used to run The Mind and Body Shop.' His voice was full of admiration.

'That's right, son. Were you one of our philosophy undergraduates?' Definitely not a credit card customer, he thought. Not with hair like that, and his shoes held together with string. It was surprising he managed to get past the Philosophical Front at all.

'I used to mop up after the Spinoza seminar,' Baxi explained. 'Though I made a bit extra on the side sometimes, pumping up the rubber doll for Mr Skillicorn's lecture.' He hacked reflectively at a carrot until it grew smaller and smaller. 'Hm. So now you're a nightwatchman?' he said neutrally.

Mr Shanker folded away the application form with fastidious care, as though it were a letter of reprieve signed personally by the King. 'Security Operative, actually,' he sniffed. 'We're trying to overcome the cloth-cap image.'

35

Colin Lumsden stood preening himself in front of what until recently had been Hambro's wardrobe mirror. In his brown floor-length robes his short body seemed even shorter, as though it had been sliced off at the ankles. Each time he bent forward his *keffiyeh* tilted over his eyes, despite the newspaper padding tucked inside the headband. He took it off and folded in Hambro's vasectomy certificate. It's ruining my quiff, he thought.

Margery was hovering at his shoulder. She picked at loose threads of cotton and tried to adjust the robes at the back to prevent them trailing along the carpet. The previous week she had tried unsuccessfully to make him a set from two of Hambro's thermal nightshirts. Most of the large department stores now stocked them, although there had been a sudden rush on them ever since Dirk Oesterbroek had appeared in the Royal Enclosure at Ascot wearing a set in his jockey's colours.

'I tried everywhere to buy myself a chowder,' Margery sighed. 'Nobody stocks my size.'

Lumsden frowned at her in the wardrobe mirror. 'It's not a chowder, it's a *chadhor*. Chowder's a fish soup eaten by Yanks. How many more times must I tell you?' He did a double pirouette, causing his robes to billow up above his luminous pink ankles.

Margery drew away from him, hurt by the unnecessary sharpness of his tone. He never used to talk to me like that, she thought. Ever since they'd been through that communal ceremony in the university mosque, with women and students lying down on one side and professors on the other, he'd changed in a way she couldn't quite put her finger on. She could tell something was wrong when he'd started walking differently. Instead of taking his usual short quick strides he now took long slow loping ones, as if he was trying to avoid the cracks in the pavement. And he always got cross if she walked by his side, instead of two or three paces behind with the shopping bags. He'd even begun to talk in a funny nasal accent.

She half sat, half lay on the unmade double bed. The bed was now placed at an awkward angle between the chest of drawers and the door, so that the door wouldn't open wide enough to let her through without a squeeze. Colin said it had to be at that angle for the headboard to be facing Merseyside. She reached unthinkingly for the box of chocolate brazils stored beneath her pillow. Before she was able to bite into the first one, Lumsden's voice rang out in reprimand.

'Oh no you don't. Put that back at once.' He pointed at her accusingly in the mirror. 'You know very well it's Ramadan. Nothing to eat or drink before the seven o'clock pips.'

Margery held the forbidden chocolate an inch in front of her open mouth. 'Oh Col, surely one won't hurt? I'm famished. Anyway, who's going to know apart from you?'

Lumsden kept his reproachful gaze fixed on her until she replaced the chocolate in its little paper cup. 'In any case,' he objected, 'you shouldn't eat chocolates with your left hand. In fact you shouldn't eat anything with that hand.'

'But Col, you know I'm left-handed.'

'That's beside the point. It's unclean.'

Margery gave a spluttering laugh. 'Don't be so soppy. Look, I've just had a bath and a manicure.' She showed him the back and front of both hands.

Lumsden closed his eyes in exasperation. 'The Arts Faculty Imam explained all that to you. Don't you ever listen? Your left hand is for wiping your bum with.'

'Well I always wipe mine with my right,' Margery sulked. 'So there.'

Lumsden stamped his foot irately on the hem of his robes. 'But Marge, you're not supposed to do that,' he cried. 'You can't just use any old hand you like. You're not a Methodist any more.'

Margery climbed into bed fully dressed and pulled the covers over her head. If he's going to be like that, she thought, he can cook his own rotten dinner. He doesn't appreciate my cooking anyway; he always moans that the cous-cous is too gungy, or that the Sainsbury's sheep's eyes haven't been properly defrosted. All he ever seemed to do these days was grumble. Yesterday he'd yelled at her because she'd spilled a tiny little drop of Ovaltine on his prayer mat. And this morning he went bonkers because she let the gasman in to read the meter and forgot to cover up her face. She couldn't breathe properly with that thing over her mouth anyway. She much preferred her Dad's balaclava, when he wasn't using it.

Her stomach was rumbling like an underground train. She felt as though she hadn't had a meal for weeks. She closed her eyes and fell asleep dreaming of eating pineapple doughnuts off a conveyor belt . . .

'Marge? Marge, are you awake?'

She woke with a start to find Lumsden clambering on top of her. 'Come on,' he said. 'It's seven o'clock. We can do it now.' He put his hands under the covers and proceeded to squeeze and pull on her breasts as though kneading a pizza dough.

Margery forced him away and turned on her front for protection. 'Get off me. I don't feel like it.'

Lumsden pulled up his robes and knelt astride her in the hollow of the bed. His face was sweaty and flushed beneath the oversize *keffiyeh*. 'You can't refuse. I'm allowed to have you whenever I like.'

'Says who?'

'Marge, it's in the Koran, for Christ's sake. The Prophet taught that woman was created for man's pleasure. You can't argue with the holy book. Get your drawers off.'

Margery poked her head out of the covers. 'But I don't fancy it yet. Not on an empty stomach.' She saw that Lumsden was naked from the waist down. How could such a small man have such a great big thingy, she wondered; it always looked so red and angry, and it was always

197

pointing at her. It wasn't a bit like Duggie's little winkle.

'I keep on telling you, Marge. What you want has got nothing to do with it.' Lumsden punched the pillow in angry frustration. 'It's the satisfaction of the man's needs that counts. That's what you're *for*.'

Margery gripped the eiderdown in her fists and rolled herself up inside it. Lumsden found himself sliding off the bed. 'All right,' he muttered grimly. 'Be like that. I can always take another wife. I'm allowed up to four.' He sucked on his lips in anticipation of having his full entitlement. Maybe I'll take Denise Mason, he thought; and that big black nurse in the fever hospital. That still left him one in reserve.

'I'm really married to Duggie.' Margery's voice could only just be heard inside the eiderdown.

Lumsden shook his head knowledgeably. 'Marriage to an infidel isn't recognized as lawful.' He leafed through his copy of the Channel Four publication on Islamic England for the exact reference. 'It says here that all former conjugal ties are now invalid. You belong to me. The contract was sealed when I paid your father the bride price.'

Margery's voice rose to a muffled squeak. 'My dad? He didn't say nothing to me.'

Lumsden knelt on his prayer mat. 'Half a lamb was the stipulated price. It's a whole lamb for a virgin.'

'But Dad never eats lamb. He's got a sentimental streak.'

'So he told me. He settled for a kilo of rump steak and a crate of Guinness instead.'

36

Baxi was digging the eyes out of King Edward potatoes with a pointed knife and lobbing them into a large vat at the far end of the kitchens. Earlier he had baked three hundred sausage rolls and decorated three hundred side plates with tiny curls of butter, using a special instrument. He tossed another knobbly potato in a high arc, giving it plenty of backspin with his middle finger. It struck the edge of the vat, bounced off at an acute angle, and landed with a plop in a tureen of cold banana custard fielding at forward short leg. Baxi flung his arms in the air in jubilation. 'Howzat!' he cried. By his own reckoning he had now bowled out the entire West Indies touring side in less than a dozen overs. He was about to take on the Australians when the internal telephone rang.

'Catering,' he intoned grandly.

'Is that Professor Grogan?'

Baxi stiffened at the sound of Hedda Hagstrom's voice. 'No,' he said, in a hurriedly concocted accent. He ran his hand nervously across his savagely cropped head. Despite his shortage of funds, he had finally been forced to visit the barber because of the rapid multiplication of Darwin's fleas in his own more hospitable hair. They had a bad habit of jumping into the scrambled egg.

'Get him for me,' Hedda Hagstrom commanded. Her tone had the hard edge of newly acquired authority. 'Tell him it's the Dean and tell him it's important.'

Baxi glanced across at the small glass-partitioned office where the prostrate figure of the Head of Catering lay snoring among a pile of empty bottles. 'He's not here. He's lecturing the Prison Officers' Federation.'

'Prison Officers?'

'On methods of forced feeding. He's a world authority on the subject.'

There came a deep sigh that lasted several seconds. 'When will he be back?'

As he spoke Baxi could hear his accent slipping from Belfast to Bronx. 'I doubt if he'll be around before tomorrow morning.' Beads of sweat were gathering on his upper lip and falling into the jam roly-poly. If she recognized his voice she would have him frogmarched off the campus in a flash.

'Who exactly am I addressing?' she demanded. He sounds like a mental defective, she thought. He would have to go.

"Deputy Assistant Vegetable Chef.'

'Oh my God. Let me speak to someone more senior. Anyone at all.'

'I'm the only one here. The salmonella's been playing havoc with the duty roster.'

Another protracted sigh made its way down the line. 'Very well, I suppose you'll have to do. Now listen carefully, this is of the utmost importance. I'm sending a messenger round with detailed instructions for next Thursday's banquet in the Khomeini Centre. I want you to see that Professor Grogan gets them the minute he returns. I shall hold you personally responsible if there's any delay or a mishap of any kind. Do I make myself quite clear?'

Baxi drew his potato knife suggestively across the telephone cord. 'I think I've got the general drift.'

'Good. What did you say your name was?'

'Ndambarharjonghi,' Baxi said, and hung up.

Ten minutes later the messenger arrived on his tricycle. He handed Baxi a long brown envelope addressed to Head of Catering and stamped 'Confidential' on all four corners, back and front. 'Sign here, mate,' he wheezed.

Baxi took the proferred ballpoint in his fist and scribbled what appeared to be a crude profile of the Manhattan skyline. He waited until the messenger had pedalled off before steaming open the envelope over a bubbling vat of minestrone.

Inside was a twelve-page memorandum headed 'Khomeini Centre Opening Ceremony – Banquet Arrangements and Seating Plan'. Baxi ran his eye down the long list of items on the principal menu: spit-roast lamb on saffron rice; clay-baked chicken with cashew nuts; poached turbot in lemon and coriander; aubergines stuffed with goats' cheese; fried peppers in cinnamon; honey and almond cakes; fresh pineapple in yoghurt; persimmons, mixed nuts, dates and figs; Vichy water, still and sparkling; After Eights. There followed nine pages of detailed instructions on the ritual observances

200

for animal slaughter, and approved methods for the preparation, cooking and presentation of every dish. The last two sentences read, 'These culinary rules have been laid down by the university Imam and must not be departed from in the smallest particular. By Order of the Dean of Faculties.'

Baxi screwed the memorandum into a loose ball, set light to it in the sink, and flushed the ashes away. Professor Grogan was still snoring methodically beneath his desk. His head was partially in the upturned waste-paper bin and one arm was crooked protectively around an empty flagon of home-made schnapps. Now and then he gave a series of small kicks and grunts, as though dreaming he was a farmyard animal struggling for a place at a crowded trough. Baxi stepped between his splayed legs, lifted him by the ankles, and dragged him like a broken wheelbarrow to a corner of the room. He cleared the bottles and rubber tubes of the makeshift still off the desk and plugged in the electric typewriter. He spent the next hour and a half of the evening shift tapping away with two fingers. The only other time he had used an electric typewriter was to provide his father with a character reference for a job with the Luton Philharmonic.

When he had finished he put the typewritten sheets in the confidential envelope and re-sealed it with a thin application of macaroni cheese. He then fastened the envelope securely across Professor Grogan's bare chest with long strips of Sellotape.

Darkness had fallen over the campus by the time he returned to his duties as Deputy Assistant Vegetable Chef. He moved the tureen of cold banana custard from forward short leg to silly mid-off, placed another pan of béchamel sauce in the outfield, and resumed his leg-spin attack on the Australian opening batsmen.

37

Hambro screamed in agony as the electric current surged through his broken body. His back was arched like a fully-drawn bow. At any moment his backbone would snap in two, releasing the spinal fluids. He let out another piercing scream as the voltage was increased from thirty-five to forty.

'Try again, Winston,' said the Vice-Chancellor. 'What were you *really* doing in Paris? And Wigan, and Hampstead, and Barcelona?' His porcine eyes glinted evilly behind the unfamiliar metal spectacles. 'We've been watching you all the time.'

Hambro was barely able to speak through the pain. 'I've already told you a dozen times.' How many days and nights had they kept him here, in the infamous Room 101 of Admin II?

The Vice-Chancellor signalled to Hedda Hagstrom seated at her instrument panel. Hambro saw her hand move fractionally before the unbearable pain intensified.

'Come now, Winston,' murmured the Vice-Chancellor. 'Try again. You were passing philosophical secrets to other universities. We've been monitoring you on the telescreen.'

Hambro managed to raise his head. 'No. I swear I'm innocent. Please stop the pain. Do it to someone else. Do it to Skillicorn. Skillicorn's the one you want. He's been microfilming my lecture notes on remedial logic.'

The Vice-Chancellor put his face close to Hambro's, as if he was about to kiss him. 'The truth, Winston, the truth.' He spoke gently, lovingly, like a father to a favourite but wayward son. 'You'll feel so much better if you confess.' He made a sign to Hedda Hagstrom.

'Forty-five,' she laughed.

Hambro felt his body dance an involuntary Charleston.

'Stop!' he cried. 'Stop, stop, stop! I'm guilty. I confess. I'll tell you everything.'

The Vice-Chancellor's eyes softened as he wiped Hambro's tormented face with a spotted handkerchief. 'Who are you working for, Winston?'

Hambro wanted to kiss his tormentor's hand in gratitude. 'Consolidated Tractor Fuels,' he sobbed.

He woke up at the foot of his camp-bed covered in sweat. His heart was thumping in his throat. As his eyes grew accustomed to the dark he could make out the shapes of the beloved objects surrounding him on the shelves of his outhouse sanctuary. He put on the light and sat for a while looking at his collection until his heartbeat returned to normal. Each item had its own unique meaning that filled him with a special kind of joy. How foolish he had been not to move in with them long before. The days he had spent eating, sleeping and working in the midst of these cherished artefacts were among the happiest he had ever known. How odd, he reflected, that other people, rather than himself, had made it all possible. And how privileged he now was in being able to spend his days doing nothing but the one thing he wished to do. No more essays to mark, no more clocking on and off, no more meetings of the Illiteracy Committee, no more unseemly wrangles over the chalk allowance. There were times when he felt he could cry out in sheer exultation at his own good fortune. He gave a sigh of profound content-ment as he reached for his Burmese policeman's truncheon.

38

The Vice-Chancellor alternately flexed and unflexed his but-tocks on the seat of his swivel chair. He was wearing his interviewing suit with a sponsor's yellow tie and matching banana-shaped cufflinks. 'We'll have to be quick about this,' he said. 'I've got to dash in five minutes. I can't keep the Imam of Balliol waiting.'

The Professor of Fisheries Science and the Fellow in Hotel and Casino Management nodded in concurrence. Between them, his grey head slumped forward on his chest, sat the Dean of Divinity.

'Don't wake him,' whispered the Vice-Chancellor. 'He'll only slow things up.' He opened a buff dossier containing a single sheet of paper, gave it a cursory glance, and passed it along the desk.

'No references?' queried the Professor of Fisheries Science. He had one small slit eye and one large round eye that moved independently of one another.

'I'm afraid not.' The Vice-Chancellor was studying the dials on his shatterproof watch. 'The Registry's being re-organized by the Business Efficiency School as part of a teaching exercise. It seems that all the files have been shipped off to the Azores by mistake.'

The Fellow in Hotel and Casino Management looked momentarily troubled as he stroked his goatee beard. 'Is there only one candidate? I'd have thought that the Chair of Metaphysics would have attracted a few more applicants.'

The Vice-Chancellor waved his hand airily. 'Remember, it's just a temporary post. We only advertised it in the free local paper.' Pity there's even one applicant, he thought. He put his face unnecessarily close to the intercom and said, 'Miss Pollins, send the candidate in.'

The door opened and a wiry man in a seaman's jersey and white sneakers came soundlessly through. 'Morning gents,' he beamed, knuckling his forehead.

The Vice-Chancellor pointed to an upright chair isolated in the centre of the room. 'Do have a seat, Professor Shanker.'

Mr Shanker inclined his head in surprise at this unexpected courtesy. He sat on the very edge of the chair, as though ready to spring away. Why was he being interviewed in a gym, he wondered?

The Vice-Chancellor locked his hands together, leaned

across the desk, and said in his overpitched interviewing voice, 'You realize, Professor Shanker, that this post isn't a permanent one. What we're looking for is someone to run things until the merger with Horticulture. It's really a sort of . . . nightwatchman role.'

Mr Shanker winked affirmatively. 'Just my cup of tea,' he said. 'You'll never catch me dozing on the job.'

The three conscious members of the selection committee chuckled at this witticism. 'Unlike the previous holder of the post,' the Vice-Chancellor muttered. He went on to give details of the salary, commission, and overtime payments, and the concessionary use of library facilities and university car wash, all of which Mr Shanker found entirely to his satisfaction.

'Now, tell me, Professor, which institution are you with at present? It doesn't seem to say on your application form.' The Vice-Chancellor turned the crumpled sheet of paper over and picked at a hardened lump of mulligatawny soup above the candidate's date of birth.

'None right now,' Mr Shanker admitted. 'As a matter of actual fact I only just finished a three-year spell.' He knew from experience that it was best to come clean about his past; they probably knew anyway, and were just testing him. They didn't have three computers for nothing.

The Professor of Fisheries Science looked at the wallbars with one eye and at Mr Shanker with the other. 'And where exactly was that?' he enquired.

'Reading. In the Oscar Wilde wing.'

'I see.' He made a note of it. 'And you say that was for a three-year period only?'

Mr Shanker cleared his nasal passages. 'A bit less than three in actual fact. I got eight weeks' remission for good . . .'

'Splendid place, Reading,' interjected the Fellow in Hotel and Casino Management. 'I was there myself a few years back. It would have been a bit before your time.'

Mr Shanker was unable to contain his surprise. 'Well I be blowed.' He didn't look the type, with his floppy bow tie and

205

Gordounstoun lisp. It only went to show how deceptive appearances could be. What would it be for – tax evasion? Art fraud? He did a quick mental calculation. 'That means you must have known Tinderbox Turvey,' he said. 'He was in Reading for seven.'

The Fellow in Hotel and Casino Management put back his head and contemplated the volleyball marks on the ceiling. 'Turvey? Turvey? Wasn't he the Senior Lecturer in Pharmacology who used to spend the whole time in Senate meetings squeezing his blackheads and flicking them at the Assistant Registrar? If I'm not mistaken he emigrated to America a few years back and eventually got the Chair in Arkansas State. He well deserved it, too.'

Mr Shanker shook his head decisively. 'No, no. Not Tinders. He never went to the chair. He's still alive and kicking. I saw him not long ago in his tattoo parlour near the Elephant . . .'

'Gentlemen, gentlemen, *please.*' The Vice-Chancellor rapped on the desk with his commemorative matchbox holder. 'We must press on, there'll be time enough for reminiscences later.' How these academics like to rabbit, he thought. He turned to the Professor of Fisheries Science and invited him to pursue a different line of questioning.

'Professor Shanker,' the latter piped, 'as you are no doubt aware, we at this university are keen to emphasize the applied and practical approach to things. We prefer, as it were, the nitty-gritty to the airy-fairy. Now, where do you think your own line of work would fit in here? If you don't mind my saying, it doesn't seem to have much practical use, does it? To be perfectly blunt, would it make the slightest bit of difference if it was done away with altogether?' He sat back grinning smugly. Got you there, he thought. Philosophize your way out of that one if you can.

Mr Shanker was sucking hard on his back teeth. What was the silly prat on about, he asked himself? Surely they weren't thinking of making him redundant before he'd even got the lousy job? What a bunch of wankers. 'It's absolutely essential work,' he said, with evident conviction. 'Just think what would happen without it. There'd be anarchy. You got to have someone keeping an eye on things while everyone else is kipping. It's obvious.' A fat lot these people know about security, he thought.

The Fellow in Hotel and Casino Management pressed his fingertips together thoughtfully. 'Extremely interesting,' he said, stressing every syllable. 'What you're saying, if I'm not mistaken, is that you see your role as one of upholding and safeguarding basic moral principles in the face of general apathy and indifference. And that without someone to re-affirm these basic principles we should soon sink back into a state of nature. Do I read you correctly?'

Mr Shanker sniffed non-committally. 'I suppose that's one way of putting it,' he said. 'What I know for a fact is that people can get up to some very dodgy numbers after dark.' He leaned forward as though to impart information that he wished to go no further. 'Without your nightwatchman, it would be bang to property rights, believe you me.'

'Ah.' The Professor of Fisheries Science seized his cue. 'Property rights? Is that your field of special philosophical interest?'

'I'd say more practical than philosophical,' replied the candidate.

'Excellent,' the Vice-Chancellor put in. 'Excellent. That's the kind of language I like to hear.'

'But what about the philosophical side of it?' persisted the Professor of Fisheries Science. 'Does philosophy have anything useful to tell us about property?'

Mr Shanker stared at him in wonderment. 'Philosophy? About property?' Someone should have tipped him off that a university security operative was expected to know his onions. Lucky for him he was up to it. 'Course it does. Think of Locke, think of Thomas Hobbes. And what about Montesquieu, and our old friend Rousseau? Practically everything that Jean-Jacques wrote . . .'

The alarm on the Vice-Chancellor's watch went off with a

207

strident buzz. 'I'm afraid we'll have to call a halt there, gentlemen,' he said, trying to shut it off. 'You can continue your discussion of German philosophy some other time.' He held a rapid, whispered discussion with his two colleagues while still struggling with his noisy watch. Moments later he was on his feet and extending his hand across the glass-topped desk. 'Congratulations, Professor Shanker. The selection committee recommends your appointment unanimously.'

'*Nem con*,' corrected the Fellow in Hotel and Casino Management. He gave the Dean of Divinity a gentle nudge. The Dean's lifeless body toppled sideways and slid to the floor in a crumpled heap at the feet of the Professor of Metaphysics elect.

'Oh, no,' groaned the Vice-Chancellor. He struck his forehead with the heel of his hand. 'That's all I need. Another salmonella victim.'

39

The day of the opening ceremony began with a cloudless dawn. Seagulls soon appeared in the brightening sky, squawking in pursuit of the early cross-channel ferry, and wheeling and dipping above the small fishing boats unloading their catch by the submerged pier. A lone beachcomber picked his way among the rockpools, watched by stranded day-trippers unable to sleep on the damp shingle. Further inland, Tozer Place was bathed in a melancholy glow by the rising sun. Its pale rays fell upon lifeless neon signs and shards of broken glass that still littered the closed-off street. Stray cats stalked among the ruins. Rooks had nested in the exposed beams of the Hermeneutics Wing of The Mind and Body Shop and a colony of frogs had made their home in the brackish water of the Jacuzzi.

Further inland still, high on its windswept promontory,

the campus was cloaked in silence. Giant cranes, bulldozers and yellow mechanical diggers stood motionless in the mud like once lordly creatures made impotent by a sudden whim of evolution. Surveillance cameras had been placed at strategic points around the main piazza and on the roof of Senate House, and signs in several languages now directed visitors to the VIP car park, the foreign press marquee, and chemical latrines. The grebe, coot and mallard splashed aimlessly about on the artificial lake as though it was just another day.

Baxi's radio-alarm came on shortly before six. A tinny voice began chattering excitedly about the June sales and contraflow systems and the dramatic resolution of the abdication crisis following the meeting of the Royal Family, the Archbishop of Canterbury, the Imam of Merseyside, and the President of the Boilermakers' Union on the Dirk Oesterbroek Celebrity Show. Baxi mumbled something in his sleep and pressed the snooze button.

'Wakey, wakey,' Denise murmured in his ear. Inside the single sleeping bag she might have found it difficult to disentangle her limbs from Baxi's had she wished to do so. She kissed his neck and ran her practised hands down his chest and across his lower abdomen. 'Now you're awake,' she observed. 'That part of you at least.' She took hold of it as though it were a hand-brake. 'Nice,' she purred.

With his eyes still shut Baxi prised away her fingers one by one. He unzipped the sleeping bag and clambered out. He felt about for the matches and lit the kerosene lamp.

'Oh, Baxi,' Denise pouted, 'you're not going to waste that erection?'

'It'll keep.'

'You've been saying that for days.'

'Don't be silly, it's not the same one.' He was fumbling about for his cook's whites in the jumble of clothing piled high against the door. His head was throbbing and his throat felt as if it had been sprayed with paint-remover. There's not enough air in here for two, he thought. No wonder the lamp

209

doesn't burn properly. Even his parents slept under healthier conditions – the air in Regent's Park was bound to be fresher than this. He lay on his back, legs in the air, and pulled on his white cotton trousers. That reminds me, he thought: I still haven't finished paying their vagrancy fine.

When he was dressed he rubbed his face on a strip of towelling and ran his finger around his teeth and gums. Normally he did his ablutions in the kitchens, but today all the vats would be in use. He put his head round the door and looked along the dark passage. The overhead pipes hissed and rumbled inside their asbestos wrapping. 'Don't forget,' he said quietly, 'be there at one o'clock pronto. And bring both bags.' He edged his way out.

'Don't I even get a kiss?' Denise called from the sleeping bag.

Baxi pushed his lips forward and smacked them together the way Herbert Spencer used to do when someone landed on his property. He closed the door softly behind him.

The three surviving second-year catering students were already in the kitchens when he arrived. They were playing an improvised version of baseball, using hard boiled eggs and a stale French loaf.

'All right, you lot,' Baxi commanded, with a clap of his hands. 'Enough pissballing about. Today's the big day.' He pointed at each of them in turn. 'You, get the carcases out of cold store. You, light all the ovens. And you, stop flicking your fag-ash in the cabbage soup, that's your breakfast, lunch and dinner.'

The kitchens soon echoed with the sounds of chopping, scraping, pounding and dicing. Water bubbled in vats, fat spluttered in baking trays, and blue smoke leaked from the ovens and snaked around the malfunctioning air vent. Presently Radio Free Campus came on the air. The loudspeakers above Professor Grogan's office crackled with the massed voices of the Security Police choir singing the university anthem. This was followed by the regional weather forecast and the announcement of this week's winning num-

210

bers in the Science Faculty lottery. At eight o'clock sharp, normal transmission was interrupted for a special address by the new Dean of Faculties. She began by reminding her listeners that this was the most important day in the history of the university, and that everyone, from the most distinguished professor to the humblest student, should be on his or her best behaviour, and should be formally attired in accordance with the regulations laid down in her illustrated pamphlet. Her audience were further reminded to assemble at the appropriate sites in the piazza at the duly appointed time, not to drop litter, not to speak to television crews or members of the press, and not to block the portable latrines.

'I want you all to bear in mind,' she concluded, 'that the eyes of the world will be on the university today. It is up to each and every one of you to act as personal ambassador for our noble institution. Remember, too, that leading dignitaries from many countries will be our guests. Most of them will be accompanied by their own armed security squads. For your own safety do not, I repeat do *not,* attempt to approach them for autographs. Nor should you make any sudden movement towards them or raise your hands in the air. In the event of any mishap, let me remind you once again that an emergency operating theatre and blood transfusion unit has been set up in the snooker hall. Please ensure that you have sufficient cash or university medical stamps on you to pay for any treatment you may require. Credit facilities will not be available.

'Finally, after all formalities have been concluded, and our guests have departed, please disperse in an orderly fashion to the Designated Picnic Zone where biscuits and mineral water will be available at nominal cost. Have a good day.'

The Dean of Faculties' address was followed by selections of light operatic music played by the Maintenance Staff brass band. Baxi whistled the tunes between his teeth as he bustled about supervising the preparation of the banquet. He issued his instructions with firmness and precision and was quickly earning a reputation for himself as a stickler for detail. The

Head of Catering had recognized his leadership qualities from the very first. It was Baxi who, in the nick of time, had prevented the heating engineers from inadvertently lagging the hot water tanks with a freshly-made batch of sausage toad. It was Baxi, too, who had been in the right place at the right time to administer mouth-to-mouth resuscitation to the first-year student discovered at the bottom of the Irish stew. Again, when Professor Grogan had accidentally tipped a tray of grilled kippers into the tapioca pudding, it was Baxi who had saved the day by mixing it all together, sprinkling it with cockleshells, and serving it as paella. In the space of three weeks he had progressed from part-time pot-scrubber to Deputy Assistant Vegetable Chef to Senior Chef, aided in part by the timely decimation of the regular catering staff. He now pushed a wooden spatula into a bubbling vat, stirred it, and fished out an elasticated jockstrap.

'Sheldrake!' he bellowed. 'I've told you before. Do your dirty washing in the sink. Look at the colour of this saffron rice.'

Shortly after twelve-thirty the Head of Catering appeared through the steam. He was wearing one left boot and one left sandal and had somehow managed to put his head through the armhole of his string vest. He stood rocking backwards and forwards on his heels as though on the deck of a small boat in a turbulent sea.

'Everything under control, Baxi?' he was able to say. He held one arm out to steady himself as he went about the kitchens squinting into ovens and probing at pans of spitting fat, ostensibly checking the things he saw against his long, typewritten list. 'Bloody wogs,' he grimaced. 'How can they eat this foreign muck?'

Soon he began to cough. It started as a succession of short separate barks but then gradually developed into a single unifying convulsion that brought every part of his face and body into play. Thin sprays of saliva flew in many directions and his normally bright red face became a deeper and deeper burgundy. His typewritten list fell to the floor as he seized the rim of the nearest vat and held his head low over the contents. Baxi took him by the arm and steered him over to the glass-partitioned office. He lowered him onto the canvas bed and poured him a tumbler of schnapps from the illicit still. The Head of Catering took it in both hands and swallowed it without once taking his lips from the glass. Before long his eyelids dropped shut like those of a china doll. Baxi laid him down, wiped his face, and covered him with his MA gown.

It was twelve fifty-five by the office clock. Through the tiny porthole window he could see columns of students marching from different directions towards the main piazza. Each column was led by a professor carrying aloft the departmental banner emblazoned with the insignia of commercial sponsors past and present. Two helicopters clattered overhead, not quite drowning out the sound of a ladies fife-and-drum band practising an unfamiliar national anthem. Suddenly, a black vehicle came racing along the access road. It screeched to a halt and four uniformed men jumped out, accompanied by four sniffer dogs. They ran in single file down the muddy embankment and, after some initial confusion, surrounded the Arts Faculty ice-cream van that was parked alongside the *mullahs'* bicycle shed. Seconds later a man holding a double scoop was led away under escort.

Baxi looked at the clock again. It was seven minutes past one. 'Where the hell are you, Denise?' he said aloud. He lit one of Professor Grogan's cigarettes, took a few nervous puffs, and stubbed it out in the empty schnapps glass. His hands were trembling. He thought to himself, if she's having a quick tutorial with Mr Poulter-Mogg . . .

She came hurrying in carrying two canvas holdalls, one of which contained a number of long cardboard tubes. 'Sorry I'm late,' she said. 'It was all the fault of the security guards. They wanted to take it in turns to give me a body search.' She rolled her eyes lasciviously. 'They weren't interested in the bags.'

'No wonder,' Baxi grunted, disguising his relief. 'You could have been arrested in that skirt.' He unzipped both

213

holdalls and checked the contents. 'Okay, follow me.' His anxiety had quickly given way to a sense of nervous elation, such as he had felt as a small boy the first time he had accompanied his father on the zither outside the Albert Hall.

'I hope you know what you're doing, Baxi,' Denise said, as she followed him along the carpeted passageway that led directly from the kitchens to the banqueting room. In the centre of the principal room, polished mahogany tables had been arranged in a T-formation. The red leather dining chairs had high backs embossed in gold leaf with the letters KCPI. Shafts of sunlight streamed through the windows onto the silver cutlery and Wedgwood bone china and the tall vases of orchids and white lilies. At each place-setting was a commemorative menu printed in gold on black, and a name-card in matching colours. At the far end of the room, between the two long windows, hung a portrait of the Ayatollah in a baroque gilt frame. Next to it was a silver plaque bearing the inscription 'Khomeini Centre for the Propagation of Islam' beneath a crescent moon.

Denise pushed her foot experimentally into the carpet to see how far it would go. 'Wow,' she gasped in awe. 'This place must have cost a bomb.' She stroked her fingers tentatively down one of the silk wall-tapestries. 'No wonder the university can't afford books.'

Baxi was dragging one of the throne-like dining chairs to the far wall. He stood on the seat and took down the portrait of the Ayatollah. In its place he pinned up a full-length poster of Golda Meir wearing a red and white polka-dot dress. She was shielding her eyes from the sun with one hand and making a victory salute with the other. Denise unfurled two more posters from the cardboard tubes and held them up in readiness.

'How should they go?' Baxi asked. 'Moishe Dayan to her left, and Menachem Begin to her right?' When all three posters were positioned to his satisfaction he covered over the silver plaque with a rectangle of stiff card that had recently served as a notice board in the refectory advising

214

students to beware of unauthorized additions to the Hungarian goulash. It now depicted, in Oxford blue on a Cambridge blue background, a slightly asymmetrical Star of David.

'Baxi, hurry, they'll be coming in soon.' Denise glanced apprehensively at the long double doors of the main entrance. Outside, television crews were standing about like unemployed dockers, complaining about the heat and the lack of alcoholic drink. The ladies fife-and-drum band could be heard playing selections from Gilbert and Sullivan, and from further afield came the sound of organized cheering.

Baxi ran back along the corridor to the kitchens and began piling steaming dishes onto a trolley, aided by the three catering undergraduates. 'Well done, lads,' he said. 'As a special treat you can have the leftovers.' He trundled the loaded trolley back to the banqueting room at great speed, like a contestant in a peak-hour television game.

At the head of the table he placed a whole roast sucking pig. Stuffed between its jaws was a large orange with the Jaffa label outermost. At regular intervals along the table he then set out platters of grilled streaky bacon, boiled hams, fried pork chipolatas, and jellied pigs' trotters. Denise worked her way along in the opposite direction, distributing bottles of Scotch and Irish whisky, Kentucky bourbon, Dutch gin, Professor Grogan's home-made schnapps, and litre carafes of Israeli wines, red, white, and rosé.

Limousines were approaching the forecourt. Those leading the procession had pennants flying on their bonnets and were flanked by motor-cycle escorts sounding their sirens. As the cars drew towards their destination, men in tight suits got out of the rear doors before the wheels had stopped and ran along at the side.

'Something's missing,' Baxi announced, just as the ladies fife-and-drum band struck up a martial air. He dashed back to Professor Grogan's office. The Head of Catering was on all fours, trying to crawl out from beneath his desk, apparently unaware that his string vest was caught in the buckle of his sandal. Baxi took from the cupboard a Jewish candelabra which he had acquired from an acupuncture student earlier in the week in exchange for certain items of Denise's soiled underwear. He ran back to the banqueting room, trying to light the candles on the way. He was lighting the fifth one as the double doors were flung open.

The Vice-Chancellor was standing on the threshold. He was smiling fixedly at the cameramen while trying at the same time to talk to a thick-set man in black robes. Hedda Hagstrom was immediately behind. On either side of her were men whose beards were of almost identical hue, length, shape and texture. She was wearing a *chadhor* of white samite with a half-veil. She seemed to Baxi to glide along without moving her limbs. Her pale blue eyes shone above the veil with a bright triumphal radiance. She moved into the room, talking to someone on her right, hesitated as though sensing some unseen danger, and then stood completely still. The buzz of conversation gave way to a sudden chilling silence. Baxi watched in fascination as the light in Hedda Hagstrom's eyes burned with a fierce intensity, flickered, dimmed, and finally went out. She was staring at him across the long, sunlit room. With slow deliberation she removed her veil, as though to let him see the expressive lineaments of shock etched into her face. As the first guttural cries rang out on every side, he saw her lips come together to shape his name, curiously like a lover's parting kiss.

40

These events passed unnoticed in the tranquil middle-income suburbs on the slopes below the university. Here the rhododendron bushes rustled in the soft summer breeze and herbaceous borders were alive with blue tit and chaffinch hopping among fallen rose petals and French marigolds and slug pellets. Local foxes basked in the sun on garage roofs, licking their chops, while small children played constructively on newly-mown lawns or threw handfuls of dirt at the neighbours' washing.

Hambro dithered in the doorway of the outhouse wondering whether he would be too warm in his prisoner-of-war greatcoat and chunky rollneck sweater. His erstwhile gardening trousers were tied below the knee with lengths of green string, causing the bottoms to end several inches above his hobnailed boots. He adjusted the straps of his rucksack, hooked his arms through the loops, and engaged in an energetic struggle to hoist it on his back, like a man fighting off a much more powerful assailant. He put on his khaki mittens and battered cloth cap and took a final farewell glance around the bare walls of his sanctuary. Cardboard boxes containing his collection were stacked in orderly piles reaching almost to the ceiling. On each box was a sticky label itemizing its contents; the labels were in five different colours, each colour representing one of the five politico-biographical epochs that now formed the basis of Hambro's revised classification. He locked the door with his burglarproof device and lumbered up the garden path.

Mr Shanker was sitting at the kitchen table writing on a pad of university notepaper. He wrote in a tiny bunched-up script, from the very top left-hand corner of the page, in the manner of someone accustomed to squeezing the maximum number of words on a permitted monthly postcard. 'Douglas, just the man,' he said, without looking up. 'All this malarkey about Free Will versus Determinism. What's your line on it?'

Hambro took two Cox's orange pippins from the fruit bowl, washed them under the tap, and stuffed them in his greatcoat pocket. 'I am delighted to say that as from the thirteenth of last month I have not been required to have a line on it.' Not that I had much of one before, he confessed to himself.

Mr Shanker put the tip of his ballpoint in his mouth and

rattled it against his teeth. 'You see, what I reckon is,' he said pedagogically, 'is that we got to accept the argument for Free Will because we got no other choice.' He put out his tongue and inspected the mauve inkstain on the tip of it.

Hambro was cutting two thick wedges of wholemeal bread. He spread them liberally with beef dripping and wrapped them in a sheet of kitchen roll. 'Is it really worth bothering about?'

Mr Shanker looked deeply affronted. 'Douglas, what a diabolical thing to say. Course it's worth bothering about. It's the theme of me inaugural lecture.'

Hambro propped his foot on a kitchen chair and tried to tug his trouser-bottom closer to his boot. Mr Shanker seemed to notice him for the first time. 'You're all dressed up to the nines. Where you off to then?'

Hambro could not quite conceal his elation. 'I am going to the spike. I believe there is a very good one outside Tunbridge Wells.'

'The spike? The doss-house? I thought you liked living in your garden shed?'

Hambro took off his check cloth cap, wiped his domed head, and replaced it. 'There are urgent things I need to do,' he explained. 'Things I should have done long ago. I am finished with the bourgeois life.'

Mr Shanker seemed deep in meditation. He tilted back his chair until it was balancing precariously on two legs. 'It's a rough life on the road, Douglas,' he warned. 'I had a taste of it once myself. I tell you, I was almost glad when they picked me up.' It might have been easier if Spiro hadn't been with him, demanding three hot meals a day. 'What about your collection? It must be worth a bob or two.'

Hambro picked abstractedly at the Commando flash on his coatsleeve. 'I have donated it all to the newly-formed Orwell League. In fact, I've bequeathed them my entire estate. I am severing all links with the Royal Eric Blair Society. Restricting life membership to Old Etonians was going a bit too far.'

It was two-fifteen by the kitchen clock. Time to begin a new life, he thought. He took off a khaki mitten and put out his hand. 'I shall say goodbye.' He tried not to wince as Mr Shanker's grip responded to his own. 'I hope you are more comfortable in the Chair of Metaphysics than I ever was.'

Mr Shanker laughed. 'I'll be in me element. I've already got the guvnor eating out of my hand – he's dead keen on my sponsorship proposals.' He talked enthusiastically about his plans for revitalizing philosophy while he accompanied Hambro to the garden gate. The street was deserted except for a Carmelite nun pushing a pram and the dog-licence inspector hammering at the door of number seven. In the distance they could hear fire engines and police cars howling in unison. A pall of smoke was rising over the hill, partially blocking out the sun and filling the air with smuts.

'Looks like a fire on the campus,' Mr Shanker observed. He flicked a speck of grey ash off his university tie. 'It's probably the library,' he added knowingly.

'The library? Surely they remove the books before burning them?'

Mr Shanker glanced cautiously up and down the street. 'The insurance, Douglas,' he said in a low voice. 'The guvnor's got it covered for a very handsome sum. About as much as he needs for his heliport.'

Hambro's bushy eyebrows jigged beneath his cap. 'I find it hard to believe that even our, or rather your, Vice-Chancellor would deliberately set light to university premises.'

'Course he wouldn't,' Mr Shanker confirmed. 'That's a craftsman's job. I put him in touch with Tinderbox Turvey. All the big companies use him nowadays.' He winked confidentially. 'If he makes a decent job of it he'll be up for an honorary degree. Doctor of Civil Laws, I reckon.'

Hambro was about to speak, but stopped, his attention caught by a sound carried down the hill on the summer breeze. It was an insistent, rhythmic chant whose single word could only gradually be made out.

'*Jihad! Jihad! Jihad!*'

Mr Shanker made a face as though he had swallowed a mouthful of sugarless Earl Grey. 'The Merseyside Shites,' he groaned. 'Seems like they beat Tinders to it. I wonder what set the bleeders off this time?'

Hambro sighed uncomprehendingly. 'Let's hope that young Skillicorn is nowhere on the campus. His new eyebrow was just beginning to take.' First it was The Mind and Body Shop, he thought, now the university itself. Where would it all end? Wasn't it Merleau-Ponty who said that whatever happened to philosophy today would happen to the world tomorrow? Or was that Bulkowski? He loosened one of his shoulder straps where it was beginning to chafe. Soon he would be far away from all these local troubles. It occurred to him for the first time that he had no very clear idea of where, and under what circumstances, he would be waking up next morning. The more he thought about it the less it seemed to matter.

Voices were being raised in anger inside the house. He looked up at the open window of the master bedroom and caught a glimpse of his former second wife swirling about in her home-made purple *chadhor*.

'I don't care,' she cried, 'I don't want to go and live in your mother's rotten caravan. I hate caravans. They make me feel big and clumsy.'

'I keep telling you,' Lumsden shouted back, 'you're not supposed to argue with me. You're meant to obey me. I could have you chastised.'

The voices grew more shrill and soon solid objects were being thrown about the room.

'Those two are at it again,' Mr Shanker remarked. 'Things have never been right between them since Colin's circumcision went wrong. I warned him not to go to that cowboy outfit by Tozer Place.' He stepped nimbly aside as a prayer mat came flying out of the window followed at once by the leather-bound edition of *Slimming Through Prayer*.

There was a howl of pain or anger before Lumsden's voice rang out in desperate finality. 'Right, that's it. You've had

220

it. I divorce thee. I divorce thee. I divorce thee. Sod you.'

The two men standing below exchanged glances but made no comment. They walked together to the end of the street and said their last farewells. Mr Shanker could not help noticing how different his ex-son-in-law seemed. All of a sudden he had stopped looking like an East German defector who had tunnelled into Poland by mistake. His cheeks were glowing with bliss and perspiration. He was smiling as he walked jauntily away, his bedroll bouncing against the small of his back, and a chipped enamel mug swinging from a strap around his waist. In his long khaki greatcoat he could have been mistaken for a volunteer marching to the front in a just cause. He paused outside the Pakistani grocer's on the corner, turned, punched the air gleefully with his small fist, and was gone.